# BACK TO YOU

A SWEET MILITARY ROMANCE

JESS MASTORAKOS

Cover Photography By: Edith Barfield, Uno's Photography

Edited By: Amanda Horan, Let's Get Booked



This story is adapted from its original version, written by the author.

***To get a free copy of the prequel, Forever with You, visit:*** http://jessmastorakos.com/forever-with-you

## SIGN UP FOR JESS'S SWEET ROMANCE SQUAD

Sign up for my newsletter at http://jessmastorakos.com/forever-with-you to get the free ebook version of Forever with You: A San Diego Marines Novella. You'll also get bonus content, sweet romance book recommendations, and never miss a new release!

instagram.com/author_jessmastorakos
bookbub.com/authors/jess-mastorakos
goodreads.com/author_jessmastorakos

# 1

## ELLIE

I deserved a medal.

The light from the fire danced across the features of our friends as I wormed my way through the crowded party on the beach. I'd just refilled my cup from one of the dozen two-liters we had on ice in the back of someone's truck, so I took care not to spill it as I walked barefoot through the sand.

Spencer was standing near the fire, surrounded by girls in their smallest bikini tops and shortest shorts. He was easy to spot, with his tall frame and shaved head. He caught my eye over the heads of our friends around the fire. I beamed and lifted my plastic cup in salute. He grinned back at me as a hot but fake bottle-blonde leaned in close to speak to him over the country music pumping from a nearby car.

The closer I got to the fire and the crowd, the more stuffy the air got. There had to be at least a hundred people there. Or, maybe not that many, but it sure felt like a lot. I headed to the waterline for some fresh air. Wading through the mob, I received several nods and hugs from the friends I passed along the way. I thanked them for coming with a smile I knew didn't quite reach my eyes. While I was grateful for such a good turnout, I couldn't help but be sad that we were all there to say goodbye to Spencer.

The party was his last hurrah. It was Saturday night, and come Monday morning, he'd be boarding a bus for Marine Corps boot camp. I wouldn't be able to see or talk to him for three months. It would be awful, considering we'd never gone more than a few days without talking. No one knew me like he did. There was about to be a Spencer-sized hole in my life.

I pushed my way through the crowd until I reached the wet sand where the water had touched it. Eyes closed, I took a deep breath of the hot, July air, enjoying the taste of the Pacific Ocean on my tongue. The gentle waves from the bay couldn't be heard over the loud music and noise from the crowd, but the glow from the fire and moonlight allowed me to watch them roll in. I felt calmer from here, the steady rhythm of the waves going out and always coming back to me. I glanced around, looking for my boyfriend, Tim. I hadn't seen him in a while. Admittedly, I wasn't looking very hard.

He didn't get my relationship with Spencer, and if he picked up on my sadness over my best friend leaving, he would probably take it the wrong way. I wasn't in the mood to deal with whatever jealous remarks he might come up with about our "history" or "lack of boundaries." Tim's parents were psychologists, so he used all kinds of technical terms in casual conversation. It really got on my nerves.

Taking a few steps along the wet sand and peering into the night, I could see the shadowy form of a couple sitting in the surf, making out. Not wanting to interrupt them, I shook my head and made my way over to a long log in the sand, sitting down and giving up. I'd find Tim, eventually.

As I lowered myself onto the log, I wished I could just stop being so mopey. I wanted to enjoy my last night with Spencer, even though I hadn't seen him much. He was a bit of a playboy, and he was on a mission to have one more fling before boot camp. Big surprise there.

I smirked into my cup, thinking about how he wouldn't have to work hard to accomplish that goal. There were many girls at the party ready to be on his arm at the first opportunity. Spencer had always been good-looking, but it was also his happy-go-lucky nature and sense of humor that made him appealing. The fact that he was about to become a U.S. Marine didn't hurt either.

He loved all the attention, and never tired of it, unlike me. The spotlight wasn't my favorite place to be. I took another drink and grimaced as the bubbles tickled the back of my throat, making it hard to swallow. I scanned the horizon, not even sure what I would be looking for in the dark. But it was just more peaceful to look into the night ahead, than worry about what was going on in the crowd behind me.

I sipped my drink and stared into the night, trying

unsuccessfully to get my best friend out of my head. Was he getting nervous? He wasn't the type to pour his heart out about his emotions. Still, it must have freaked him out at least a little. I couldn't imagine how I would feel if I were in his shoes. Tonight, at least, I hoped he wasn't thinking about it at all.

"Hey." A voice made me jump and almost spill my drink, but when I realized it was Spencer, my whole body warmed. I swallowed, surprised by my reaction to his approach.

His new buzz cut made the angles of his jaw look even stronger and sexier than usual. If I were being honest with myself, I understood why girls fawned over him constantly. He had that swagger that came with his tall and lean frame, and his deep blue eyes made him look like an Abercrombie model.

Well, actually, it was his abs that made him similar to those guys. And they were prominently on display for all the world to see, as he wore only his black swim trunks. We'd all been in the ocean earlier, but the sun had set long ago and the fire became the new focal point of the party. Apparently, Spencer hadn't felt the need to put a shirt on. I cleared my throat and looked away from him.

"What are you doing over here by yourself?" he asked, sitting down on the log beside me.

I felt the heat from the fire radiating off him. "It was getting kind of hot over there."

"You're telling me." He fanned his face with his hand dramatically. "Those girls are too much."

"Oh, please," I laughed, draining the rest of my drink

and dropping the empty cup on the ground next to the log. I took the fresh one that Spencer held out and we touched our cups together in a toast. "Don't pretend you don't like it. This is what you wanted, right?"

Spencer looked at me then, his lip twitching into a smirk. "Yeah, guess so."

Spencer's behavior didn't surprise me by any means. I'd known him since middle school. He never had "girlfriends," only girls he was "hanging out" with. It only amused me rather than bothered me because he somehow managed to stay friends with every girl. If he'd been running around stomping on hearts, I wouldn't be as close to him as I was. Spencer wasn't the typical bad boy with a hidden heart of gold. You didn't have to dig too deep to find his best qualities; they were right on the surface and within reach to all he encountered.

"Thanks for the going away party, E. You look great tonight," Spencer said with a smile. "What'd Timmy say when he saw the new suit?"

I raised my chin haughtily. "He doesn't like it when you call him that. But anyway, he was just as impressed as you thought he'd be."

"You always act so surprised when I'm right. Even a broken clock is right twice a day." He wagged a finger and smiled at me with a lopsided grin.

I swatted his hand out of the air with a laugh. Spencer had gone shopping with me earlier in the day to find a new swimsuit for the party. He went with the basic black pair of board shorts, but he wouldn't stop pestering me until I agreed to buy the red bikini and white shorts to go over it. He'd insisted that the color went great with my long, blonde hair, and on a hot summer night at the beach, the whole look would be perfect. I had to admit he was right. I felt amazing.

"Have you seen him, by the way?"

Spencer frowned. "Who?"

"Tim."

"Oh. No, I haven't seen him for a while, actually. You haven't either?"

I shook my head.

"He'll turn up."

"Yeah," I agreed. "I just hate how he does that, you know? Disappears for most of the party and then magically reappears when it's time to leave."

Spencer patted my knee. "Well, that's what you have me for. I'm much better company than Tiny Tim."

"He hates that name too, you know."

"I bet he does. So, listen, there's something I've been meaning to talk to you about," Spencer began, looking at me somberly.

I nodded in encouragement for him to continue.

"My recruiter told me about the phone call we're supposed to make when we get to the depot. It's not a big deal; it's just this script we have to read to let our families know we made it there alive or something."

"Okay..."

"Well, you know how things are with my dad..."

I gave him a small smile. "Yeah."

"So, I'd like to call *you*, instead of him."

"Of course," I answered with no hesitation.

"Cool, thanks. I don't want you to get freaked out though. I heard we basically just pick up the phone and yell this couple-sentence thing and hang up. It's not like we'll get to chat or anything."

"That's fine, I don't mind. I'll let your dad know you got there safely." I put my hand on Spencer's knee, knowing how much he wished his mom were still alive so he could call her instead.

"Thanks," Spencer said, putting his arm companionably around me. I rested my head on his shoulder and closed my eyes. We sat in silence for a few minutes, both just letting the ocean breeze waft over us. When I stayed uncharacteristically quiet, he squeezed my arm. "You're moping. I told you, this is a night for fun, not being sad. Be sad all day tomorrow for all I care since I'll be busy packing and I won't have to see it."

I opened my eyes and took a breath, smiling at his teasing words. "I wasn't moping."

"You absolutely were."

"Okay, okay," I conceded, looking him in the eye. "I'm just going to miss you, that's all."

"I'll miss you too, but you need to cheer up or you're gonna ruin my night. Too many feelings." He swallowed. One side of his mouth twitched upwards and he squeezed my shoulder again before getting up from the log. He took a step toward the wet sand and dug his toes in. "Besides, we're about to be pen pals. You'll need to entertain me with stories about your adventures on the outside."

"On the outside? It's not prison, Spence."

"Might as well be," he laughed.

"Well, either way, I wouldn't get too excited about letters from me. Who would I have adventures with if not you?"

"That's true. Your life is pretty boring. But that's what you want, isn't it? A white-picket-fence, a boring husband, and a couple of messy but well-mannered kids?"

I laughed and rolled my eyes. "My future husband doesn't need to be boring. Just stable... like my dad."

"Your dad is boring," Spencer countered, before sticking his hand out to pacify my move from the log. "Easy, easy, I'm kidding. Your dad's not boring. He's predictable. Your parents remind me of a fifties sitcom... you know... 'Leave it to Beaver' style."

"Whatever, I love my 'Leave it to Beaver' parents."

Spencer nodded solemnly and looked out at the lawn behind him. "I love your parents, too. I don't know what I would have done these last few years without Carol and Tom. And *you*."

I met his eyes then, seeing more emotion swimming in them than I expected. I swallowed past the lump that had formed in my throat, unsure of what to say. If I said anything too deep, he would just brush it off. Too many feelings.

"So, I guess that makes you the adopted son of the Cleavers. If they'd had one, that is." I said, knowing how lame I sounded.

He cocked his head and narrowed his eyes a bit. "Adopted son, huh? Nah. I'll stick to being the kid from down the street. No relation."

I blinked, once again at a loss for words. I watched him

as he stared out into the darkness. The light from the fire behind me was just close enough that I could see him but not so close that I could feel its warmth. The shadows of the partygoers danced across his bare chest and broad shoulders. When my gaze met his face, I found him looking at me. Why did he suddenly look so different?

Spencer cleared his throat, looking uncomfortable. "Speaking of your dad, I can't believe you'll be working for him soon."

"I know." I was grateful for the break in the tension. "Only a few more weeks. I wish this summer could have lasted forever. I already miss the beach trips and parties."

"Same."

"Soon, you'll be a slave to the military, and I'll be a slave to the law firm." I winked at him, knowing the two situations were worlds apart.

Spencer wrinkled his nose. "Yeah, I know you're not super stoked about that."

"His expectations are just way too high. Just because I take this job in his office doesn't mean I'm going to suddenly fall in love with the legal field and follow in his footsteps."

"It probably makes him nervous that you don't know what you wanna do yet," Spencer offered, gesturing with his cup. "Like, maybe if you had another plan, he'd lay off."

His words stung a little. Mostly because they were true. I didn't have a plan. I knew I didn't want to be a lawyer, but that was pretty much all I knew. I got good grades in high school because I knew I wanted to do *some-*

*thing* worthwhile. I was just taking my time deciding what that something was. I had always expected that I would develop a passion for something and then follow my dreams. Nothing had given me that feeling yet.

"You're right." I allowed. "I'll figure something out. When I have a better plan, I can at least have the receptionist job on my resume. I want something stable, something I can rely on. I can picture my life as far as the family and the house and all of that, but my actual career plans are a total mystery right now."

Spencer nodded. "You'll be fine, E. Just do whatever makes you happy."

I paused. "This feels so..."

"Heavy."

"Yeah."

"Listen," he said, stretching one long arm across his chest before switching to the other, "I hope you find your white-picket-fence and stuff. I'm glad you know what you want in that area at least. The job stuff will come, and I'm sure having the office job with your dad will help you figure it out. I'm not joining the Marines just to get out after my first enlistment, so I want to know when I come back to visit, you'll be happy and living life on your terms."

I smiled. "Thank you, Spence. I'll try."

"You might not want to thank me yet. The last thing I wanna say is... I'm pretty over this thing you've got going on with Tim."

"Excuse me?" I shook my head, unsure if I'd heard

him right. We'd been dating for over a year. Why was he speaking up about it now?

Spencer came over to where I sat on the log and crouched down in front of me, hands on my bare knees. My skin lit up when he touched me and I met his eyes, not sure where this was going or how I felt about it.

"Ellie, he wants what you want on paper, but he's not good enough for you. In fact, I think he's kind of a tool."

"I-I don't know what to say."

"You don't have to say anything. Just think about it. Where is he right now? This happens everywhere we go. I don't know what he's up to, but I think if your boyfriend was really that into you, he'd be with you right now."

"What makes you so sure?" My voice caught in my throat as I stared into his bright blue eyes.

"Because that's where I'd be if it were me."

The intensity of his stare messed with my already jumbled brain. What was he saying? Before I could form a response, two cheerleaders Spencer had been talking with earlier skipped through the sand in our direction, calling his name. I leaned away from him and felt a fake smile reflexively spread across my face as they glanced between us. My stomach turned slightly as I watched him go from a laser focus on me to flirting with the girls.

"Hello, ladies. Did you miss me?" He rose from his position in front of me and headed their way.

The duo giggled and held out their hands for him. I rolled my eyes. He playfully swatted the shorter one on the butt as she danced toward the fire. He followed them back over to the crowd, quickly blending in with the rest of the shirtless guys and bikini-clad girls.

I gazed out toward the dark water again, trying to gather myself. Why would he wait so long to speak up about Tim? And what was that part about how he would act if it were him? Did he mean for that to sound so... inviting?

"Hey..." Spencer said, having jogged back over to my log and crouching down at the end of it.

I threw a smile on my face to hide the turmoil I felt. "Yes?"

"Stop being a baby and have fun. You know I always come back to you."

With a wink, he rose from the sand and went back to the party. I stared at the space where his face had just been. Was he talking about leaving with the girls just now, or the three months he'd be in boot camp? Maybe he was referring to what he said about coming home to visit over the course of his career. Whatever he meant, my smile turned genuine that time. Maybe I should just go ask him what he meant. Feeling bold, I rose from the log to go find him. It was now or never, right?

"Well, you two sure looked cozy..."

I rolled my eyes and sunk back onto the log. Apparently, I'd get to hear a lecture on Freud instead. "Hi, Tim."

## 2

## SPENCER

I felt for my phone in the dark, hurrying to silence the obnoxious ringing of my alarm before it woke my dad in the next room. Through the haze of waking, I realized what day it was. It was Monday, and I was about to leave for boot camp. I lay in my bed wide-awake, staring at the ceiling. I hadn't expected to feel so nervous. How had I been so calm and confident yesterday, only to wake up this morning feeling like I was on death row?

Eventually, I rolled out of bed and adjusted my boxer briefs. I'd left my window open overnight, and the breeze felt nice on my slightly damp skin. Why was I sweating? Was I really that nervous?

It was just past three in the morning and the world was still quiet. I tiptoed to the bathroom. My dad had to be up for work in a few hours, so I doubted he would get up early to see me off. Just as well, since my interactions with him were rarely anything but awkward, anyway. I stared at my reflection in the mirror, noticing the hard expression in my eyes.

When I was twelve, I watched some movie at school that showed Marines raising the flag over Iwo Jima. I told all my classmates that my dad was a Marine like those guys and that I would be one someday, too. I rushed home from school that day and told my parents about my plan. My mom's eyes got all teary as she looked at my dad. He smiled like he'd been hoping for this moment. Like I'd just made his day or even his week. They were both so proud.

Maybe my mom was looking down on me and was still that proud. Hopefully, she didn't hold my dating habits against me though. As for my dad, I wouldn't know if he was proud of me now or not. We barely spoke anymore. Part of him died with my mom, and our relationship hadn't been the same ever since.

I shook my head abruptly, vowing to put the past behind me. These were exactly the kind of thoughts that would distract me from success in boot camp. I needed to focus on what *would* be, not what *had* been.

I'd been practicing the art of speed showering for a few months now. In record time, I'd washed my entire body and what was left of my hair—post-buzz-cut. I'd also taught myself how to shave at speed without cutting my face. There was a lot of bloodshed until I'd mastered that particular skill. Now I was a pro.

On my desk chair, there was a dark gray button-up shirt, black slacks, and dress shoes. My recruiter had once told me Marines always looked sharp. That was something I could get behind. I studied my reflection in the long mirror on the back of my bedroom door. The last time I'd worn this outfit was the day I'd sworn in, over nine months earlier. I'd raised my right hand and swore an oath to God and country, signing over my life to the United States government. In a matter of hours, I would box up these clothes and replace them with whatever they issued me.

With nothing left to do to get ready, I grabbed my phone off the nightstand and opened my text messages. I went to the folder of conversations between Ellie and me and paused with my thumb hovering over the on-screen keyboard. There were so many things I wanted to say to her, but I closed my eyes to block them out. What could I possibly say without coming off as a total creeper?

I felt dumb enough already after my confession about my thoughts on her relationship with Tim. On the one hand, she seemed totally weirded-out. On the other, there was a chemistry between us that was hard to miss. Screw it. She had probably already forgotten about it. Why make it awkward now?

I settled on a simple text. "Be back soon."

I quickly powered off the phone and threw it in the top drawer of my nightstand. I didn't want to wait for Ellie's reply. She was probably still sleeping, but I didn't want to take the chance of seeing something that would make leaving harder.

In the kitchen, I checked the time. My recruiter wouldn't be here to pick me up for another thirty minutes.

I grabbed a bagel out of the bag by the fridge and popped it into the toaster. I leaned against the counter and crossed my arms over my chest, settling in to wait for my breakfast to pop. I grew restless within seconds and paced the kitchen. I tucked my hands in my pockets, then withdrew them again. *Gotta get used to keeping my hands out of my pockets. Can't be doing that in uniform.*

There was a picture on the fridge of Ellie and me at high school graduation. I'd put it there because it seemed like the right place for it. Isn't that where parents displayed the accomplishments of their children? I stared at the smiling face of my best friend. I had my arm around her shoulder, and she was leaning into me. Her body fitted mine like a puzzle piece. The fact that I'd spend the foreseeable future without her was sinking in, and I didn't like how it felt. I shook my head and turned my back on the photo.

We were friends. It wasn't a big deal for me to know how much I would miss her. It made sense that the closest person in my life was the only person I was thinking about as I was getting ready to leave. It meant nothing.

I sighed heavily. *Lies.* I knew anything more than friendship with Ellie wasn't a good thing for either of us. She may not know what she wanted as far as a career went, but she knew what kind of man she wanted. And it wasn't me. Regardless, the way she'd looked the other night in that red bikini was frozen in my mind. She'd been my best friend for the better part of the last decade, but the closer I got to leaving, the more I realized my feelings for her weren't as simple anymore. Just thinking about her now made my entire body hum with nervous energy. The more I acknowledged it, the worse the feeling got. How had I let it get this far?

"Were you going to wake me up or just leave?" Dad's gravelly voice from the doorway made me jump.

"Just leave," I answered bluntly, cursing myself for showing how anxious I felt. I heard the note of challenge in my voice as I stared at my father. He had barely bothered to talk to me lately, and now he acted like he cared if he slept through my exit. I tried for a casual expression and leaned against the counter again. "Didn't think you'd mind."

Mike grumbled incoherently and tightened the belt on his robe. He crossed his arms and leaned against the counter opposite me. Something in his face changed as he looked at me, and I watched as he uncrossed his arms and then crossed them again with a self-conscious expression. He looked conflicted. I had no idea why, or what he was thinking.

"You hungry?" he asked me.

"I'm making a bagel." As if on cue, the toaster popped. I turned to put it on a plate and went to the fridge to get some butter. I ducked my head into the cool air and came back up frowning. "No butter?"

"Try cream cheese," my dad suggested.

I glanced around in the fridge again, coming up empty once more. I went to the pantry and found a jar of peanut butter. It was probably a good thing to get some protein in my system since it might be a while before I got to eat again. I set to work spreading the peanut butter over the halves of my bagel. I never took my eyes off my meal, but I was fully aware that my dad was still standing at the counter watching my every move. I refused to be the one to break the silence.

After putting a huge helping of peanut butter on my bagel, I held the plate in my hand and leaned against the counter once more to eat. We weren't really a 'sit-down-like-civilized-people' kind of family anymore. That was just another thing Dad stopped caring about after Mom died.

"So, I bet you're gonna miss Ellie," Mike said, obviously trying to get me to open-up to him. "She gonna write you?"

"Probably. Are you?" I asked, biting into my bagel.

My dad nodded. "Yeah, sure, kid."

"I'll write you first, so you have the address. It'll probably take a couple of weeks though. I heard it's pretty crazy when you first get there."

"It is. Receiving Week is a trip, man. They put on a big show to shock you, but it gets better with every day. I know it's changed since I was there, but that part's still true, I'm sure of it. And one more thing."

"Yeah?" I asked.

"They'll treat you like something on the bottom of their boots. But it's all part of the head game. The point is to break you down until you're a whimpering little boy, so they can build you back up and make you a warrior. They want to strip away every bad habit you've ever had and give you a new identity. Let them do it. It's how they make a Marine, a Marine."

"Thanks." I nodded, swallowing a mouthful of bagel. My mouth was suddenly dry. I hadn't expected him to say anything worth knowing. It was a shame we didn't have a better relationship, or I would've been able to ask him about everything else I wanted to know. Like, how bad was the food? Would we get to sleep much? What was the craziest thing that happened while he was in recruit training?

Mike pushed up from the counter and crossed the kitchen to where I stood. He extended his hand for me to shake. "Good luck, son."

I hesitated for the briefest moment and then shook my father's hand. I instinctively wanted to go in for a hug, and that shocked me more than Receiving Week probably would. I hadn't felt any kind of affection for my dad in years, so maybe it was just a clear sign of my nervousness. I looked at the man in front of me and swallowed past the lump in my throat. Had he been this nervous when he went?

"Were you nervous?" I asked on impulse.

He nodded. "Yeah, but it was better than the alternative. You know. Back in those days, I didn't have a choice in the matter. Even the Marines seemed more appealing than jail."

"Was anyone there when you left?"

"Nope. I left before that last foster lady woke up."

My dad had been in the system since he was a kid. His parents were both druggies and gave him up to the firehouse when he was a baby. My mom was an only child and so were her parents. Between his past and hers, that didn't leave me any relatives to speak of. After my mom died, it was just me and my dad. And Ellie's family.

"All right," Mike said, awkwardly. He nodded once more and then retreated out of the kitchen without another word.

My bagel tasted dry in my mouth, the lump in my throat tightening further as I watched my father round the corner and leave me standing alone in the kitchen. I threw the bagel in the trash, not able to stomach another bite. I took a seat at one of the four chairs around our kitchen table and waited alone for my recruiter.

Sergeant Moore's excited demeanor was infectious as he drove me to the processing center downtown. I had always liked my recruiter for his laid-back attitude and sense of humor. There were several recruiters in the office where Sergeant Moore worked, and I was glad I hadn't been recruited by any of them. I didn't need much selling though since I'd already made my mind up about joining long before I stepped into their office that day.

"I wish they would let me drive you guys around in the Charger," he said with a shake of his head. He weaved in and out of traffic in his 'government car,' the Chevy Malibu that he drove whenever he had work-related errands to run. "This car is lame."

"What, powder blue isn't your color?" I jabbed, laughing.

"No, and thank you for proving my point. Plus, it has a camera that turns on if you speed."

"I can't complain, I don't even have a car."

Sergeant Moore smirked. "Yeah, just do me a favor—talk to me before you let some idiot sell you a brand-new car with 'great military rates.' I'm so sick of seeing young Marines making stupid decisions."

I chuckled at his passion for the topic. "Will do, sir. I probably won't need a car for a while, though."

"That won't stop you from being dumb and buying one anyway."

I laughed and looked out the window. "Any other words of advice for after I'm a Marine?"

"Don't get married on boot leave."

"Not a chance. Next."

He side-eyed me. "I know you and Ellie are just friends... but are you sure you don't have some chick ready to write you letters and convince you to elope while you're home for ten days? It's plenty of time."

"There's no chick, trust me." I swallowed at the mention of Ellie though, not liking the way her face was the one that came to mind when he'd first said it. "Is that really a thing? Getting married on boot leave?"

"Of course it's a thing." He changed lanes and attempted to put the pedal to the metal, then dialed it back after glancing at the speedometer. "I've been in for seven years now and I've seen plenty of military marriages fall apart. Most of them started on boot leave. Or, worse, right before the dude ships out to boot camp."

I shook my head, confused. "Why is that worse?"

"Because then I have to do all kinds of ridiculous friggin' paperwork. Anything, like getting tattoos, or married, or even piercing your belly button, requires paperwork on my part if you've already signed up but just haven't left yet."

"At least I didn't cause you any extra paperwork."

He laughed. "You were a model poolee, Hawkins."

After you swear in and before you leave for boot camp, you're in the Delayed Entry Program or the DEP. Each kid in the DEP is a 'poolee' and part of their recruiter's pool of kids waiting to ship out. Sergeant Moore had been new when I'd first met him, but over the course of the year I'd spent in the DEP, he'd built the biggest pool in the office. It didn't surprise any of us. He was a cool guy. Plus, part of being a poolee was going out and helping your recruiter get more kids, and I was pretty good at it.

"Hey, can you put in a request for me to come back on Recruiter's Assistance sometime? I brought in a few guys for you while I was in the DEP."

It was a long shot, but totally worth asking for. Especially considering the number of guys I helped him recruit. Recruiter's Assistance was a temporary duty assignment where you could come back after you were a Marine and help the office get more kids. A few guys came back on RA were in the pool with me and it was cool seeing them go from the high school kid to the Marine. They got all kinds of chicks while they were home visiting.

"Yeah, I'll ask if they'll let you come out for a couple of weeks. We'll see what your schedule's like after boot.

What job program did you get again? Aviation Support, right?"

I nodded. "Yeah. When do I find out what my specific job will be?

"You find that out in boot camp. That's where they'll tell you if you're Crash Fire Rescue or Aviation Ordnance."

"Cool. And then when do I find out where I'm gonna get stationed?"

"Much later. Get through these next thirteen weeks, then your combat training. You'll figure out the rest in your career schools."

I was grateful for the conversation with Sergeant Moore. It kept me from thinking about my dad. Or Ellie. I wondered if my text had woken her up this morning and if she'd replied. I clenched my fist in my lap and tried to stop that 'crazy-train' of thought before it went off the rails. I couldn't help it though. The closer I got to leaving the more I thought about what—or *who*—I was leaving behind.

Ellie had been there for me when my mom was sick and stuck by me through the worst parts of my life when she finally passed. I understood why she wanted stability so badly. She was *my* stability. No matter where I went or what I did, I could always go back to her. We were more like family than anything else, especially since Ellie's parents practically adopted me when they saw how bad my dad was doing. But, as I'd told her that night on the beach, I was glad there was no relation.

I chewed it over in my mind. Yeah, we were *like* family,

so it made sense I loved her. I just didn't want to consider what *kind* of love it was turning out to be. That was another distraction I didn't need for the next three months.

"Are you wearing a belt?" Sergeant Moore asked.

I jolted, not having heard him. "What?"

"I asked if you were wearing a belt."

I checked my waist, just to be sure. "Yeah, shouldn't I be?"

"Yes, you should be. I swear, I'm gonna lose my mind if I have to give mine to another kid with no belt on ship day. I should start stashing some in the car instead of giving them mine if they don't have one."

"Is it really that big of a deal?"

He glanced at me. "If you're told to do it, it should be treated like a big deal."

I nodded. "Check."

Sergeant Moore's phone buzzed in his pocket. He pulled it out, glanced at the screen, and barely concealed a smile before clearing his throat and silencing the call.

"Is that her?" I asked, thinking of the hot brunette who worked at the bookstore next to the recruiting office.

"Yeah," he replied, "I'll call her back."

Sara's parents owned the independent bookstore and café and she ran it for them. They met because they both work insanely long hours, so it made for a convenient relationship. Since I'd been one of Sergeant Moore's first contracts and since Ellie loves Sara's store, we'd been there to witness the whole thing.

"How are you guys?" I asked. I kinda felt invested after

watching it all go down.

"Great. Probably gonna propose to her."

I took a breath. "Seriously?"

"What?" He raised a brow.

"Man, I'll never understand wanting to be married and still be a Marine."

"I mean, I'm sure being married and being a Marine is hard. And being married and being a Marine Recruiter is probably total garbage. I literally never get time off. If she didn't work right next door, we wouldn't even be together, guaranteed." He checked his blind spot and then changed lanes.

"Recruiting Duty doesn't seem that bad. You don't even deploy, and you get to work in an office all day instead of sleeping in dirt holes."

Sergeant Moore tilted his head back and laughed out loud. "Bro, let's talk about it in six years after you've actually slept in some dirt holes yourself, deal?"

"Deal," I laughed. "Anything else about boot camp I need to know? Now that I've been put back in my place?"

He chuckled. "I try to prepare my guys as best as I can during the workouts while you're in the DEP. You're in decent shape, so if you work hard, maybe you'll get Honor Recruit. That looks great on me, so you should do that."

"I'll do what I can," I promised. I saw the building looming ahead and knew I was out of time for pep talks. Sergeant Moore pulled into the lot and found a spot in the back. We got out of the car and I checked my pockets to make sure I had everything I needed.

"What'd you bring?" Sergeant Moore moved around

the car to stand beside me.

"My I.D., social security card, and cash," I answered.

"No smokes?"

I shook my head. "No, I quit a few months ago."

"Man, when I was leaving, I chain-smoked like crazy right up until the last second. I even got chewed out by my recruiter for asking if I could smoke in the car on the way." Sergeant Moore laughed at his memory and walked toward the entrance. "Okay, when you get in there, you're gonna go into a room with a bunch of other kids that are just as freaked out as you are and listen to some guy try to motivate and scare you at the same time. They're gonna ask you *again* how many times you've smoked pot, so if you mess that up, you're not going. And I'll get in a world of trouble, so just stick to what you put on your paperwork and we're all good. Then they're gonna have you swear your oath again, and you'll all head to the airport to meet some DI's and go from there."

"The airport? Isn't the Recruit Depot right here in San Diego?" I asked, confused.

"Yeah, but other recruits are coming in from around the country and it's easier for you local kids to get in line at the airport with the rest of 'em. The DI's take you from the airport to the Depot on their busses. And the bus is a trippy feeling, my friend. You're on a big white chariot to hell, led by some pretty scary mother effers. You ready for this?"

My head swam with all the information. I forced a shaky smile and gave him the thumbs up, hoping I looked sarcastic and not terrified.

"Very convincing." Sergeant Moore held the door open for me to pass through. We wove through hordes of other recruiters with their poolees in tow. Sergeant Moore told the clerk behind the desk he was checking me in, and we both signed the clipboard on the ledge.

"Here, take this." He handed me my service record book full of paperwork from the DEP. "Any last words?"

I shook my head.

"Okay, kid. I'll see you when you're a Marine."

The USO at San Diego International Airport was a place for military and their families. The elderly volunteers who staffed the facility were nice and welcoming. I thought I saw a hint of pity in their eyes when they found out we were about to go to MCRD or the Marine Corps Recruit Depot. I brushed it off. They were old, probably just had watery eyes all the time or something.

"You can relax here until it's time for you to go outside. The rest of these young gentlemen will be joining you. Good luck, honey. You're gonna need it." The old lady patted me on the shoulder and went back to the front desk, leaving me with a handful of future recruits playing video games in plush leather recliners. They looked calm, just like I probably did.

The kitchen counter had baskets full of snacks, Crock Pots full of soups and chilis, a hot dog grill, and a panini maker. There was a row of coolers with all kinds of bottled drinks. There were shelves packed with candy, jerky, and various other things. I eyed the jerky and wondered if I had enough time to eat some before the DI's showed up.

"All of this is free?" I asked a kid leaning against the nearby counter eating chips.

He tipped the bag into his mouth to eat the crumbs. "Yeah. Pretty sweet, huh?"

I nodded. I would definitely enjoy this perk of being in the military.

"If you're going to MCRD, get on your feet and get outside," a voice boomed from behind me.

I whipped around to find a DI standing in the center of the room, his Smokey the Bear-lookin' campaign cover making him even more intimidating than he already was with his near seven-foot frame. He hadn't screamed, but his voice commanded an instant response from the room. Hordes of guys, including myself, dropped whatever they were doing and made a beeline for the door.

Outside, everyone was milling about and looking at each other to see if anyone knew what we were supposed to be doing. The DI came charging out of the USO and gestured to the bus with one rigidly straight arm, pointing with his whole hand, like a knife.

"Form one line alongside my bus. Do not talk. Look straight ahead. When you get to the front you will hand me your service record book and board my bus. Do you understand?"

There was no organized answer from the crowd as we hustled over to the big, white bus and lined up. He wasn't screaming when he ordered us out here from inside the USO, but he was sure screaming now.

"The correct response when I say, 'do you understand?' is 'yes, sir.' Do you understand?" he yelled.

"Yes, sir," we yelled back, somewhat in unison.

His nose was about a centimeter away from the cheek of the guy in front of me when he screamed, "Eyeballs straight ahead, DO NOT LOOK AT ME." I made a mental note not to look at him.

When it was my turn to board the bus, I handed the DI my service record book and got out of his reach as fast as I could. Everyone on the bus sat two to a seat, so I rigidly sat in the seat next to the guy who had been in front of me in line. We didn't speak, but we had the same thoughts. This was gonna suck.

By the time everyone had boarded the bus, we were all scared silent. The DI hopped aboard and put a hand on the vertical metal bar next to the driver's seat. "Put your head in your lap and do not lift your head until you are told."

We lowered our heads with no response.

"That rates a response, say 'aye aye, sir' *now*," he screamed.

"Aye aye, *sir*," we replied.

The bus ride was only about five minutes long since the airport was right next to the recruit depot. When it lurched to a halt, I waited for the command to lift my head before I moved an inch. I wasn't stupid. I stared at my black dress shoes, unblinking, telling myself over and over again that the mind games hadn't even begun yet and I would make it through. I would make it through, and then I would be a Marine.

"EYEBALLS." The DI boarded the bus and yelled the word at us, and we all snapped our heads up and looked at him. "Yes. When I say 'eyeballs' you stop what you're doing and look at my face. Aye aye, sir."

"Aye aye, sir," we said.

"You will get off my bus and find the yellow footprints on the ground outside. You will not talk. You will keep your eyeballs straight ahead unless otherwise instructed. Aye aye, sir."

"Aye aye, sir."

"When I tell you to get off my bus you will move to those footprints as fast as humanly possible do you understand?"

"Yes, sir."

"GET OFF MY BUS!"

"Aye aye, sir!" There was no confusion about what to do next. We tripped over each other and scrambled for the exit, frantically trying to find the footprints and not get singled out by the DI.

I looked down at my dress shoes again, this time as I stood on the iconic yellow footprints of Marine Corps recruit training. I'd heard so much about these footprints in preparation for boot camp. I'd always wondered how this moment would feel. I'd assumed I'd be proud and excited and ready to be a Marine. Instead, I felt sick. As awesome as I'd always believed myself to be, was I good enough for this? Would I make it?

After teaching us the position of attention, they ordered us off the footprints and into the building. We gave up all our possessions and accepted what they issued us. I looked down at the pile of stuff in front of me as I sat cross-legged on the floor with the rest of my platoon. There were five sets of cammies, two pairs of boots, and one pair of running shoes that we now had to call "go fasters." They'd supplied us with skivvies, or underwear and undershirts, sweats, socks, and two olive green sea bags to store it all in. In a mesh laundry bag, I'd been given two canteens, first aid items, toiletries, glow belts, hand sanitizer, insect repellent, laundry pins, and several more items that had new names. Pens were now 'ink sticks' and a flashlight was now a 'moonbeam'. Everything I came in with was marked with my name and set aside until after graduation. This mountain of gear, the same stuff as the guy next to me, was all I had now. Whoever we were when we showed up at the airport was replaced with our identities as recruits. And that meant you had no identity.

I now understood what my dad had warned me about. Receiving Week had only just started, and it was already insane. I stood in a line of recruits, all waiting to use the phone for our arrival calls. The DI's screamed from all directions. They screamed so loud their voices were cracking and straining under the effort. Veins popped out of their necks and foreheads. I wondered how long they'd be able to keep it up before they lost their voice entirely. Then I remembered that they did this for a living and were probably conditioned to handle it.

I looked to my left and right and noted the sullen expressions of the guys beside me. By now, I was sure we are all thinking the same thing: *What have I gotten myself into?*

I rushed forward and white-knuckled the receiver when it was my turn to use the phone. I felt the body heat radiating off a sweaty drill instructor as he yelled at the kid to my left. I prayed that he didn't turn his attention on me next. In a moment of panic, I was afraid I didn't remember Ellie's number. *619...* I recovered quickly and dialed. She answered on the second ring.

"Spencer?"

"I have arrived safely at Marine Corps Recruit Depot, San Diego," I read from the script posted on the wall in front of me. "Please do not send any food or bulky items. I will contact you in three to five days with my new mailing address. Thank you for your support. Goodbye for now."

Before I hung up, I waited a beat to see if she would say anything.

"Ellie," I breathed into the phone without thinking, bending my head and squeezing my eyes shut tight. I wasn't supposed to deviate from the script at all. I didn't know how much time I had before the DI turned on me. I didn't know what I planned to say, but my breath caught when I heard her melodic voice on the other end of the line.

"Love you, Spence. Be safe." Her voice was so quiet compared to the melee around me. I couldn't be sure if I'd heard her correctly, or if I'd heard what I'd wanted to hear. I felt the DI shift towards me, so I slammed the receiver back on the cradle and took off for the line of waiting recruits.

## 3

## ELLIE

I walked through the door to the ladies' room and wrinkled my nose. Public bathrooms are awful, but they're even worse when you have to stand in line. I peered around the women in front of me to gage how long I'd need to take in the foul air. Tim and I had just seen the latest rom-com. I usually got the 'warm and fuzzies' from movies like that, especially at the end when everything finally fell into place for the on-screen couple. This time, I felt a little empty. I couldn't put my finger on it specifically, but it kind of felt like my real-life relationship just didn't measure up to the fake one in the movie. Even though Tim and I have been saying those three little words for months now, our relationship seemed miles away from an epic love story. I hated the thought of wishing for a love found in fiction. Real love should be better than fiction.

The line moved slowly, and I silently prayed that the women in the stalls would hurry it up a bit. Two women in front of me chattered excitedly. They were clearly in a better mood than I was. I inched forward and eavesdropped on their conversation as they fawned over the shiny engagement ring decorating the brunette's left hand. Her friend complimented the groom's taste, and the bride winked conspiratorially.

"I think my mom must have had a hand in this," she said in a hushed voice. "It's exactly the one I wanted."

"Girl, please," the friend said, waving her hand, "give the guy some credit. Andrew knows you better than anyone. I bet he just got it right."

The bride sighed. "Yeah, maybe you're right."

"Seriously," her friend said, putting an arm around her and squeezing, "that man loves you like nothing I've ever seen. I secretly hate you for it."

The bride looked like she was about to cry just thinking about her guy and how much he loved her. It was enough to make anyone roll their eyes and gag. I wanted a love like that...

"Long line?" Tim asked when I finally exited the restroom. He offered me his arm and led me out of the packed theater.

"Very," I confirmed, suddenly annoyed with myself for being in such a funk. Here I was, on a date with an attractive and smart guy who cared about me, and I wished I had it better. I sighed and pulled him to a halt before he could get in the car. "Let's go for ice-cream. I'm not ready to call it a night."

Tim smiled at me with his pearly whites and clear green eyes. "Sounds good to me."

I stood on my toes and pressed my lips to his. He was a great kisser, there was no denying that. I felt his arms come to rest on the small of my back, and I wove my own around his neck. Running my fingers through the short brown hair at the nape of his neck, he gently pressed me against his car. His lips were warm and soft, his breath mingled with mine as our lips moved together. As the heat between us intensified, Tim pulled back.

"What?" I asked, slightly breathless. This was one area of our relationship that didn't need any work.

"Nothing. We should probably go get that ice cream now."

"I'll just text my mom and tell her I'm gonna be home late." Disentangling myself from Tim's arms, I pulled my phone out of my back pocket.

When I turned the lock screen on, I found that I'd already missed a call and a text from my mom. I opened the text, sucking in a sharp breath when I read the words on the screen. She'd text me to tell me I had a letter from Spencer. My heart immediately pumped faster, and I exhaled in what was almost a laugh. Just knowing there was a letter waiting for me at home felt like I could finally breathe... even though I hadn't known I was holding my breath. I bit my lip and looked up at Tim. His eyes were questioning.

"Tim... I'm sorry. I have to go home after all."

I racked my brain for an excuse, knowing he would flip if he knew I'd cut our date short for a letter from Spencer. I didn't care though. I hadn't heard from Spencer since that crazy phone call almost two weeks ago. There had been so much chaos in the background, and he sounded so different when he read the script to let me know he'd arrived. All I wanted was to know that he was okay. I had to keep myself from literally bouncing on my heels with excitement to get home.

"What happened, Ell?"

"My mom needs me to help her with something. It's important," I lied.

Tim cocked his head and frowned. "It can't wait until tomorrow?"

"No, I'm sorry. Will you take me home?"

Part of me was kicking myself, knowing I would never feel better about my relationship with Tim if I made a habit out of lying to him. The other part, the part that missed Spencer like a phantom limb, couldn't get home fast enough.

"Yeah, sure."

"Sorry again," I said, kissing him on the cheek. "Rain check, for sure."

He smiled and walked me around to my side of the car and opened the door for me. "Definitely."

We listened to music and kept it light on the short drive to my house. Thankfully, I lived super close to the movie theater. I jumped out of the car as soon as Tim pulled into my driveway.

"Thanks, Tim. See you tomorrow!" I called as I

rounded the car. I stuck my head through his open window and gave him a quick kiss. He reached for me, but I turned and bounded up the porch steps and through the door without looking back.

My mom was sitting on the couch reading a travel magazine when I came in. "Hey honey, how was your date?"

"It was fine," I answered with a wave of my hand. "Where's the letter?"

"On the counter," she replied with a chuckle.

I darted into the kitchen and snatched the letter off the marble counter with greedy hands. I took it outside and went to the swing set in the backyard. Spencer and I had spent countless nights hanging out on the swings when we were younger. I swung back and forth for a few minutes, staring at the outside of the envelope. Above the return address, the name read, 'Recruit Hawkins'. I traced my thumb over the ink, feeling the indentation of where the pen met the paper and tried to picture him writing it out. His handwriting was almost as familiar to me as my own after all these years.

With shaky fingers, I opened the letter and pulled out two separate papers, each with a number on the outside. I unfolded the letter labeled with a number '1'. The text was almost illegible... It was clearly written in a hurry. I smiled as I read.

*Dear Ellie,*

*It's Wednesday, and I haven't slept since I woke up on Monday morning. I can honestly say this has been the strangest experience of my life. It's probably five or six at night right now, and I think we might get to sleep soon. I haven't been able to keep track of the time very well. These other recruits were getting yelled at all day for falling asleep. It's so weird not being able to call you and tell you about everything. It's weird not to be able to take a minute and do anything I want to do. There's been some funny stuff happening, but it's hard to remember everything right now since I haven't slept in two days. Hopefully, I remember and can tell you when I see you. Obviously, since I've mentioned sleep three times now, that's all I'm thinking about.*

*Just so you know, recruits are treated like the absolute stupidest, scummiest, filthiest beings on this planet. But I guess if we all have to go through it to call ourselves Marines, I'll do what I have to do. Each week is called something different based on what we're doing, and this week is called Receiving Week because we've just arrived and we're getting all our stuff. The real work starts on Black Friday. That's when we meet the DI's that will be with us for the rest of boot camp. All right, I'm passing out as I'm writing this, and I'm still not supposed to sleep yet. I hope you're doing well. (And you're not too bored without me.)*

*Be back soon,*

*Spence*

I sighed as I folded the letter along its creases. I took a calming breath and unfolded the next one. It was dated a week after the first one and wasn't as hastily scrawled. Maybe he'd settled in better by then. I took a breath before reading it, not ready to start it because then it would end.

*Dear Ellie,*

*I haven't had time to write in the last week. Receiving Week was crazy, but every day gets a little better than the last. One day closer... that's what I keep trying to remember, anyway. When we first met our DI's, I was in a rough place. One of them reminds me of Will Smith (in a cool way) though, so I just pretend I'm in a movie and this isn't really happening. Sometimes it doesn't feel like reality anyway.*

*I don't understand why they would issue us recruits so much nice stuff only to have it dumped on the floor and mixed with other people's stuff, then shoved in our footlockers, not giving us time to organize it for days. Then they expect us to pull it out in a second and we don't even know if we have it. I found my rack mate's stuff in my footlocker, and he found some of mine. Those are some of the mind games they play, but they say boot camp is 90% mental crap and 10% physical. Most of it leaves you wondering why you have to do it, or even why you made this decision in the first place. I think they're trying to beat the word 'why' out of us. Doesn't matter why... just do it. It's a weird feeling.*

*But anyway, I don't have much time to finish. I'm writing this during square-away time, and I still have a lot of stuff to do before I go to bed. Including shaving my* face, *which I am already sick of having to deal with every day. I'll write you again when I can. Tell your family I say hi.*

*Be back soon,*

*Spence*

I folded the second letter and put it back in the envelope with the first. I had no idea what to write back. He was going through this crazy culture shock, and I had just gotten home from a movie. I wondered if it would come off as bragging if

I told him about all the mundane things in my life, knowing he wished he could be doing stuff like that too. It all seemed so pointless compared to what he was going through.

I groaned out loud. What was wrong with me? I was second-guessing how to talk to Spencer—*my* Spencer—when he had always been the one person I didn't have to worry about that with. Why was I over-analyzing every little thing?

"Ellie?" Mom stood in the doorway that led to the kitchen, squinting into the night. "What are you doing out there?"

"Reading Spencer's letter. I'm not sure how to respond," I admitted, my shoulders sagging against the chains of the swing.

"Well," Mom began, crossing the porch and into the grass, "you and Spencer have always had an easy friendship. I don't see why things would be any different now."

"I don't know why, but I feel like it *is* different somehow. He's off serving our country, and I'm here, still doing the same things I always do."

Mom reached for my hand and gave it a quick squeeze. "You're living your life and he's living his. You're heading to great things too, you know. Starting your new job with your father next month is exciting."

"Yeah, I just wish he wasn't so bent on me going to law school. I'm not sure if that's the right path for me."

"That's why it's so great you get to work at the office with him while you decide. You can get exposure to law and decide from there."

I nodded. "I know. We'll see how it goes. I don't want either of you to get your hopes up."

Mom gave my shoulder a pat and stood from the swing. "Treat Spencer like nothing's changed. Talk about the things you normally would, like how annoying your parents are. He'll welcome some normalcy, I'm sure."

As I watched her walk away, I took a chance. "Mom?"

"Yes?" She turned and came closer.

"Spencer said something weird at the party before he left. That's why I thought things might be different between us."

My mom tilted her head. "What did he say?"

"That he didn't think Tim was good enough for me."

"Hmm." She could barely conceal her smile.

I raised a brow. "Hmm?"

"How did that make you feel?"

"Bad," I answered, not sure how else to describe it, or why she was smiling.

"Because you care about how he feels about your choices?"

I dug the toe of my boot into the dirt in front of me. "Yeah..."

"I'm sure he just wants to make sure you're happy while he's gone."

"Okay, but I've been with Tim for so long. Why pipe up about it now? What changed?"

My mom pursed her lips, seeming to choose her words carefully. "Maybe he was afraid your friendship wouldn't be the same after he left, so he wanted to make sure he told you how he felt about Tim while you two were still close."

I shook my head. "That won't happen. I'm not going to let this pull us apart. He's my best friend."

"Then you really need to relax, sweetheart. Be normal with him, don't create drama or pressure where there doesn't have to be any. You know Spencer's been through a lot. He's protective of you."

"I guess. Thanks, Mom." I gave her a small smile and looked away as she walked back into the house. My mom was right, I just needed to act normal with Spencer. But in the back of my mind, I couldn't help but think there was more to our changing friendship than I wanted to admit.

"Hey, how was last night?" Tim greeted me with a kiss.

"It was fine, just helped my mom." I felt guilty for lying to him again. I sat on a barstool at the counter and watched him help himself to a glass of soda and a bag of chips.

Tim brought his snack to the couch behind me and sat down, picking up the remote control. "Ready to watch some football?"

"Sure." I crossed the room to sit beside him, not sure what to say next. It would be weird if I apologized for the previous night again, so I settled on saying nothing at all.

"What time will your parents be home?" he asked.

I checked the clock. "She said right before dinner. Are you staying to eat?"

"Yeah. Do you have any salsa for these?" Tim asked, gesturing to the tortilla chips in his lap.

"I think so, want me to check?"

Tim shook his head. "I got it, babe. Here, you find the game."

I took the remote from him and surfed through the sports channels.

"You got a letter from Spencer?" Tim asked. He stood at the kitchen counter holding my letter.

I shrugged and continued flipping through the guide. I silently prayed he wouldn't ask when it arrived. I found the game we'd planned to watch and selected it, tossing the remote down on the couch next to me. I'd rather have done something else with my time than watching Tim's favorite football team play against another team I didn't care about. I only liked sports when my team was playing.

I glanced toward the kitchen and balked when I saw Tim unfolding one of the letters. There was nothing in it I wouldn't mind him knowing, but it still felt like an invasion of privacy for him to open it without asking. I jumped up from the couch and took the letter out of his hands.

"That's not very nice," Tim said, narrowing his eyes. "Do you have something to hide?"

"No," I answered. "I just don't know why you would read it before asking if you could. It's not addressed to you."

Tim raised a perfectly kempt brow. "Ellie, are you sure there isn't something I should know about you and

Spencer? Did something happen that night at Fiesta Island?"

I laughed without humor. "Spencer is my best friend. I care about him a lot, but I'm not the girl for him. He's not the guy for me. So, once again, there is *nothing* going on between us. And besides, I wouldn't cheat on you."

"Well, I can understand why he wouldn't be the guy for you."

I surprised myself with how defensive I felt at that moment. It was one thing for me to occasionally mock Spencer for his womanizing ways, but I didn't want anyone else doing it. "You know, Tim, green's not a very good look on you."

He cocked his head at me with a hint of challenge. "It's not jealousy. He's a tool. And he treats girls like objects he can just throw away when he's done with them."

"Spencer's complicated. You just don't know him like I do."

"Clearly, but none of that excuses how he treats girls."

"Those girls never get involved with him thinking they'll end up in a relationship. He tells them up front that he probably won't call them again."

Tim shook his head and laughed. "Yeah, he's a real prince. Look, all I'm saying is that I can see why he's not the right guy for you. You're looking for the type of guy who can give you a future and take care of you. As soon as I'm done with school, I'll be that guy for you. You deserve better than someone who runs off to join the military because they don't have the grades for college."

I felt heat rise to my cheeks as he took my hand,

rubbing his thumb over my knuckles, intending to soothe me. Who did he think he was? Telling—not asking—me about my future with him, all the while insulting someone I cared about very much. He made it seem like Spencer *couldn't* give me the life I wanted, but it was that Spencer wouldn't *want to.* He had always been clear about his feelings on marriage and being with one woman for the rest of his life. That didn't mean he wasn't as good of a guy as Tim, just that he wanted different things out of life.

"Look, Tim," I pulled my hand away and rested it on my hip. Realizing it probably looked a little too combative, I let it fall to my side with a huff. "First of all, I don't want a man to 'take care of me.' I'm planning on taking care of myself. I want a man who would support me no matter what I wind up doing. Second, Spencer's grades were perfectly fine. In fact, he scored in the top five percent on his placement exam for the military. He joined the Marines because he wanted to make a difference and fight for his country. I could do a lot worse than Spencer Hawkins."

Tim started to speak, but I held up my finger to shush him. "And last, this isn't a freaking love triangle where I have to choose between the vampire and the werewolf. He's my friend, and you're my boyfriend. But if you don't knock off this jealous act then you'll probably lose your title."

He looked fittingly abashed as he placed his hands on my shoulders. "You're right. I'm sorry. I don't know what kind of grades he got. But listen, let's stop talking about this, okay? I'll even write him a letter to thank him for what he's doing if that makes you feel better."

I wrinkled my nose. "It's fine. Don't bother. You wouldn't mean it anyway."

"Is this going to be an issue?"

"What, that you keep insulting my best friend?"

He nodded. "I'm sure you don't like all of my friends. I don't have to like yours."

I stared at him, not sure how to respond. "What now?"

"I don't know, maybe I should take off."

"Maybe." I shrugged.

"What do you want, Ellie? Do you even want to be with me anymore?"

I looked past him out the sliding glass door that led to the backyard. I could see the swing set. It looked lonely and forgotten, swings gently swaying in the breeze. It represented years of memories... and not just with Spencer, with other friends, too. But of course, I saw none of those friends when I looked at it. I only saw him. And he was gone, living the life he'd always wanted to live. I needed to do the same.

Tim cleared his throat. "Ellie?"

I shook my head to clear my thoughts. "You're right, let's stop talking about this."

"Okay... but you didn't answer my question."

I put my arms around his neck and sealed my lips over his. He used one hand to cup the side of my face, and I soon lost myself in the feel of his mouth on mine. He took control of the kiss and responded to my actions over words.

This wouldn't be the last time we'd fight about Spencer, since I would never stop defending him against Tim's insults. But at the end of the day, Spencer wasn't my boyfriend. We were on separate life paths. I needed to let go if I wanted peace in my relationship, and maybe I just wasn't destined to have an epic love story, after all. I let the letter from Spencer slip from my grasp and back onto the counter and tugged Tim over to the couch.

"C'mon," I said, grabbing the remote again, "let's watch that game."

## 4

## SPENCER

"Hawkins," the surly drill instructor called my name and threw a letter in my general direction. I followed the letter with my eyes as the recruit nearest to where it fell began passing it back to me. We were all sitting on the ground in our usual formation for mail call, cross-legged and eagerly awaiting word from our loved ones. The letter finally made its way to me. I smiled broadly when I saw that it was from Ellie. We weren't allowed to open the mail until every piece was passed out, so I fidgeted with the corners of the envelope as I waited. The DI called my name again, and when I got ahold of this one my eyebrows nearly flew off my forehead.

It was from my dad.

The DI dismissed us a few minutes later and I headed back to my rack to read my mail. I decided to read the letter from my dad first. It was only a few sentences, but somehow it meant more than he probably would ever know.

*Spencer,*

*How are you? Is it as hard as you thought it would be? Hope the food is better than when I was there.*

*Dad*

I shook my head as I stuffed the note back in the envelope and put it aside. I grabbed my notepad and pen, figuring it was best to just write him back now, so I didn't have to worry about it later. Yeah, it meant a lot for him to write me. It would be dumb for me to pretend that it didn't. But we still didn't talk much... so I wasn't sure how to write more than a couple of sentences in response.

*Dad,*

*I'm fine. It's not that hard. The food is probably just as bad.*

*Spencer*

With much more enthusiasm than when I opened my dad's letter, I moved on to Ellie's. Hers was considerably longer. My heart hammered in my chest as I saw her familiar handwriting on the page. Then I got a whiff of something distinctly feminine. I glanced around the room, seeing only the same smelly recruits I'd been with the whole time. Looking down at the paper, I wrinkled my nose and gave it a discreet whiff. It was *scented.*

*Dear Spence,*

*I read online that recruits can get messed with pretty bad if they get a letter with perfume on it, and just because I love you so much, I decided to test that theory. Let me know how that goes for you.*

*It sounds like this is going to be pretty crazy. I don't know when you're going to get this letter, but hopefully, you've adjusted pretty well by the time you do. That's absurd that they made you stay up for so long in the beginning. I would have been giggling like an idiot... you know how weird I get when I'm really tired! And yes, I agree that it's weird not being able to talk to you all the time. I'm going through sarcasm withdrawals!*

*By the way, Andi and Ashley both asked me why you weren't answering their calls. Did you forget to tell some girls about boot camp? I'm not your secretary!*

*Have you heard from your dad? I gave him your address. Actually, he was the one who called me asking for it. I wonder if he regrets being gone the whole weekend before you left. My family says 'hi' back and hopes you're doing well. My mom asked if she could send you some cookies, so I told her I'd ask you. If it will have a similar effect of perfume on a letter, I'm all for it.*

*In response to your question, nothing new is happening over here. Tim and I are doing fine, as usual. He's leaving for Sacramento soon, so I guess we'll be doing the long-distance thing. I'm not gonna lie... I'm not looking forward to it. I feel like I probably won't be good at maintaining a relationship like that, but I guess we'll see. At least I'm getting practice writing letters to you, so thanks for that.*

*Come back soon,*

*Ellie*

"Is that a letter from your girl?" A voice from behind me made me jump. I looked over to see my rack mate looking at me from where he sat on the floor, leaning against his footlocker.

"No, just a friend."

"Smells like more than just a friend."

I widened my eyes, hoping the letter didn't attract too much attention in case what Ellie said was true. "You can smell it from there?"

Mills grinned. "Yeah, and it smells like it came from a girlfriend."

I rolled my eyes. "Shut it. She's not. Did you get a letter from your girl?"

"Yes, thank God. I was starting to think she already forgot about me. The drill instructors keep telling me that some other dude is back home keeping her company while I'm here."

"I wouldn't be surprised. I've seen the Vienna sausage in your pants. It's sad. That poor girl needs to move on."

Mills glared in mock fury and turned back to his letter without another word. I picked up my notepad and pen to write Ellie back. I hesitated for a moment, trying to figure out how to start. I settled on keeping it light, even though hearing from her was the best thing that had happened to me since I'd gotten there. It was strange how disconnected from reality I felt, and I welcomed every mundane detail from the outside world.

*Ellie,*

*Your attempt at sabotage with the perfume didn't work at all. It was just awesome to smell something other than these nasty recruits. Nice try though. You can send whatever food you want, as long as it's healthy. The other catch is that you have to buy enough for the entire platoon, or they won't let me have any. There are eighty guys in my platoon, so have at it.*

*One dude got a huge box of granola bars and Gatorade packets from his mom, so we all got to have that.*

*Tell Andi and Ashley (and anyone else who asks) that I died. That way, when I come back from the dead, they'll be super impressed. Speaking of my phone, will you bring it to graduation with you? It's in my nightstand.*

*Of course you and Tim are fine. You're always fine. Dump him, E. He's not right for you and you know it. He's like the evil character that infiltrates the sunny neighborhood in 'Leave it to Beaver'.*

*All right, I'm gonna go. I'll be expecting a big box of civilian food before the week is out.*

*Be back soon,*

*Spence.*

*P.S. Thank you for writing me. You have no idea how good it was to hear from you.*

I put away my writing materials with a sigh. I re-read the part of my letter about Tim and wondered if I should scratch it out. I really didn't like that guy. I meant every word I said to her that night at Fiesta Island. Just because I wasn't right for her didn't mean she should be with just anybody. My new (and so far, pretty well-suppressed) feelings for her had nothing to do with it. Tim didn't care about Ellie. He wanted a hot trophy wife lined up for when he was a doctor. If he wasn't already cheating on her, he probably would in the future.

No matter how I felt about Ellie, I refused to make something more than friends out of our relationship. We wanted different things, and our friendship meant too much for me to start something with her and then leave her behind. I couldn't offer her the stability she deserved, so it wasn't just jealousy that made me want her to break things off with Tim. She could do better.

I looked back over at Mills. "Are you still pouting?"

"No, I'm over it. You only make jokes like that to make yourself feel better." Mills grinned at me.

"You're right," I conceded jokingly.

Staff Sergeant Ferguson, our senior drill instructor, entered the squad bay and loudly announced that we were to commence field day. Mills and I went to the whiskey locker to grab our rags. Each week we had a day where we cleaned the squad bay from top to bottom, including raking the rocks outside.

"I really hate that they refer to cleaning as 'field day.' When I was a kid, 'field day' was the best day of the school year." Mills said, wiping the windowsill with the dry rag.

I snorted. "We're only three weeks in, bro. Think positive."

"It's not that easy," he replied. "Olivia is pretty good about staying positive in her letters, but I know this sucks for her. I'll make it up to her with a big fat ring when we get out of this hellhole."

"Wait. Are you proposing on boot leave?" I stuttered, absolutely stunned.

Mills smiled like a fool. "Not on boot leave, at graduation. My mom picked the ring up and I'm gonna pay her back for it. I'm gonna ask Olivia if she wants to go see a judge over Christmas if I get to come home, that way everything'll be squared away before I get stationed somewhere and she can come with me."

"Duuuuuude," I drew out the word. "We're only eighteen."

"Yeah, so what?"

I grunted. "You're crazy, that's all."

"Hey, man. We've been together for five years now. Plus, I want her to come with me wherever I go. She can only do that if we're married. And, you know, I love her."

"You don't have to plead your case to me, Mills. It's none of my business. All I know is, I'm never getting married." I resumed wiping the window I had been neglecting.

I took a few glances over my shoulder to make sure a DI wasn't in the room to slay me for talking. I couldn't believe Mills was getting married at eighteen. Not to mention the fact that he was planning on ripping that poor girl away from her family and everything she knows to follow him around wherever they send him. Who knows, maybe his girl is excited by the unknown. Ellie would never go for something like that. Life in the military was the opposite of stable. She'd be packing up her white-picket-fence life every three years or so.

"You say you're never getting married now, but when the right girl comes around, you'll feel differently," Mills said.

I snorted. "Wrong."

"I'm serious. You don't know what you don't know."

The problem was, I did know. There couldn't be anyone more 'right' than the girl I was purposely steering clear of. "I'll take your word for it, man."

Mills rolled his eyes in response, not bothering to

comment further.

We worked in silence for a few moments, both of us cleaning the same places over and over again to make sure it looked like we were working hard. I peered around the room and noticed that none of the DI's were there. I dropped the rag and stretched each of my arms across my body. I was sore, but I was no stranger to aching muscles. I had worked out with the Marines at the recruiting office for almost a year before I stepped foot in this place, so I knew what to expect from boot camp as far as the physical stuff went. I was glad I'd spent so much time training before I left, or else I'd probably be struggling.

I stooped to pick up the rag again and resumed cleaning the already spotless window. I peered at Mills, who was still working on the same windowpane as when we first started. I glanced around the room. The rest of the platoon seemed to be working hard though, poor bastards.

The door at the end of the squad bay slammed open so hard I bet it left a dent in the wall behind it. Three DIs charged in, screaming their heads off. We dropped our rags and ran to the end of our bunks, falling in line with the rest of the recruits. We had no idea what had set them off—maybe nothing did. I imagined they all stood outside in their little huddles and planned random attacks on us just for fun.

"You call this a field day?" The kill hat, or DI in charge of discipline, asked no one in particular.

"Yes, sir!" we replied.

"This room is already spotless! Let me see you clean

up a dirty room."

And with that, we spent the next two hours destroying our squad bay. We tossed the contents of our footlockers, unmade our racks, and flipped our bunk beds upside down. Then we TP'd the whole place better than any high school prankster could even imagine. After creating a war zone out of our sleeping quarters, the kill hat started a timer for thirty minutes and told us to make it shine. Thank God there were eighty of us.

"So," Mills started during our square-away time the next day.

"So, what?"

"So, who was the 'friend' with the smelly letter?" He used his fingers to make the universal sign for quotations.

I let my shoulders droop in defeat. "That was Ellie."

Mills wagged his eyebrows. "What's the story with Ellie?"

"There is no story. Like I keep saying, she's just a *friend.*"

He laughed. "You seem like the kind of guy who has a lot of girls who are just 'friends.' So, fine, I'll drop it."

"What do you mean by that?" I mocked his finger quotations.

"Nothing, I just know you don't do the relationship thing. So she must just be another girl, right?"

I nodded in understanding. I didn't like the way my life sounded coming from Mills. It sounded... cheap. I knew he probably had a different view because of his relationship with Olivia, but my habits with girls still sounded worse when he put it that way. I could be vain and shallow, but I never pretended to be anything other than who I was. Still, I felt the need to defend myself. And Ellie, since she was definitely *not* just another girl in the way he meant it.

Just as I started to say something about it, our senior DI entered the squad bay. We weren't technically doing anything wrong because they allowed socializing during square-away time. It was the only time in our long day when we could do whatever we wanted. Well, almost whatever we wanted. It was in the recruit training order for us to get an hour a day to decompress. I nudged Mills and tilted my head towards the DI. We watched him carefully, both ready to hop up and look productive if he headed to our end of the huge room. A few minutes later, the DI left the squad bay and let the door slam on his way out.

"Listen, Mills." I kept my voice low. "Ellie is just a friend, and she always will be. I'm not in the market for a girlfriend, and Ellie wants a legit boyfriend who will eventually marry her and settle down with her. I don't want that, and I don't pretend to. When I hang out with a girl, she knows what she's getting herself into, unlike Olivia, who probably thinks all of this crap is romantic but doesn't realize she'll be alone more often than either of you think."

Mills recoiled, the hurt plain on his face.

I hung my head and squeezed my eyes shut, taking a

beat before I faced him again. "I'm sorry, that was messed up. I shouldn't have said that."

Mills narrowed his eyes at me. "Yeah, no kidding."

"I've got some stuff. Like, past stuff. It's not personal towards you."

He shrugged. "We all do."

"Look, my dad did twenty in the Marines. I was born when he'd been in for like five years or something. He was gone on deployment a lot when I was little. I remember him telling my mom all the time that things would be different after he got out, but she always just said she was happy with the way things were. Then she got cancer."

Mills cringed.

"Yeah."

"How old were you?" he asked.

"Thirteen. And instead of getting out right then, he had to put in the full twenty. I don't know, retirement or insurance or whatever. Maybe just because he wanted to. They let him stay back from a deployment once because she was sick... but he missed a lot of her good years."

Mills' eyes softened. "I'm sorry, Hawk. That had to suck."

"It did. But I shouldn't have said that stuff to you. It's just that I watched my mom struggle like a single parent and move around all the time, and I would never do that to a girl I cared about."

"Yeah," Mills allowed, "but Olivia's dad was a colonel in the Air Force. She grew up in this life just like you did, except she liked it. I've heard so many stories of cool things they got to do because of the military. If she's willing to put up with this situation to be with me, I'm all in. And it's pretty messed up for you to act like I'm doing something bad to her."

"You're right. I'm sure you and Olivia will be happy, Mills."

"I'm gonna go hit the head," he said with a nod, walking to the bathroom without another word.

The next day, we stood in the chow line after a brutal morning of physical training. The drill instructors stood in a huddle a safe distance away from us, so I risked whispering to Mills in front of me. I figured now was just as good a time as any since we wouldn't be able to say much before we got blasted for talking.

"Hey, sorry again about yesterday."

Mills whispered back without moving his head, and I could barely make out the words. "It's fine."

"I'm just a little on edge," I whispered.

"We all are, bro. Now shut up before they hear you."

I glanced at the imposing men with their campaign covers and green cammies with their sleeves rolled tightly around their biceps. The campaign cover was the 'Smokey the Bear' hat worn by drill instructors, and I thought it definitely added to their look of authority. I peeked down at my boots, annoyed instantly by the fact that my cammie pants were hanging down over the laces. It wasn't until the initial drill competition that we could use boot bands to roll our pants up to where they should be at the top of our boots. We looked like idiots, but I supposed that was exactly the point.

The back of Mills' head had become very familiar to me. I still felt bad for jumping down his throat the day before, but I was glad we'd worked it out since we'd just found out we were heading to the same job school after boot camp. We were both going to be aviation ordnance technicians. In short, we got to load bombs on some type of aircraft or build the bombs that someone else would load. We'd find out later what the aircraft would be and whether we'd be turning wrenches out on the flight line or fixing parts in a hangar. I'd hoped for the flight line, but Mills wanted I-Level, which meant the hangar.

After standing in line for what seemed like forever, we marched into the cool air of the chow hall. Sweaty recruits rushed through their meals at large circular tables. I scanned the room and blew out a breath. I absolutely couldn't wait for graduation.

I stared out at the field in front of me, squinting through the smoke. Gunfire rang in my ears and I could barely hear myself think. We were six hours into the fifty-four-hour hell that was The Crucible. Recruits screamed in fake-agony all around me, pretending to have been wounded in combat and needing rescue. Their screams would be comical if it weren't for the sound of the machine guns. Machine gun fire and heavy smoke made the screams seem real to my frazzled brain.

The guy in front of me slung his rifle over his shoulder and stooped to pick up one of the injured recruits. He hoisted him over his shoulders and took off down the field. About five beats later, another recruit jumped in front of me and sprawled out like he was dying. Like the guy before me, I repositioned my rifle and hunched down to lift the fake-dying recruit into a fireman's carry.

I launched forward into the field, the recruit on my shoulders screaming the whole way. I tried to be conscious of every step I took, dodging squares of barbed wire so I didn't trip and hurt the guy for real. Sweat poured from under my Kevlar helmet and into my eyes, but I couldn't swipe it away without breaking my hold on my partner. I shook my head as much as I could to send the sweat beads flying. *Almost there. Just a few more feet.*

At the end of the field, the recruits ahead of me were stretching and drinking water, waiting for our group to finish. By the time my group made it to the end, my legs were about to give way under the weight of the recruit on my shoulders. I heaved him off and ran a dirty hand over my face and tried to wipe away the sweat. The exercise was over, and it was time for a much needed fifteen-minute break before our next event. I pulled out my first of three MRE's, or Meals-Ready-to-Eat and sat down with the rest of my platoon to break into it. We were only getting three meals over the course of the three days and were told to ration them ourselves.

We all dumped the contents of the thick plastic bag into the dirt in front of us, too exhausted to care that it wasn't a table and there were no plates. The meal was broken up and separated into several brown pouches and plastic bags.

"Hey," Mills scooted over to me. "What'd you get?"

I picked up the largest brown pouch with the main course inside and squinted to read the tiny print. "Cheese tortellini in tomato sauce. You?"

Mills grinned. "Chili mac. I heard it's the best one."

"It is." One of our DI's said, startling us. He'd been sitting next to us with an MRE of his own. The DI's had been showing us their normal human side on The Crucible so far, and it was hard to get used to. I didn't even know they had normal speaking voices. I thought they just screamed or glared to communicate. Who knew.

I turned back to my meal, knowing the time was ticking and we only had a few minutes before we hiked to the next event. There was another pouch with mixed fruit, an apple-cinnamon energy bar, peanut M&M's (much to my excitement), dry crackers, peanut butter, orange electrolyte powder, pepper sauce, a plastic spoon, and the Flameless Ration Heater, or FRH.

We'd been told ahead of time that we wouldn't be allowed to use the FRH to heat our meals while we were on The Crucible. That was a luxury meant for leisurely trips to the field, not a combat simulation. I tucked the heater back into the bag, along with the main course. I had too much adrenaline to eat something so heavy. I didn't want to throw it up on the hike.

"I'm just gonna go with the fruit and energy bar," I told Mills.

"I have jalapeño cheese spread for my crackers, I'm gonna do that and the grape drink."

"Ah," I lamented, picking up another pouch from my pile. "Mine's peanut butter."

"Sucks to suck," Mills replied, grinning and pouring the cheese sauce on one of the crackers. They were basically four Saltine crackers attached to make one bigger square. Peanut butter or cheese sauce, at least they included something to make them taste less like cardboard.

We finished the rest of our snack in silence, packed the rest of the MRE's back up, and got into formation as instructed. I didn't know how many miles we'd already marched since beginning The Crucible earlier in the day, but I knew we'd do a total of about forty-five by the end of the three days.

We started the short hike to the next event, and as one of the DI's passed me on the left, I noticed his pack bouncing a little more than it should if it weighed as much as ours did. I wondered if they got to stuff them with pillows or something. The weight of my pack, sleeping roll, and rifle suddenly felt twice as heavy.

When we got to the next warrior station, we crowded around the post with the information about the event. Before each event, we sat and listened to our DI's tell us about the purpose of the exercise and what they wanted us to learn. Each event was named after a deserving Marine and the challenge was similar to what the Marine went through.

"This warrior station is dedicated to Corporal Larry D.

Harris, Jr.," our senior DI began when we were all seated in the dirt in a semi-circle around him.

Staff Sergeant Ferguson proceeded to read the Citation posted on the sign, which told the story of Corporal Harris. He'd served in 2010 during Operation Enduring Freedom. They'd been on deployment in Helmand Province, Afghanistan when the enemy engaged them while out on patrol. Not only did Corporal Harris lead his team to safety and join them in firing upon the enemy, but he also saved his machine gunner's life when he was shot in the leg. With no regard for his own safety, he carried the wounded machine gunner to the medical evacuation site, continuously evading enemy fire. Corporal Harris sustained fatal wounds when he struck an improvised explosive device, or IED. He was posthumously awarded the Silver Star for his bravery.

I swallowed past the lump in my throat as Staff Sergeant Ferguson explained to us that the IED course we were about to complete would be our first encounters with the kinds of blasts we might experience while in combat. It felt real. I knew it wasn't, I knew the blasts would be simulated, but every event is designed to feel as real as possible so they can properly prepare us. The gravity of what it meant to be a Marine had been hitting me more during The Crucible than any other time in recruit training so far.

"Okay, recruits, listen up," Staff Sergeant continued. "The course itself is a trail that we will walk in combat patrol formation. Along the side of the trail will be objects. There will be a number of practice IED's throughout the trail. It's just smoke and noise, but make no mistake, an explosion right next to you isn't fun. We'll tell you how to identify them before we go. You'll use arm signals to let everyone know if you've found one, and if it explodes on you, everyone close to it needs to lie down and wait to be rescued. This is where we'll simulate Corporal Harris' bravery. Good to go?"

"Yes, sir," we sounded off.

When we had our instructions on what to look for, we set off on the trail. I held my rifle at the ready, scanning my surroundings for any sign of the enemy. My mind cycled back and forth between remembering it was all just a game and getting lost in the wartime environment. I studied the ground to my right, looking for signs of an IED. Without warning, an explosion sounded right next to me. In that instant, my heart stopped beating. I flinched away from the sound, expecting to be lifted off the ground and thrown to the dirt. I blinked, my mind not registering my surroundings. *Am I dead*? I blinked again, and someone chuckled. Nothing had happened. The bomb was fake. There was no blast or dirt or shrapnel. Just a speaker behind a bush. I swallowed past the lump in my throat, saying a silent prayer of gratitude that I hadn't peed my pants or anything embarrassing like that.

"You're dead," Sergeant Ramos tapped me and three others near me and gestured for us to get on the ground. He paused and looked at a few others who weren't as close to the blast. "Get down and scream in pain, you're not dead but you're hurt."

I got down and played dead like I was told. If I was

being honest, it felt like heaven to lie down in the warm dirt and rest my eyes for a bit. I tried not to think about how scared I'd been in the brief moment between the explosion and me realizing it was a fake. If this were real, I'd be dead. Boom, that's it. Lights out. My heart started racing and I pushed away all of those thoughts. This wasn't real, and I probably wouldn't see action like this when I was finally a Marine. My job was in the Air Wing. Air Wingers didn't patrol in Afghanistan. As far as I knew.

Part of the simulation was that the explosion alerted the enemy to our position, so the rest of my team had to recover us casualties while avoiding getting shot. I couldn't tell what was happening around me with the gunfire and my eyes closed, but when someone grabbed me and dragged me through the dirt, I kept my eyes closed and stayed limp like I was dead. The only thing I could focus on was the feeling of the dirt pouring into my pants as he dragged me along.

The next twenty-some-odd hours were brutal as we moved from station to station, learning about Marines who sacrificed it all and carrying out exercises designed to simulate their bravery. We continued rationing our little food on our short breaks, my feet were blistered probably bleeding, though I didn't take off my boots to check. My lungs burned from exertion, as trained as I thought they were from the rest of boot camp. My muscles felt like jelly, and I was sore down to my very bones. I thought I might have sprained my ankle at one point, which would have meant getting held back. The sheer terror of that possibility had me ready to cry like a little baby. But I didn't, because I was tough. But I prayed harder than I ever had to just make it through without getting kicked back. I never wanted to go through this again.

The last event before our final test was a warrior station called Dunham's Defense, in which we grappled and used hand-to-hand combat to overcome the enemy. It was dedicated to Corporal Jason Dunham, who lost his life in 2004 when he fought his opponent and threw himself on a grenade to save his fellow Marines. The heaviness of these exercises was not lost on me, and I knew I wasn't alone. As I looked at the faces of my fellow recruits, I knew we were all being enveloped into the brotherhood of the Marine Corps, one warrior station at a time.

"Some hill," Mills said as we stared at the seven hundred foot mountain in front of us.

I nodded, taking a drink from my canteen. I was too tired to speak, too emotionally spent. We'd just completed a nine-mile hike and were taking a water break before we scaled The Reaper. At the top, we'd get another water break, then take a short three-mile hike to the parade deck where we'd finally get our eagle, globe, and anchor emblem. It would be the moment we'd finally get to call ourselves Marines. It would make all of this worth it. But we had to earn our place. And that mountain was so steep, I wanted to throw up just looking at it. This experience had been a far cry from the rest of recruit training. I thought I was tough with everything we did there. Not here. Here, I was fighting for my life.

It was time to scale the beast. Mills and I formed up

without another word and braced ourselves for the climb of our lives. My pack had gotten heavier as the hours wore on. I climbed at such a steep angle that I could reach out and touch the ground in front of me without bending over. It took all of my strength not to let it pull me back towards all of the other recruits behind me.

I focused on thinking about what we'd already accomplished in the last couple of days. We'd done log lifts and rope courses. We'd low crawled through the mud under a net of barbed wire. We'd used teamwork to get ammo cans up one ladder and then down the other side. We'd crossed pits of water on boards while under enemy fire. We'd had to concentrate on saving each other's lives while getting blasted by simulated machine gun fire the entire time. After all of that, this hill and a brief hike were the last things standing between me and calling myself a Marine.

One of the guys in front of me started to slip. His feet kept losing traction and my steps stuttered a few times to keep from running into him. I looked at the guy to my right, Harris. He noticed it, too. I knew I wouldn't be able to catch him if he fell back on me at that point, the hill was too steep and I was too tired. Harris nodded at me and we both shifted so that the guy in front was between us. Harris and I each grabbed a strap on the side of his pack and lifted it slightly, lightening his load. His steps grew steadier as we helped him. None of us spoke, just continued up the hill as inconspicuously as possible. I knew more than ever about the power of teamwork.

After hours that felt like days, we finally made it near

the top. As each recruit exploded onto the flat earth at the top of The Reaper, they whooped and hollered and jumped with more energy than they probably knew they had left. We could hear them celebrating as we got closer, so our steps automatically became more urgent. Ascending the ridge of that monster of a hill was one of the greatest feelings I'd ever had in my life. I shouted and cheered with the rest of my platoon. We all looked like zombies, once dead and now very much alive... and hungry.

We had a few guys who passed out or fell out of formation on the way up, so once the rest of the DI's helped them to the top, we were ordered into formation. We counted off to make sure we were all present and accounted for. Our senior DI reported that we were all there. Then we made our way down what appeared to be the flat side of the mountain toward the parade deck.

Three miles had never felt so quick, and once we arrived on the blacktop, we broke off one platoon at a time to hear a motivational speech from our company commander. When all of the platoons of Echo Company had been properly congratulated, our DIs went from Marine to Marine, handing out our eagle, globe, and anchor emblems.

I thought I was strong walking into boot camp thirteen weeks ago. I was wrong. After what I'd learned, what I'd powered through, I felt like a completely different person. Now, I was strong. But strong or not, when Staff Sergeant Ferguson put that EGA in my hand and called me a Marine, I cried right along with the rest of my platoon.

## 5

## ELLIE

After a long, nerve-calming shower, I wrapped myself in a towel and headed to my closet. I flipped through the rack of clothes, then grabbed my phone off the desk and opened my weather app to check for rain. It was the last week of October, so it would be clear and sunny with a high of seventy degrees. I tossed my phone on my bed and went back to the closet, grabbing my favorite skinny jeans from the top shelf and a brown long-sleeved shirt off its hanger.

Tossing the clothes on my bed, I went back into the bathroom to blow dry my hair. I was impressed with myself for not agonizing over what to wear. Normally, I went back and forth between several outfits before finally deciding on one. Maybe it was because I was so comfortable with Spencer. I never felt self-conscious with him, and he always expected me to be myself. I flipped my head over to blow the underside of my long blonde tresses, and when I righted myself, I saw a girl with bright, happy eyes staring back at me from the mirror.

I checked the time. Oops. I'd spent almost twice the usual amount of time on my make-up. No big deal, I was probably just distracted or something. I dressed quickly and pulled out a pair of socks and brown boots. Being able to wear boots made fall one of my favorite seasons, and I loved to shop the sales for more pairs than necessary. This compulsion of mine had Spencer laughing every time I told him about a new pair. Did I really need them? Of course not. Did he really need the fifty million shirts hanging in his own closet? I very much doubted it. Everywhere we went, he bought a new shirt, so I rarely saw him in the same shirt too frequently. I made a mental note to buy him a USMC T-shirt at the gift shop on base.

When I was ready, I used my laptop to look up the directions to the Recruit Depot. They had a section on their website for Family Day, so I clicked the link. The page outlined what I should bring, what I should expect, and how to get there. According to the site, there was a breakfast buffet for the families, but we wouldn't get to see the new Marines until later. I bit my lip and wondered if I should even bother going to that since I was going alone.

According to the timeline of events on the website, the first time I'd get to see Spencer was during the Moto Run. I grinned. There was a picture on the site showing new Marines in tiny green shorts and green shirts running in formation, their families lined up along the track. After that, apparently the Marines would go change for the ceremony and the families would have some time to kill before they released them for liberty, or as the website explained, time off.

I opened my desk drawer and took out Spencer's most recent letter. In it, he'd had told me to be on the lookout for his buddy Mills' girlfriend, Olivia. Spencer had said Mills was planning on proposing to her that very day, and I could tell by the tone of his letter that Spencer thought the guy was a complete moron. I, on the other hand, thought it was adorable. I fully intended to be there to witness the romance of it all. Yes, eighteen was a little young to be married, but who was I to judge?

I continued perusing through the webpage, trying to see if there was anything else that I needed to know before I got there. I learned they wouldn't have to be back at the barracks for another six hours after they were released for liberty. Spencer had already told me he wouldn't be able to leave the base on Family Day, but I figured it would still be fun to hang out and explore the base with him.

I closed the lid on my laptop and leaned back in my desk chair. My workspace faced a large window with an unobstructed view of the ocean. My parents had chosen their house in La Jolla specifically because of this view, and I loved it. There was nothing more peaceful than the rolling waves of the ocean. Someday, I wanted a view of the ocean just like this one. I'd have a big bay window in my bedroom where I would sit and read books.

Before I could get lost in the view and my own imagination, I glanced at the clock on my bedside table. Time to go. I wondered idly if Spencer would be any different. He always seemed like the same guy I knew so well in the letters he wrote me. He wrote about so many new experiences, but his tone was always just the way I expected it to be. Would he think I was different? After months without him, I felt like I was.

When I hit the off-ramp that led to the front gate of the base, traffic came to an absolute standstill. My little white coupe was sandwiched between two very large SUVs, and I couldn't see anything in front of or behind me. After sitting in the exact same place for over twenty minutes, I opened the car door to see what was going on.

As I peered around the SUV in front of me, I saw that every car in the line was going on base. I got back in the car with a huff and settled in for a long wait, switching the radio to the country channel. I tried to pass the time by singing along with my favorite songs, but when I didn't move more than ten feet in thirty minutes, I put the car in park and got out again. Some people had pulled out of the line of cars and parked in a dirt lot under the freeway. It looked sketchy, but I had already missed the breakfast for the families and was getting dangerously close to missing the Moto Run, too, if I didn't hurry. I ducked back behind the wheel and followed another car over to the lot.

After parking, I checked my reflection in my visor mirror, gathered what I needed to get on base, and slung my purse over my shoulder. I locked the car and hurried to the front gate. There were a few families walking with me from the dirt lot, so I didn't feel bad about avoiding the long line of cars. I made my way up to the Marine checking I.D.s and then followed the horde of people wherever they were going. A lot of families had made T-shirts with their Marine's name and platoon number on the back. I spotted a group wearing yellow shirts printed with Spencer's platoon, 2109, and fell in step behind them.

My phone vibrated in my pocket. I pulled it out and saw it was a text from an unfamiliar number, so I swiped to open it.

Olivia: *Hey! This is Olivia, Matt's girlfriend. Matt told me you were the only one coming for Hawk, and he wanted me to find you and invite you to sit with us. :)*

I cocked an eyebrow at the reference to Spencer as 'Hawk.' His dad had gotten that nickname in the Marines, but I hadn't realized Spencer had gotten it, too. It didn't surprise me that he hadn't mentioned it, given the connection to his dad.

Another text came in from the same number before I had a chance to respond to the first one.

Olivia: *Sorry, I just realized you probably don't know my BF as Matt. His last name is Mills. I don't know Hawks' first name either! :)*

I smiled. Olivia seemed friendly. I typed up my response as I continued following the other family members of Platoon 2109.

Me: *Hi, thanks for the invite! I'm walking up now, where should I meet you? His first name is Spencer, BTW.*

Olivia responded with her location and I looked

around, trying to see any signs that would point me to the Command Museum. I saw one up ahead and veered around the family I had been stalking. Now that I had a destination, they were walking way too slow for my liking.

After what seemed like a mile, I finally passed under an arch that led to the courtyard of the museum. I looked around for a family that had a girl my age and cringed when I realized almost every group had a girl my age. Like Olivia, they were probably all eager to see their boyfriends after months apart. Just as I was about to get discouraged, I felt a hand tap my shoulder.

"You must be Ellie," a small brunette squealed, pulling me in for a hug. She looked beautiful in a long, flowery maxi dress. The deep purples and bright yellows of the design looked great with her olive complexion. Not to mention she was practically glowing. This was a girl in love, no doubt about it.

"Yeah, how did you know?" I returned the hug and smiled at the girl's tenacity.

Olivia released me and stood back. "Well, Matt told me you were blonde, and if you haven't noticed, you're the only one wandering around by yourself."

I glanced around, confirming I stood out from the girlfriends and families surrounding us. "Good point. It's nice to meet you. Thanks again for inviting me to sit with your family."

"Oh, this is actually Matt's family. Come on, I'll introduce you." The bouncy brunette headed over to a group of people all wearing matching shirts with Matt's name and their platoon number on it. I watched her skip happily over to them, remembering that little did she know, they would soon be her family, too.

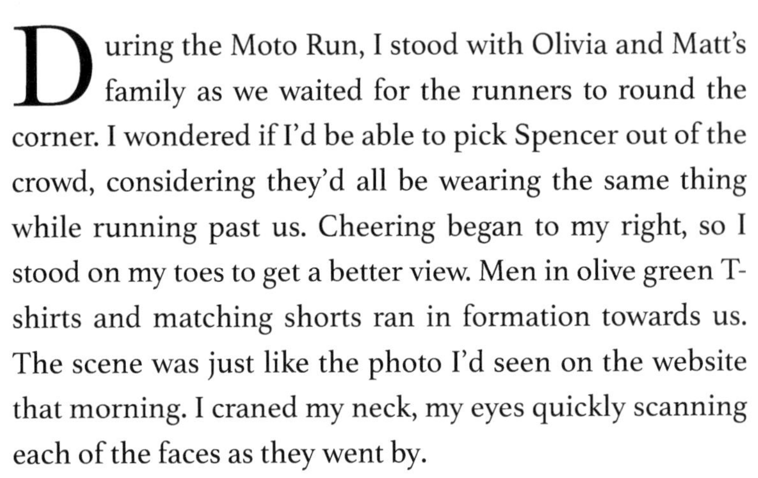

During the Moto Run, I stood with Olivia and Matt's family as we waited for the runners to round the corner. I wondered if I'd be able to pick Spencer out of the crowd, considering they'd all be wearing the same thing while running past us. Cheering began to my right, so I stood on my toes to get a better view. Men in olive green T-shirts and matching shorts ran in formation towards us. The scene was just like the photo I'd seen on the website that morning. I craned my neck, my eyes quickly scanning each of the faces as they went by.

Right in the group's middle, I spotted a familiar face. Spencer kept his eyes straight ahead; as they all did. He looked skinnier than when I had seen him last, and maybe a little taller, but other than that he looked the same. My stomach flipped at the sight of him and a wild grin spread across my face. I cheered and waved with the crowd of excited family members. Spencer's blue eyes shifted in my direction, and I could tell by the barely-there quirk of his mouth that he had seen me. It was brief, *so brief*, but it rocked me.

"Did you see him?" Olivia asked excitedly, pulling me out of my daze.

I nodded, smiling at the happy tears in the girl's eyes. My own eyes stung, ready to well up as emotions snaked through me. I clenched my hands, realizing they shook slightly. I turned back toward the Marines as they rounded another corner and disappeared behind the yellow buildings of the museum. Seeing him again shouldn't have felt so intense. Every time I'd pictured that moment over the last three months, it was happy. I was afraid of the raw emotion and turmoil swirling around inside me. It honestly made me want to run away. Or run after him. I couldn't tell which.

"Okay," Olivia said, wiping the underside of her eyes to make sure none of her mascara had run. "That was crazy. I only saw him for like, a second, but here I am crying like a baby."

I buried my own feelings and smiled at her, linking my arm through hers as we followed the crowd back to the Command Museum. It would take time for the Marines to finish the run and then go shower and change, so they'd told us to explore the museum and gift shop. You could feel the pride and excitement rolling off the crowd of families. I'd never experienced anything like it in my life. Maybe it was just the atmosphere of the day (or Olivia's feelings rubbing off on me) that made me react that way to seeing Spencer. It didn't mean anything more.

I focused on Olivia and Matt. They were the love story of the day. "I can tell you love him a whole lot. How long have you guys been together?"

"About five years. We started dating the summer before high school. He's such a great guy."

"I've heard a lot about him. Spencer's glad they have the same job, so they'll get to be in more training together after this."

Olivia smiled. "Yeah, Matt said the same thing. I'm glad he found a friend. I could tell by his letters he was really homesick, but it seemed like Spencer helped him out a lot. You've got a good friend there."

"Yeah," I agreed. "I really do."

When we reached the courtyard outside of the Command Museum, everyone split up. Some families went into the museum itself, others went to the gift shop, and some just milled around the courtyard and hung out. I realized again how strange it felt to be there alone. Spencer didn't have any family outside of his dad and my parents, who would all be at the actual graduation. It bugged me that I was the only one there for him on Family Day.

Matt's family was huge. His girlfriend, parents, three sisters with their spouses and kids, and even two cousins all came out to see him graduate. I guessed it was because they all lived right there in San Diego, so it was easy to come out and support him. Most of these families had to travel to attend the event. I'd read on the website that morning that the Marine Corps used the Mississippi River to determine which boot camp location you'd attend. If you lived west of the Mississippi, you went to MCRD San Diego. Everyone east of the Mississippi went to MCRD Parris Island in South Carolina.

Olivia and two of Matt's sisters talked and laughed as the rest of the family made plans to get dinner later. I didn't want to impose on their family time, so I motioned to Olivia, signaling I'd be in the museum. She nodded and waved, then went back to her conversation with her future sisters-in-law.

Just inside the museum, there was a sign that read, "USMC: Providing the enemies of America an opportunity to die for their countries since 1775." I chuckled. *Savage.* Continuing into the room, there were old photos of the Recruit Depot in years past. They had set up rooms with mannequins representing drill instructors and recruits so you could see what their daily life was life. I passed by an exhibit showcasing their sleeping quarters, which was called the squad bay. It had a metal-framed bunk bed with two-foot lockers at the end, and not much else. They'd definitely been living in what I imagined was a little bit homier than jail would be.

I was in awe as I made my way through all the exhibits. They re-enacted fighting holes, the shooting range, and the armory, which held all the different weapons they were trained to use. A lot of exhibits were about the history of the Marine Corps, which led to the sense that these guys were part of something much bigger than themselves. It was hundreds of years of tradition and sacrifice. It was blood, sweat, and tears over many generations of Americans. I had goosebumps just thinking about how amazing it was that Spencer was part of this now. I'd never belonged to anything so important in my life. I probably never would, along with the vast majority of our country. Only one percent of the population could call themselves Marines, according to one of the plaques on the wall. And once you earned the right to call yourself a Marine, you were *always* a Marine.

I checked my phone to see what time it was and made a face. I'd been immersed in Marine Corps history for too long and it was time to go sit on the bleachers so the Marines could be released for liberty. Making my way back out into the sunlight, I almost ran right into Olivia as she was heading into the building.

"Oops," she laughed. "I was just coming in to find you. We gotta go get seats," she said, grabbing my arm and urging me to catch up.

"Can't wait! Have you been in there, yet?" I asked her, falling into step beside her.

"Not yet, we'll probably go in there with Matt after they're released. Is it cool?"

I nodded. "Very. I got a whole new appreciation for what they're doing here."

"My dad was in the Air Force, so the Marines are all new to me. It's funny, I'm used to military-brat life, but Marine girlfriend life is way different."

We had reached the bleachers, and I followed my group as they made their way up the metal steps to an open row that would accommodate the whole family. I took a seat next to Olivia at the end of the row, right next to the stairs. The view from the bleachers was amazing. I gazed out at the beautifully maintained landscapes of the base, admiring the red-roofed buildings with the contrasting yellow hue of the exterior. It almost looked like a college campus from this angle.

I turned to look at the barracks behind the bleachers and saw a scattering of recruits cleaning windows and gazing out longingly at the families. I would bet my life they were all wishing it was their turn to graduate. I felt bad for the recruits who had their sleeping quarters right next to the Parade Deck. They had to watch families hugging and congratulating their new Marines, knowing they were weeks or even months away from that moment. Spencer had told me in a letter that there was a graduation every week, so a front-row seat to graduation was constantly torturing these poor guys.

"So, how long have you known Spencer?" Olivia asked.

"We met in sixth grade."

Olivia nodded. "Oh, wow. And you've never dated before?"

"Absolutely not." I laughed and waved my hand, but my stomach did an odd flip when I remembered how I'd felt when he smiled at me during the Moto Run. "We're great at being friends. Neither one of us wants to mess that up."

"I see."

"Besides, I actually have a boyfriend. His name is Tim. He just started school up in Sacramento, or else he'd be here."

Olivia looked confused and started to respond, but the drill instructor who had been our host all day walked onto the parade deck in front of us and tapped his microphone to make sure it was on. We immediately focused our attention on him.

"Okay, ladies and gentlemen, this is the fun part," the Marine told the crowd, speaking into his microphone. "You're going to get a taste of following orders like your Marines have been doing for these thirteen weeks. When

I say, 'do you understand' you will reply with 'yes, sir!' Do you understand?"

The crowd laughed and replied, "Yes, sir!"

"Your Marines will march in formation until their platoon is right in front of the section where their families should be. So, if you didn't follow directions and are sitting in the wrong section, you will look at the signs posted above you and move to the correct section. I will give you one hundred and twenty seconds to do that right now so get ready, and if you think that's a long time, you're not going to like how I count. When I get to zero, I will yell 'zero,' and you will freeze. Ready, move!"

I looked around and saw a few people hurrying to another section, and the crowd chuckled like it was all part of a show. The drill instructor counted down from one hundred and twenty at the speed of an auctioneer. In way less time than it was supposed to be, he yelled, "ZERO!"

The crowd laughed and the people who had been rushing to their sections picked up their speed and hustled to their spot on the bleachers.

"A few of you need lessons in freezing at zero, but overall, not bad," the drill instructor said, humor in his tone. Messing with people seemed like his idea of a good time, so I guessed he was perfect for this job. "When we release the Marines, you will hear me say 'ladies and gentlemen, they are all yours.' It is at that time that you will be able to attack the formation and hug your loved ones. Please do not attempt to leave the bleachers until I tell you to do so, do you understand?"

"Yes, sir," the crowd roared in unison as excitement built.

"Okay, your new Marines will have a total of six hours of leisure to spend with you on my base. They are not to leave my base for any reason, so please do not encourage them to do so. Do you understand? Say, 'yes, sir.'"

Again, the crowd yelled, "Yes, sir!"

"Alright let's get this party started. The last thing I need you to do is to get as loud as humanly possible when you see these new Marines in formation. I want my eardrums to burst because of the sheer volume you are producing. Do you understand? Say, 'yes, sir!'"

"Yes, sir!"

"Oh," he tapped his microphone, "is this thing broken? I said I want you to get loud! Lemme hear you scream!"

The crowd screamed and hollered in response, stomping the bleachers and clapping. The excitement was real; it wasn't like a pep rally with moody teenagers. It was a crowd full of people who genuinely could not contain their excitement over seeing their son, boyfriend, or brother again. It was infectious and my face hurt from smiling so wide. A marching band to our left played an upbeat song and I could barely hear it over the excited cheers from the crowd as the Marines came marching into view.

Their precision was something of an art, and each platoon seemed like one moving object rather than eighty men moving in unison. I counted five groups of men, each led by a Marine holding a red flag. The flag had platoon numbers printed in yellow, and I squinted as I tried to find

2109. I located the group of men that Spencer was in and cheered louder. They marched across the huge asphalt space until his platoon was directly in front of our section on the bleachers. At the direction of the drill instructor closest to the platoon, the Marines turned to face the roaring crowd.

# 6

## SPENCER

Like so many times before, I looked at the back of Mills' head with laser focus. This time was different, however, because on the other side of his head was a crowd of people cheering for us. I felt more pride at that moment than I ever had, and all I could think about was getting released from the formation and having some freedom. Even though I wouldn't be able to leave base, I was pumped to spend an afternoon without getting screamed at by a DI.

The DI in charge of motivating the crowd came over the PA system. "Ladies and gentleman, I need absolute and complete silence while your Marines are being released on liberty."

First Sergeant Meyer called out the command that brought us from Parade Rest to Attention. In one quick motion, I brought my arms from behind my back to my sides and snapped my feet together. The rest of my platoon made the action at the same time. Having seen other companies practicing for graduation, I knew seeing that many men move in sync was a powerful sight. My chest swelled with pride and excitement as I thought about what would happen next.

First Sergeant gave the order for our Senior DIs to sound off. "Report!"

The Senior DIs at the front of each platoon called out their platoon number and reported their Marines as present and accounted for.

"Platoon 2109, all present," our senior DI called when it was his turn.

"Echo Company—you are due back at eighteen hundred hours. Senior Drill Instructors - turn to 'on liberty,'" called First Sergeant.

The Seniors brought their right arms to their foreheads in salute and called, "Aye aye, First Sergeant."

They each turned and walked to the side of their platoons and gave the command for us to turn to our right and face them. As I turned with the rest of my platoon, I tried to focus on the crowd for a familiar face, but they were too far away, and it happened too fast. I forced myself to breathe and have patience. After a short pause, the Seniors released their platoons, one by one.

"Platoon 2109, turn to 'on liberty,'" called Staff Sergeant Ferguson when it was our turn.

"Aye aye, Staff Sergeant. Oorah!" My platoon sounded off and about-faced, and the crowd went wild.

Mills looked over his shoulder and I followed his gaze. The DI gave the order for the family members to make their way off the bleachers and greet us on the Parade Deck.

"I'm freaking out."

I laughed. "You'll be fine, bro. I still think you're crazy, but I'm happy for you two lovebirds."

"Here she comes," he said, shakily. "I'll meet you at the restaurant?"

I nodded. "See you there."

I watched as Mills made his way through the sea of Marines in our green Service Bravo uniforms. Ellie should be with Mills' family, so I searched the faces in that direction. I saw her through the crowd and my stomach flipped painfully. I'd known my feelings for her had grown, but seeing her after all I'd been through over the past three months cemented those feelings for me. It felt like my gut was full of rocks. Moving rocks, if that was even possible.

I made my way through the embracing families, watching her crane her neck as she looked for me. Our eyes locked, and I saw a flash of panic in her eyes. My feet stuttered slightly in response. What was she so afraid of? I'd pictured this moment a thousand times, and in it, I'd always grabbed her into a bear hug with no questions asked. Once or twice, I'd gone too far in my mind. I'd pictured myself tangling my fingers in her hair and crushing my mouth to hers. It had been torture imagining it, knowing it would never happen. Now that the moment was finally here, could I even lay a finger on her without going too far? I'd soon find out. Maybe that's the fear I'd seen in her eyes a moment ago... Was she afraid I would kiss her? Or was she afraid because she *wanted* me to?

I finally closed the space between us and reached for her, grabbing her around the waist and lifting her feet off the ground. She laughed in my ear and squeezed me tightly in response. I set her down gently but didn't break the hug. She smelled like home.

After a moment, she pulled away. There was a hint of something in her smile I couldn't place. She looked the same, but there was something different about the way she looked *at me.* I tried to shake it off, but maybe the whole 'Marine in uniform' thing had an effect on her. Secretly (and wrongfully) I really hoped it did.

"Congratulations," she said, squeezing my shoulder. "I'm *so* proud of you."

"Thank you. And thank you for coming out, it means a lot."

She bit her lip. "About that..."

"What's wrong?" I asked.

"Your dad's not here. He'll be here tomorrow though, I promise," she said, looking concerned about how I'd take the news.

I shrugged. "It's fine, it's actually a good thing he's only coming for one day. That way we don't have to hang out with him as much, right? He's bad at small-talk."

"Right," she agreed, replacing her frown with a wide smile. "It's really good to see you."

"You, too," I replied, feeling that overwhelming sense of pride again. "I'm pretty awesome now, just so you know. More than I was before, even."

Ellie laughed and rolled her eyes. "Great. Your head has gotten even bigger."

"Get *off* my parade deck," the booming voice of a DI came over the sound system.

I put my hand on Ellie's lower back and led her towards the restaurant, careful to steer her onto the sidewalk without walking across the grass. That was a big no-no on the depot. They took grass-crossing very seriously, and I had no intention of getting blasted for rule-breaking in front of Ellie.

"We're gonna get lunch at the restaurant on base, if that's cool with you. There's a lake or something over there and that's where Mills is gonna propose to his girl," I explained as we walked, keeping my voice low and looking around to make sure Mills' girl wasn't in earshot.

"She seems nice. I'm happy for her. She said they've been together for like five years."

I scoffed good-naturedly. "Yeah, they have, but they're still only eighteen. I told him he's a moron for getting married this young. Or at all."

"You're like a happiness Nazi. Just because you're content with being single for the rest of your life doesn't mean other people are wrong for wanting to settle down." Ellie's stare held a challenge in it, as if she were daring me to disagree.

"Speaking of, have you dumped Tim yet?" I asked.

She hadn't responded to that part of the letter I'd written her at the beginning of boot camp, so it had felt weird to bring it up again in a later one. That didn't mean the conversation was over though. Far from it. I saw through Tim's 'perfect boyfriend' act to the dirtbag underneath. I'd put money on the guy being a liar and a cheat, and him being hours away in college while Ellie was still here was a recipe for disaster. I'd always known Ellie was too good for Tim from the perspective of a friend, but now that I had these new feelings for her, my urge to get him out of her life seemed even more important. I worried about her on a new level now. Not just the normal protectiveness I'd always felt. Something deeper.

"No, and I'm not planning to." Ellie stared straight ahead as she responded.

The last thing I wanted was to upset her after going so long without seeing her, so I figured I would just have to come up with a better way to get through to her. Later.

We arrived at the restaurant and got in the long line for the buffet, so I reached into my sock to fetch my I.D. card and cash.

Ellie stared at me; eyebrows lifted. "Did you just pull money out of your sock?"

"Yeah," I confirmed with a shrug. "Apparently it looks better to pull something out of your sock than to have anything in your pockets when you're in certain uniforms."

"That makes no sense at all."

I laughed. "You're telling me. There are so many little rules that are absurd when you really think about them."

"Like what?"

"Well, in civilian clothes, your pants always have to fit at the waist, so you don't need a belt."

Ellie lifted a brow. "That sounds pretty straightforward to me."

"That part is, yeah, but if your pants have belt loops on

them, you have to wear a belt. If they fit, why do I need a belt?"

"I guess they care a lot about fashion in the Marine Corps."

"Yeah, I mean, I know it all comes down to us looking presentable whether we're in uniform or not. There are a lot of rules about how we look. We have to have a clean shave every day, a new haircut every week, and if our shirt has shirt tails, we have to tuck it in."

"Even if you're rocking the jeans-with-a-button-up look?"

"Yep."

Ellie shook her head. "What else?"

"We can't chew gum in uniform."

"Good, it would take away from the look."

I snorted. "What? That doesn't even make sense."

"You chew gum like a cow. It's not attractive at all."

"So, if I'm in uniform, you're saying I'm attractive? As long as I'm not chewing gum, that is."

Ellie flushed. "Moving on. What else?"

"Hmm... If we're in uniform and on a cell phone, we can't walk."

"Wait, so if you get a phone call, you're like... trapped in place until you hang up?"

I nodded. "Mm-hmm."

"Good to know. I might call you sometimes and just blabber on. It'll be like my own version of 'red light, green light.'"

"I might just ignore your calls then."

She eyed me playfully. "You would never do that."

We'd reached the buffet counter. I grabbed a tray from the stack and handed it to her before taking one for myself. "You're right, I wouldn't."

She looked down, smiling. "My parents are coming tomorrow, too. We're picking your dad up on the way. Parking was a nightmare this morning."

"I'm sure they'll be glad to see my dad again," I snickered. Our parents had been friends before my mom died, which is how Ellie and I had first started hanging out. "Did you bring my phone?"

"Yep," she balanced the tray of food she'd been filling up in one hand while she dug around in her purse with the other. She retrieved the phone and tucked it into the pocket of my green trousers since I was scooping mac salad onto my plate.

"You know I'm gonna have to move that to my sock, right?"

She laughed and watched me do it, nudging me to hurry because the buffet line had moved up while I'd been awkwardly maneuvering the phone into position under my pant leg.

Walking out into the bright sunlight, I scanned the crowd looking for the table with Mills and his family. We weaved and bobbed through the packed outdoor pavilion. Round white tables with white plastic chairs dotted the area, and I was grateful that the Mills family had chosen a table outside after being in the stuffy restaurant. When we reached the table, Mills stood and grabbed Ellie's free hand, shaking it fervently.

"Ellie, it's so nice to meet you," Mills said, his dark

brown eyes alight with his good mood. "I've heard a lot about you. Your letters smelled really nice, by the way."

I glared at my friend. "It was only that one letter she sprayed, Mills."

Mills winked at me and turned his attention back to Ellie. "Call me Matt. And I believe you already know the love of my life?"

Olivia laughed and greeted Ellie again.

"I haven't met her yet, Mills," I said, faux hurt playing across my face.

"Yeah, and for a good reason, buddy. Come, sit, I'll introduce you both to the rest of my family."

The rest of the lunch went well. I felt at home with Mills and his family and was grateful to them for welcoming Ellie and me. I caught myself feeling down about how happily dysfunctional they were. On the bright side, it didn't take much to bring my mood back up, though. I could take as long as I wanted to finish my meal and there were no DI's breathing down my neck. Not to mention that Ellie looked amazing and was finally right in front of me. Her smile could always brighten my mood.

Ellie leaned toward me and whispered in my ear, making the hair on the back of my neck stand up. "When is he going to propose?"

"It should be any minute," I responded, my mouth inches from her ear. "He's gonna ask her to take a walk with him."

As if on cue, Mills turned to his mom and nodded. She winked in reply and began telling a story to the rest of the group in an animated voice. They were hanging on her every word and laughing hysterically. It was all part of the plan. Mills wanted someone to distract his family when he snuck away with Olivia. They all knew he was planning to propose at some point that weekend, so he didn't want one of them to blow it before they even left the table.

"Take a walk with me?" he asked Olivia in a hushed voice, staring into her eyes.

She looked all too eager to get some time alone with him. "Definitely."

Mills helped her up from her chair and then took her hand. He led her through the tables, toward the edge of the water. The sun shone off the surface of the small lake behind them.

I looked down at Ellie. She was watching the scene unfold with stars in her eyes. I didn't think marriage was for me, and I definitely didn't believe in marriage at eighteen, but I had to admit that Mills was as sure as he could be. He'd been relentlessly bending my ear about how much he loved Olivia for the last three months, so if anyone could make this work, they could. The entire pavilion erupted into applause, and I smiled at Ellie's white-knuckled reaction when Mills dropped to one knee.

## 7

## ELLIE

"So, what time do you have to be back?" I asked, fidgeting with the ring on my right hand.

"Eighteen hundred, or six o'clock, to you," Spencer replied, nudging my arm as he clarified the military time.

I squinted across the man-made lake while we walked along the sidewalk that bordered the water's edge. I couldn't get Matt's proposal out of my head. It was probably the most beautiful thing I'd ever seen in real life. The sun had shone brightly on the water of the lake behind them, and between his uniform and her floral dress, the scene had been straight out of a movie. When he'd dropped to one knee, and the crowd cheered, I'd had to work ridiculously hard not to cry.

I flashed back to my movie date with Tim. That was exactly what I'd wished for that night. Matt and Olivia's kind of love story. Maybe after years apart, Tim and I would be like them, too. After everything we'd undoubtedly go through over the next few years, his proposal would surely be just as romantic and swoon-worthy. I'd cry and laugh and not even wonder if it was the right thing to say yes. I gave the ring another spin on my finger. It felt heavy and too tight. I could feel Spencer studying me intently. He stopped walking.

"What?"

I turned to face him, a fake smile in place. "What?"

"What's wrong?" He narrowed his eyes at me and paused for a long moment. "This feels weird, E."

"I know," I covered my face with my hands. "I'm sorry. It's not you."

"What is it, then?"

I hesitated. "I don't know if I want to talk about it with you. And that really sucks because we used to talk about everything."

He laughed it off and held out his arms. "I've been gone for three months, not three years. We're still us. You can still talk to me."

I bit my lip, feeling something like anger brimming beneath the surface. It surprised me, so I worked to stifle my emotions.

"Ellie." Spencer narrowed his eyes at me, almost like he could sense that I was about to place blame on him for something. "What?"

"We're not 'still us,' because you had to run your mouth about my relationship with Tim. It messed with my head. I didn't doubt my relationship until you weighed in on it. And I thought it was really weird you had an issue with him out of the blue and hadn't mentioned it before."

I hadn't realized I'd blamed him until it all came pouring out of me. It was like something snapped after months of confusion, and I needed a place to put it.

"Oh, really?" Spencer took a step forward. "You're gonna blame me for questioning an already messed up relationship?"

"It wasn't already messed up. I was fine before you stuck your nose in it. We were happy."

"Okay." He rolled his eyes and looked away.

"I'm serious! After you left, it was like everything got messed up with Tim. There's nothing wrong with our relationship. You just confused me."

Spencer threw his head back and laughed, but there was no humor in the sound. "You are a total lunatic."

"I'm not. I'm right. I didn't have any questions about Tim until you told me I deserved better and all that." I grew more confident with each word I spoke. "He's in school to be a doctor, he wants the life I want, and he loves me. What more do I need?"

My new revelation surprised me, but it made sense. Being mad at Spencer for clouding my judgment about Tim was a lot better than not having a good relationship. I was right, wasn't I? Hadn't I been happy before Spencer made me feel like I wasn't?

Spencer stared at me for a long time. He looked taller, and more still. Was he even breathing? There was a sense of control radiating from him, and he looked more machine than man at that moment. In fact, he was so composed that I almost didn't see the flash of anger in his eyes before he swallowed it back and gave me the smallest of smiles. It was almost... a sad smile.

He nodded once, as if he'd made a decision. "Okay, E. You're right."

"About which part?"

"Tim is a good dude, and you'll have a good life with him. You were fine before I stuck my nose in your relationship. I'm sorry I confused you." He sounded stiff and his eyes were hard as they met mine.

I tilted my chin up at him. "Do you mean it?"

One corner of his mouth twitched and his gaze softened. "You know I just want the best for you. We're friends, right?"

"Yeah." I fidgeted with the ring again. He looked at my hand and I watched as his jaw clenched before he looked away.

"The MCX is over there," he pointed across the base towards the area of the Command Museum. "It's a store where everything is tax-free for military. They have them on all the bases. It's kinda like a department store, I guess. Wanna go check it out, do a little shopping?"

I smiled at his attempt to bring us back to old times. "Absolutely. We both have steady paychecks now."

"That's right, you started your job with your dad. How is it?" He asked as we turned to walk towards the store.

"It's okay. I like the new dressy wardrobe and the paycheck, but I'm bored out of my mind doing the legal stuff. Just like I expected."

"So, working there hasn't made you want to be a lawyer?"

I shook my head. "Nope. If I'm bored doing the office stuff, I can't imagine having to do everything I see the actual attorneys doing all day. It's not my thing."

"I'm sure you'll find something." Spencer looked up and hurried to greet the Marine who'd been walking towards us. "Good afternoon, Staff Sergeant."

"Good afternoon."

"This is my friend, Ellie. Ellie, this is Staff Sergeant Ferguson. He was my senior drill instructor."

Staff Sergeant Ferguson smiled widely and shook my hand. "It's nice to meet you, Ellie. Thanks for coming out to support your friend, here. He did great work. I'd say he was one of the least annoying recruits I've ever had."

"Thank you, Staff Sergeant," Spencer replied. He stood with his hands behind his back with his feet apart. I remembered him calling the stance, 'parade rest.'

"Did you travel far to come to graduation?" Staff Sergeant Ferguson asked me.

"No, I'm a local. Born and raised in San Diego."

"Nice. I forgot you were from here, too, Hawkins. Are you gonna try to get stationed here after school?"

Spencer shook his head. "No, Staff Sergeant. I'm ready to see other places. Maybe try to get overseas orders, even."

I swallowed. I knew he was excited about the Marine Corps taking him places he'd never been. I'd gone with him to the recruiting office the first time when Sergeant Moore had asked him to pick his top three choices from a pile of little plastic tags with the benefits of joining printed on them. The tag marked 'TRAVEL AND ADVENTURE' was Spencer's number three pick. His first pick was the 'PRIDE OF BELONGING' tag, and the second pick read, 'CHALLENGE'.

Still, despite knowing he wanted to travel, hearing him speak of overseas orders had my heart racing. We'd been friends for so long, but always in the same school with the same friends and in the same city. Would our friendship survive the Marine Corps?

"It was nice to meet you, Ellie." Staff Sergeant Ferguson's mouth quirked slightly as he shook my hand. I wondered what he'd seen on my face when Spencer had answered his question. "Don't forget to have this guy back by eighteen hundred or he'll get to hang out with me for another week."

"I will," I promised, chuckling. "It was nice to meet you, too!"

Staff Sergeant Ferguson said his goodbyes, and I watched as he kept walking along the path toward the restaurant pavilion. He oozed confidence. Did he enjoy being a drill instructor? It seemed like a lot of pressure. From what Spencer had told me in his letters, they spent almost as much time away from home as the recruits themselves during the thirteen-week cycle. That was probably hard for his family, if he had one.

I turned back to Spencer. "He seemed nice."

"Oh yeah, he's a real sweetheart."

We both laughed, then the humor died off.

Spencer cleared his throat. "Jokes aside, he's not too

bad. Actually, he's the one I told you about who reminded me of Will Smith. Do you remember?"

I nodded. "I totally see the resemblance. So, he was your favorite then?"

"Yeah, but then the guy I hated the most actually turned out to be pretty cool during The Crucible."

"What's that?" I asked. "And do you want to sit and talk for a bit before we go in?"

We'd reached the Exchange, but I wasn't ready to get out of the sunshine yet. There were white picnic tables outside, so I gestured to one and we sat.

"So," Spencer continued, "The Crucible was a nightmare. Basically, it's how they test us on all the stuff we learned in boot camp. Hiking, obstacle courses, carrying injured Marines to safety, eating and sleeping in dirt holes... you know, the really glamorous stuff."

"I bet you smelled disgusting," I teased. He had a thing about always smelling good. He had many types of body sprays and colognes on his dresser. It was a safe bet to get him something like that for Christmas.

"We all did, for sure," he confirmed with a laugh.

"So, what happened with the DI you didn't like?"

He cleared his throat. "Ah, yeah. The Crucible was hard. By far the hardest part of the whole thing. There was this one part where we had to scale a huge wall at the end of an obstacle course, and I was just done. My arms were dead at my sides. And you know I work out, so the physical stuff here hasn't really been that bad. But that day was just, a lot."

"Sounds mentally intense, too."

"Very. Most of it is designed to feel like a real combat or survival situation. I don't know, I froze at that wall. And the dude was right there. I felt him coming. They move like they're on the attack all the time, you know? And instead of coming up and screaming at me like a DI to a recruit, he motivated me like one Marine to another. And I know I wasn't even a Marine yet, and it wasn't a real combat situation, but it just felt *so* real. I got a legit sense of what it would be like to be in this impossible situation and have brothers there, ready to catch you if you fall, ready to help you make it through. Ah, it sounds lame now since we were just at Camp Pendleton and not Afghanistan. But it made me respect him—and all of this—so much more."

I was speechless. I put my hand on his, not sure what I was trying to comfort him about. Everything he'd been through was just so much bigger than anything I'd ever done. Our eyes met across the table and we pulled our hands apart at the same time.

"But at the end," he continued, in a much lighter tone, "there was a ceremony where we got our eagle, globe, and anchor pin. That's the moment we're officially Marines, not graduation. A lot of the guys got choked up. I guess I did, too. There we were—sweaty, covered in mud, sleep deprived, and absolutely starving—being awarded the *right* to call ourselves Marines. That was one of my proudest moments... ever."

I watched as he spoke about the ceremony, gesturing with his hands, his eyes alight with the passion he had for being a Marine. It was inspiring. If I were being honest with myself, it was also incredibly attractive. Spencer had wanted to be a Marine for as long as I'd known him. Now, he finally was one. I'd just witnessed him making his own dreams come true, and I felt like I could sit there listening to him talk about it for hours, hanging on his every word.

## 8

## SPENCER

"I'll see you tomorrow," Ellie promised. We stood near the front gate of the Recruit Depot, and she was about to walk to the underpass where she parked her car.

"Thanks again for coming." I hugged her, too briefly for me, but not long enough to be weird.

"Of course," she said, waving before heading toward the gate.

"Ellie," I called after her, and she turned. "What's with the ring?"

She looked down at her hand as if she needed a reminder of what I was referring to. She closed her other hand around it. "It's nothing."

I furrowed my brow. "Try again."

"It's just a promise ring."

There was about ten feet of empty space between us, but it might as well have been a raging river, preventing us from closing the gap. We stared at each other for a minute. "What's the promise?"

She shrugged. "It's like a symbol of getting through this distance while he's in school, and then when he comes back, we'll get engaged."

If it felt like there were rocks in my gut before, now it felt like worms. Big, fat, nasty worms.

"Spence?" she asked, when I had said nothing for a moment.

"White-picket-fence, 'Leave it to Beaver,' and all that," I repeated the catchwords we always used for her ideal future.

She nodded. "Yeah, that's what I want."

A million thoughts flew through my head all at once. I wanted to argue with her. I wanted to tell her she didn't want those things. I wanted to tell her that *I* wanted her. I wanted to grab her and kiss her until she forgot what the heck a white-picket-fence even looked like.

Instead, I just nodded back. "I'll see you tomorrow, E."

"How was your day, man?" Mills reached the door of the squad bay at the same time as me, so we entered the room together. We were about fifteen minutes early, which in the Marine Corps, was on time.

"Not nearly as good as yours." I put my arm around my friend.

Mills laughed and brushed me off. "Well, obviously."

"Seriously, I'm happy for you. You guys seem really good together."

"Look at you, not even being sarcastic about it."

"Hey, I'm not always a jerk."

"Just sometimes."

"Yeah." I rummaged through my footlocker, getting things packed and ready to leave tomorrow. Words could not describe how glad I was that it was our last square-away hour of recruit training, and this hell was finally over.

"So how did it go with you and Ellie today?"

"It was rough." I rubbed my hand over my head and sighed.

I wasn't sure how much I wanted to talk about it, but it was the last night. Might as well. I'd already told Mills about my feelings for Ellie's boyfriend. Not so much about my feelings for her exactly, but just that I didn't think Tim was good enough for my best friend. Which is true, regardless of the rest of it. He'd hassled me at the time about secretly being in love with her, but I never admitted anything. Just gave him crap right back, saying he was just looking for love everywhere like the sap he was.

"How so?"

"Right before I came here, I told her how I felt about Tim. Today, she got all up in my face about it. She said it was my fault she was doubting things with him. Apparently, after I said all that, things got weird between them."

"Or, maybe things got weird between them because you *left*, not because of what you said about Tim."

I rolled my eyes. "I highly doubt that. She completely blamed me for confusing her with what I said."

"Did you tell her you meant it, though? That you don't think he's good enough?"

"Heck no. She clearly wanted me to apologize and make her feel better about it. So I did. Told her I wanted the best for her, which I meant. And I apologized for confusing her and told her she'd have a good life with him, which I definitely did not mean. But it's what she wanted to hear."

Mills wrinkled his nose. "Ugh, why would you say all that?"

I held out my hand and counted the reasons on my fingers for him while I spoke. "Because he's in school to be a doctor, wants the life she wants, and he loves her. Those are all her reasons why I'm wrong about him."

"Lame. So, are they on the rocks, then? Because of you?"

I shook my head. "Doesn't seem like it. She has a promise ring from him."

"Huh, so that's like the ring you give before the real ring? I skipped that step." Mills chuckled.

"Yeah, no kidding. I'm just glad this tool didn't skip a step. Then I'd have to break his nose."

Mills raised a brow. "Hawk."

"What?"

"You sure there's nothing between you and Ellie? For real."

I rolled my eyes. "She's my friend. I told you."

"Yeah, you told me... But I don't buy it. It sounds like a

lot more than friendship. Either you're lying to yourself about it, or you're lying to me. One or the other though, man."

My shoulders sagged. "It doesn't matter how I feel or who I'm lying to. It's not what she wants. *I'm* not what she wants. Which, she confirmed again tonight when I asked her about the ring. I'm telling you, man, we're friends. Nothing more."

"Let's just leave it at this," Mills patted my shoulder, "I know you're in love with her. *You* know you're in love with her. But you don't have to say it out loud if you want to keep pretending it isn't true. Word?"

"Gee, thanks."

"Sorry 'bout the ring, though." Mills offered.

"So, Spencer, what was your favorite part?" Carol asked.

I laughed. For as long as I could remember, every time we did something with Ellie's family, whether it was going to the zoo, a movie, or a day at the beach, Carol always asked the same question as we were leaving. We'd been required to answer with our favorite part of the day, no matter how old we got or how cool we thought we were.

"Probably meeting my buddy, Mills. He was chill, made the whole thing bearable," I replied.

Carol's eyes twinkled. "I'm glad you had a friend, honey. I know *this* friend of yours was lost without you."

Ellie flushed. "Mom."

"Oh, Carol." Tom reached over and stole one of his wife's fries. "Don't make her sound co-dependent."

We were at In 'N' Out Burger, at my request. It was the first place I wanted to eat following the graduation ceremony. Again, we'd chosen a table outside in the perfect San Diego weather. After three months of eating in stuffy chow halls next to a bunch of smelly guys, this meal tasted like SoCal and freedom.

"These kids are glued at the hip. It was a long three months!" Carol laughed, swatting Tom's hand away as he went for more fries. "Stop that! You had plenty."

"It was definitely long," I agreed, throwing a fry at Ellie, who giggled. The sound of it made me want to groan out loud. Man, she was cute.

My dad shifted in his seat next to me and I remembered he was there. He'd been so quiet while we were all chatting and catching up. There was once a time when my parents and Ellie's parents hung out a couple of times a week. My mom and Carol had met at a school thing and had hit it off, and the rest was history. They stayed close while my mom was sick, but drifted after she died. My dad seemed to push everyone, including me, away. Carol and Tom always had room for me at their dinner table or whenever I wanted to get away from the quiet at my house. They were my family, and it really had been a long three months without them, too, not just Ellie.

"How's everything for you, Mike?" Tom asked his former friend. "Work going well?"

My dad nodded. "Can't complain."

"That's good," Tom replied, glancing at Carol, then

shifting his focus to me. "Anyway, kid, what happened to Honor Grad?"

"I tried, but this guy from the rack next to mine got it," I said.

When I was about halfway done with training, I'd gotten a letter from Tom. He'd asked lots of questions, and I'd told him about Sergeant Moore wanting me to get Honor Grad. It meant a lot that he'd remembered. My dad glanced between us, then went back to his burger without a word.

"Ah, well, you did great, we're all proud of you," Tom said. "And I hate to cut this short, but I need to get back to the office. Are you taking the rest of the day off, dear?"

Ellie laughed. "Yeah, and can I have next week off, too? Spencer's only here for ten days before he has to go to his next training thing... TCM."

"MCT," my dad and I corrected her at the same time.

She looked between us and laughed. "Yeah, that."

"A whole week?" Tom looked appalled, but I could tell he was joking.

Carol piled our paper dishes and napkins onto our trays to clear the table. "Oh, Ellie, you know he's already asked Phyllis to come in for you next week."

Ellie stuck her tongue out at her dad and helped her mom pile up the trash on the tray. My dad stood and reached for the tray to bring it to the trash can. When he'd gone, Ellie made a face at me and I knew exactly what she meant. My dad had gotten a front-row seat to the ease of my relationship with Ellie's parents. It was nothing like my relationship with him. If that bothered him, he didn't show it. Either way, that lunch would go down as one of the most awkward of my life.

"Thanks again for inviting us to come out with you guys," Olivia said as she and Mills climbed into the backseat of Ellie's car.

"No problem. It's great we're all from San Diego so we can hang out." Ellie replied, practically buzzing with excitement.

I knew she planned to hang out with Olivia more often. She didn't have very many girlfriends. It wasn't because she didn't want girlfriends, but all the girls she hung out with from high school were catty and always finding some way to cause drama. I hoped Olivia wouldn't be like that because the last thing Ellie needed to deal with was stupid girl drama.

"So, what's the deal with this restaurant? It's new?" Mills asked, settling into the seat next to his new fiancée.

Ellie beamed. "It looks really fun. You sit outside on the patio and they have games like cornhole and horseshoes and giant checkers. Seemed like it would be more entertaining than just going out to dinner."

"It'll have to do, I guess," I joked. "I thought Ellie would throw me a welcome home party, but apparently not."

She playfully swatted my arm across the center console. "Hey! I put a lot of effort into your going away party at the beach, so don't act like I don't care."

"Yeah, yeah, yeah." I rolled my eyes. "I'm just glad to have ten whole days before we have to go to combat training."

"I hear that bro," Mills said.

"So, Ellie, is your boyfriend gonna be in town soon?" Olivia asked, leaning forward.

She shook her head. "Not for a while. I think he's coming down for Thanksgiving though, so I'm excited for that."

I'd be lying if I said I wasn't happy to hear Tim wouldn't be around for a while. However, I'd hoped to see Ellie over Thanksgiving weekend if I had a break. If Tim came to town, there would be little to no shot of making that happen. Plus, I hadn't been around him at all since I'd realized how much I didn't want him to be with Ellie. Would he feel that vibe from me? Guys are pretty good at that stuff. Who knows, maybe I'd already been putting off that vibe to him and didn't even know it. I hoped so.

"Well," Olivia continued, pulling me from my thoughts, "I'd love to meet him sometime. Maybe he'll be here at some point when Matt is here, too, so we can double date."

"Yeah, and I'm sure Hawk can find a girl to bring and we can make it six," Mills added, reaching forward to pat me on the shoulder. "Right, buddy?"

I grunted in reply.

"No, Matt," Ellie chimed in, glancing at him in her rear-view mirror, "Spencer doesn't date like that. Sure, he'll take a girl to dinner, but bringing a girl on a date with other couples isn't really his thing."

"Matt's been filling me in on your dating style, Spencer." Olivia smiled at me and then turned to Mills. "I'm just glad you put a ring on this finger before he could corrupt you!"

Mills laughed and kissed Olivia's cheek. "Don't worry babe, he tried to talk me out of proposing, but it didn't work."

"Hey!" I called out, defensively.

"No, Spencer," Olivia giggled, lifting a hand, "it's fine. I know people think we're crazy for getting married so young. But when you know, you know."

Ellie sighed. "You guys are adorable. I was freaking out when I saw that proposal, and I'm sure every girl there was staring daggers at you after that."

"Yeah, it was pretty romantic," Olivia said, blushing with the memory. "He was so cute. He had this whole speech about how he knew marrying a Marine would be different from just marrying any guy, but he would do whatever it took to make it work."

I stared out the window. I already knew Mills was willing to put the work into his marriage with Olivia. We'd talked about it constantly at MCRD. In fact, we'd talked about it too much for my liking. But if any couple could make a military marriage work, it was the two of them.

We filled the rest of the ride with good-natured ribbing, loud music, and lots of laughter. I was almost disappointed when we pulled into the parking lot of the restaurant. It was in Point Loma, near an old military base that was now the site of trendy shops and restaurants. Super touristy for my taste, but the place did sound like it would be fun. Ellie drove around in search of an open parking spot. She'd successfully managed to parallel park between two large trucks, despite being harassed by me the whole time about how close she was to the bumper of the first truck.

"Okay, you win," I conceded.

She winked at me, making my stomach twist uncomfortably. "You owe me fifty bucks."

"I'll PayPal you," I replied, chuckling with her. Our eyes met, and the laughter awkwardly faded before we both looked away.

We piled out of the car and made our way toward the restaurant. It was busy, but didn't look like there was much of a wait thanks to the expansiveness of the outside seating area. Ellie told the hostess how many were in our party and she led us straight back to the patio. We wormed our way through the few tables in the indoor bar area, and my hand naturally gravitated to the small of Ellie's back. Fire blazed under my fingertips as soon as I made contact, but I didn't pull my hand away. It was a perfectly innocent touch, right?

"Spencer!" We stepped onto the huge patio, and a group of girls in skin-tight dresses and sky-high heels stood in a group around a fire pit. They took turns hugging me, tossing their hair and giggling. Out of the corner of my eye, I noticed Ellie motion for Olivia and Matt to follow the hostess to our table with her and leave me behind.

I recognized two of the girls I'd gone out with, but the other two were new to me. Maybe. Hopefully. Either way, I felt awkward staying there with them while the rest of my friends kept walking, so I promised the girls I'd stop by later and I jogged to catch up with Ellie and the lovebirds.

"We can't go anywhere with this guy," Ellie called over her shoulder to Olivia, referring to me, but she didn't know I'd joined them yet.

"It's a good thing you're just friends, or I can see that being really annoying for you." Olivia didn't even try to hide the sarcastic tone as she said this, and Mills chuckled slightly behind her.

Mills turned and grinned when he caught sight of me next to him. "You're sure..."

"Drop it, Mills," I said under my breath, secretly happy that little scene with the girls got to Ellie. She didn't want me, fine. But that didn't mean nobody wanted me, and I didn't mind her seeing that.

We made it to our table, so the hostess put our menus down and we all took our seats. All of the tables outside were either high tops or a coffee table with two loveseats on either side, like ours. Mills and Olivia sat on one, so Ellie and I sat on the other. It wasn't weird, no one was making a big deal out of it, but I'd be an idiot not to have one small thought about this being a double date. Ellie had been right before. I didn't double date. Ever. I hung out with girls, but we never acted like a couple or anything. Would it be too wrong of me to imagine us on a date?

Wrong or not, it was easy to do. Ellie looked adorable in her white shorts and royal blue top. Her blonde hair was pulled into a casual bun, with wisps of hair falling around her face. I watched as she studied her menu, her lashes long and curled as her eyes moved around the page. She considered her choices, pursing her lips. I couldn't help but notice how soft they looked.

Mills pushed my menu off the table, making me jump as it hit the floor at my feet. I looked up and met his questioning look with a frown.

"Oops," he said. "My bad."

I picked up the menu and smiled slightly at Ellie and Olivia, who were looking at us with raised eyebrows.

"Spencer? Ellie?" Our server approached the table and it was a face we recognized. The quarterback of our high school football team, Jesse, towered over us with a notepad and pen in hand. "Hey, girl. You look *hot.* Come here."

Ellie stood from her spot on the love seat and gave Jesse a hug, and I narrowed my eyes as his hands wrapped low around her small waist and squeezed. With a clenched jaw, I looked away, working hard to control my expression.

"Hey, Jess," she responded, hugging him tightly. She turned in his arms to introduce our friends. "This is Olivia and Matt. Spencer went to bootcamp with Matt and he and Olivia just got engaged!"

Jesse shook Mills' hand and nodded at Olivia. "It's nice to meet you both, and congrats, that's cool. Spencer, welcome back, bro. How's military life?"

I shrugged, shaking his hand. "So far, so good, man. Are you working here full-time?"

"Just a few nights a week to get some extra cash. Going

to UCSD and living that college life." Jesse winked at Ellie to punctuate his statement, making my skin crawl.

They'd dated briefly before Ellie had started seeing Tim. It hadn't lasted long and they'd ended things on good terms, clearly, since he still flirted with her like crazy. It never used to bother me, but everything was different now. We made small talk for a few minutes, put our order in, and then collectively decided to get up and play some of the outdoor games while we waited for our food.

Mills and Olivia were great to hang out with. Totally easy-going, didn't bicker or fight like most couples I knew, and always kept up with the sarcastic banter Ellie and I tossed around. The whole night had me wishing – briefly – that we weren't about to leave for more training in less than a week. But at the same time, it actually kind of made me mad that I even thought about that. This was supposed to be my dream. I didn't want to regret it. I didn't want to wish I could stay. My new feelings for Ellie were messing everything up.

## 9

## ELLIE

After dinner, we dropped Matt and Olivia off and Spencer drove toward his dad's house. He always drove when we were together, even though it was my car. We passed the time fighting over radio stations and laughing about entertainment news. It was just like normal. It was easy. It was us. But every now and then, I would catch him looking at me, and when our eyes would meet I had to work not to blush. It must be because of my joy over seeing him again after so long apart. It couldn't mean anything more than that, surely.

We pulled up to the house and I got out, intending to say hi to his dad if he was around. Spencer jogged up the driveway of the dark house and peered through the windows that lined the top of the garage door. He turned back to me and put his hands in his pockets, a smirk on his full lips.

"Not home?" I guessed.

He shook his head and tossed me the keys to my car. "Nope."

I glanced toward the front door. The porch swing looked lonely as it sat in the dark, unmoving. Spencer didn't deserve to be alone in that house right now. I wished more than anything that his mom was still alive. He should be around family right now, to celebrate what he'd already done and to support him before he left again. My eyes shifted to him. He was staring at the empty house with an expression that said he felt the same way.

His hands were still tucked into the pockets of his jeans. My gaze traveled up the length of his arm, noticing the way his bicep strained against the hem of his shirt before it met his broad shoulder. He'd always been tall and strong, but his posture had improved so much during training that he looked even taller now. He'd lost what little fat he'd had, making his muscles seem more prominent than ever. He looked *good*. And, he was looking right at me. I wanted to look away, but something in his eyes held mine as we stood there on the moonlit driveway.

His phone dinged in his pocket, breaking the weird trance. He exhaled with a laugh and pulled out the phone, looking at the screen. "Mills. They had fun tonight."

"Cool, same here." I said, tilting my head at him. Something about the way he said it had me doubting that was all Mills had sent in his message, but it was none of my business.

"Well, goodnight, I guess." Spencer gestured to the house, but didn't move.

"Do you want to come over?" I asked.

Again, it just felt weird to leave him there alone. He was only home for six more days and I wanted them to be as full and fun as possible before he headed back to training and sleeping in the dirt. He'd spent many nights on my couch over the years, always welcome by my parents. Our house had become something of a second home to him when his dad kind of dropped the ball on their relationship after his mom passed.

He narrowed his eyes at me, considering. "I don't know."

"What's not to know?"

Spencer chuckled then shook his head. "I don't know."

I walked toward my car and opened the door, one foot in and one foot on the sidewalk. "I just felt bad with you going home to an empty house, is all. Up to you."

He looked toward the house again as I climbed into my car and shut the door. He made up his mind and jogged over to my door, opening it and holding his hand out. I laughed and took his hand, letting him help me out so he could drive.

The ride to my house was short. We lived walking distance apart in the La Jolla neighborhood. It was a rough walk, though, from his house at the bottom of the hill to mine at the top with the ocean views. On second thought, I was probably the only one who'd have trouble with it now, after the hills he'd climbed in bootcamp.

We walked through the side gate to the backyard and headed for our swing set. I took a seat on a swing, and Spencer lifted himself onto the platform and took a seat. We sat in silence for a few minutes, not awkwardly, just both deep in thought. It wasn't unusual for us to be together without having to fill the silence with chatter. Maybe it was just me, but I felt like this silence held a little more brooding than normal from Spencer.

"Are you okay?" I asked.

"Yeah, just thinking."

"Does it hurt?"

He chuckled. "Funny."

"No, but really, what's up?"

"I was just thinking about how much has changed." He hopped off the swing set and paced in front of it. "And how much hasn't. I guess I thought being a Marine would magically make my dad and me closer. So far, not so much. Ah, never mind. I'm being lame. Let's just go inside."

I sighed, choosing my words carefully. "Spence, you didn't do this just for your dad. Remember why you wanted to be a Marine in the first place. Think about what got you through training when it was too hard or too much. Your dad might not ever come around, but you did this big, important thing, and I don't want you to feel like it's not good enough. Because it is."

He looked down at his hands. "Come here."

I stood from the swing and went over to him, almost automatically, without having to tell my body to move. When I got close enough, he reached for me, slowly, tentatively. I held my breath as he looped one of his strong arms behind my back and pulled me against him, his other hand coming to rest on the side of my head as he held me to his chest. I fit perfectly there, with my head just a few inches lower than his shoulder, and with his arms curled around me. Like a puzzle, we just stood there fitted together for a long moment. I had no idea how good it felt to actually be in his arms like this. We'd hugged before, of course, we were friends. But he'd never once *held* me.

I risked a look at his face, tilting mine up to meet his eyes. They swam with emotion. He must be wrecked over his dad. Or thinking about his mom. Or nervous about leaving home again. Whatever he was thinking about had him visibly working to control his feelings. If we weren't such good friends, I would think it was about me. About this hug. About the way my skin hummed in all of the places where it connected with his. But that couldn't be it. Because we were just friends.

## 10

## SPENCER

My hand twitched as I reached for her, cautious, trying not to spook her. She didn't flinch. In one swift move, I pulled her against me. She curled her arms around my waist and pressed her cheek to my chest. We stood there, fitted together like a puzzle, unmoving. Somewhere along the line, the dam had broken. No matter how hard I tried, I couldn't scoop up my feelings and lock them away. It was too late.

I swallowed hard as she tilted her face up to look at me, bracing her chin against my chest. I lowered my forehead to hers, using every ounce of self-control to steady myself. I was perilously close to kissing her. I couldn't move my eyes from her parted lips, so I squeezed them tightly closed. We were friends. We'd never, in all our years of friendship, been in this position before. Hugged, yes. But this? Never.

"Spence," she breathed out my name.

At the restaurant with Mills and his girl, I'd let myself pretend on multiple occasions that we were a couple, on a double date. It was dumb, I knew, but I couldn't help it. It just felt so easy and right. And now, with my body pressed up against hers, I could hardly think past the sound of my heart racing. I'd never wanted anyone the way I wanted Ellie, and it wasn't even in a physical way. It was in a cheesy, double-dating, falling in love with your best friend kind of way. Maybe if I just told her how I felt...

"Spence," she said again, this time making me realize I still held her tightly against me, thinking things I had no business thinking. I released her as if her skin burned me, holding my hands in front of me.

"I'm sorry, I shouldn't have..."

Ellie fidgeted with her ring. "It's okay."

I stared at her hand, shook my head, and headed for the house. "I'm going to bed."

The next morning, I awoke with a splitting headache. The bright San Diego sunlight cascaded through the floor to ceiling windows of the Burton's living room, blinding me from my position on the couch. The memory of what happened outside last night came back to me in a rush. I'd left Ellie standing out there, alone. I'd been so wrapped up in my own feelings. First, pretending we were something we weren't at the restaurant. Then, tempted to risk everything and tell her how I felt, and finally, crushed by the weight of her promise ring.

I crossed an arm over my eyes to block the sun. In the light of day, I was grateful I hadn't ruined everything last night. She still wanted that suburban, stable life. She wanted to marry her tool of a boyfriend who was in school to be a doctor. And I'd rather be alone than give her a life like my mom had. Always acting as both parents, never able to count on her husband to make it to stuff because the needs of the Marine Corps came first, and moving around every three years in the beginning. It would be fine for me as long as no one relied on me. I just needed to get back to training so I wasn't tempted to mess it all up.

"Good morning, sunshine." Carol said in a sing-song voice as she came down the stairs. "I've missed having you crash on our couch, Spence."

I rolled into a seated position on the couch, then stood to hug Carol. "Thanks, Carol. I've missed you guys, too."

"Morning, Ellie," Carol said over my shoulder.

I twisted toward the kitchen. Ellie sat on a barstool, a cup of coffee in one hand and a book in the other. She smiled in greeting. I couldn't tell what she was thinking from the look on her face, but I knew if I had any chance of restoring some normalcy to our friendship, I needed to act cool. Giving her a small smile, I went into the kitchen and poured myself a cup of coffee. Carol busied herself in the fridge, pulling out ingredients for breakfast.

"Morning," Ellie said when I sat at the counter next to her.

"Morning," I parroted.

I fidgeted slightly in my seat, not sure what to say. What would I say if this were any other morning?

"Black coffee?" Ellie asked, eyeing my mug.

"I got used to drinking it black in the field. There was powdered cream and sugar in our MRE's, but we didn't get much time to eat so I never wanted to waste the time on it."

She tilted her head. "What's an MRE?"

"It's a pouch full of food you can eat in the field. Kinda reminds me of space food or something. MRE stands for Meals-Ready-to-Eat. Most of it's pretty nasty, but you get some good ones here and there. We ate them a lot. The good ones had a little bottle of Tabasco in them. Some of them even had Skittles."

She nodded and turned her attention back to her book, sipping her coffee. She'd always used an absurd amount of sugar and cream, but never finished the last few sips because all the sugar was settled at the bottom of the cup. Her promise ring caught the sun as she raised her cup and it caught my eye. I spitefully wondered if Tim knew her as well as I did.

"Still like your eggs over-medium and your bacon extra crispy?" Carol asked from the stove.

"Yes ma'am," I replied with a grin.

My stomach growled in anticipation, the scent of bacon wafting through the room as it sizzled on the pan. There was a newspaper on the counter next to me, and I picked it up and browsed the pages, curious. I'd never been one to read the newspaper, but after being at MCRD for over three months, I figured I might as well see if anything was new in the world.

"What do you want to do today?" Ellie asked.

I put down the paper, considering. "How about... lunch at In 'N Out?"

"Really?" Ellie raised a brow. "We just ate there the other day."

"I might be an East Coaster soon. I'll probably want it a few more times before leave is over, just in case."

"That's right, I forgot they don't have them over there. East Coaster, huh?" She eyed me over the rim of her coffee mug as she took a sip.

"Oh, that's so far." Carol set our plates in front of us on the counter with a pout. "Will you really get stationed all the way over there?"

"There are a few bases I could go to on the East Coast. Plus, there's Hawaii and Japan if I want to go overseas. I think I heard they count Hawaii as overseas even though it's still America. I'm down."

"Travel and adventure," Ellie said, her tone flat.

She'd been there the day Sergeant Moore had used benefit tags to ask me what Marine Corps benefits I was most interested in. Travel and adventure was an easy choice. I'd never even been on a plane. Mom and I used to travel when I was a kid, but it was just stuff within driving distance... Palm Springs or L.A. And Ellie's family brought me to the Grand Canyon the summer between middle school and high school. Leaving San Diego with the Marines was never a question. Ellie had encouraged me before, and I'd been excited. Now, I was getting the impression she didn't want me to go.

"Well, we'll definitely miss you, Spencer. But I have to say, I wouldn't be upset if I had an excuse to visit Hawaii." Carol winked at me. She put the pans and bowls from our breakfast into the sink, turning on the water and rinsing them out.

"Supposedly there's a beach right on the base there," I told her.

Ellie scoffed. "Okay, but we have beaches here, too."

Carol raised a brow at me, but I wasn't sure if I understood what she was trying to say. She dried her hands and then patted me on the shoulder as she left the room. I glanced at Ellie out of the corner of my eye. The vibe between us was making me edgy. I knew I should say something about what happened between us last night, but I had no idea what to say. What even happened? I'd hugged her. Nothing happened. But it definitely felt like something happened. Should I start with an apology? Should I ask what she was thinking about?

"Spencer," Ellie began, a smile playing on her lips, "we're fine."

I looked up at her, startled. "What do you mean?"

"I mean, I can tell you're freaking out about how awkward this is, and it's fine. We're fine."

"Are you sure?"

She nodded. "I'm sure. It was just a hug."

I wondered briefly if she didn't remember the part where I came close to kissing her. Or, maybe she thought the hug was simply a hug. A hug between friends. Friends who hadn't seen each other in a long time and were happy to be together again.

Thank God I hadn't kissed her. She wouldn't have wanted me to. Even if she did, which she *didn't*, it wouldn't be right to make a move on her when she's got a boyfriend. And a promise ring from said boyfriend. I date around, sure. But I had morals. I had standards.

"I'm gonna go upstairs and shower," Ellie said, getting up and placing her empty cup in the sink.

I nodded in reply and couldn't help but stare as she walked out of the room. I was in trouble. Big trouble.

## 11

## ELLIE

I hit save on the document I'd just finished reviewing. After two months working there, I finally had the hang of most of my duties. In fact, I kind of enjoyed it. Not enough to want to be an attorney, but enough to keep the job and not be miserable while I figured out what I wanted to do with my life. I checked the clock on my monitor. It was almost time for me to leave for the day, but I had a few things left on my list. As I glanced over the tasks in my planner, I heard my cell phone buzz in the top drawer of my desk.

Olivia: *Hey, do you have plans for tonight?*

I smiled at the text. Spencer and Matt had been in combat training for a few weeks now, and I was glad Olivia and I had continued to hang out even with them gone. The distance was hard for my newly engaged friend. I made it my mission to help by providing girl time whenever I could. Plus, I enjoyed having a girlfriend.

Me: *No plans. What do you have in mind?*

I put the phone back in the drawer while I awaited Olivia's reply. Turns out, my dad was a bit of a stickler when it came to texting on the job. Just as the phone vibrated again, a man sauntered through the front door of the practice. He was probably only a few years older than me. He was wearing a perfectly tailored black suit, a red tie, and carried a briefcase. His hair was short and dark brown, styled in an effortless way that added a boyish charm to his professional demeanor. I couldn't deny it. The guy was *gorgeous*.

"Welcome to Burton & Associates. How are you today?" I asked, smiling politely at the man.

"Doing well, thank you. And yourself?" He approached my reception desk as he spoke, placing his briefcase on the ledge that ran along the outside of my workspace.

"Fine, thank you. What brings you in this afternoon?"

The man opened his briefcase and pulled out a manila envelope. "I have some paperwork for Mr. Burton. Please see he gets it as soon as possible."

I stood and took the folder from his outstretched hand. "Yes, sir. Is he expecting them, or would you like to add a note?"

"I would hope he's expecting them since I'm supposed to start work tomorrow and he requested those papers before I start. I'm Eric Moore."

I nodded in understanding. I'd almost forgotten my father had hired a new addition to the team. I hadn't expected him to be so young. Or attractive.

I extended my hand for him to shake. "I'm Ellie Burton. It's nice to meet you."

"Ah." Eric nodded with a quick grin, shaking my hand. "The boss' daughter."

"That's me." I gave a small curtsy.

"I thought he said your name was... Elizabeth. Why do you go by Ellie?" Eric asked, looking genuinely curious.

I tilted my head at his question. "I'm not sure, it just happened."

"Hmm. Well, it was nice to meet you. Please tell your father to call me if he has any questions about those docs. See you tomorrow, *Elizabeth*."

I watched as he sauntered out the door without giving me a chance to reply. Was he flirting with me? My phone buzzed in the drawer to remind me of the unread message, so I shook my head and pulled it out.

Olivia: *Let's do dinner around seven at that new sushi place in the Gaslamp. It's a weeknight so it shouldn't be too busy.*

I thought for a moment. Parking in downtown San Diego is expensive no matter when you go. It would be best for us to carpool and split the price of parking. I suggested this to Olivia, along with offering to pick her up after I got off work.

"Ellie," my father admonished as he rounded the corner of the reception area. "Get off your phone."

"Sorry, Dad. The new guy brought these for you," I said as I swapped the phone for the manila envelope, handing it to my father.

Dad glanced over the documents in the folder with a nod. "Thanks. What did you think of him?"

"He seems... nice."

He nodded again. "He is. Just graduated with honors from UCLA. I'm glad we got him; I know he had a lot of offers. He's not much older than you, you know."

My brow furrowed. "So?"

"So," my father started, resting his elbows on the ledge, "I'm merely pointing out that if you'd made plans to go to university right after high school you could have been a lawyer as young as he is."

"True, but since I haven't even decided if I want to be a lawyer it doesn't matter, does it?" I asked in a singsong voice.

His reply was cut short by the buzzing sound of my cell phone signaling Olivia's reply. I glanced guiltily at the phone and then back up at my father.

"Be discreet," he warned with a wag of his finger and then walked back down the hall.

Seeing that Olivia had agreed to my idea about carpooling, I hurried to organize my desk and get through my list as quickly as possible. A mid-week girl's night out was exactly what I needed.

At the restaurant, we took our time choosing from the expansive sushi menu. We got two rolls to share, along with some edamame and miso soup. After we placed our order with the server, a very kind-looking older woman, Olivia got down to business.

"Okay, so, next weekend is their last libo weekend before graduation," she announced, referring to Spencer and Matt. "I was thinking maybe we could ride up there and stay at a hotel on base for the weekend."

I pursed my lips. "Sorry, what's a libo weekend again?"

"Oh, libo is short for liberty. It's basically like time off. I figured we can split the hotel between the two of us and then we'd be able to hang out with them for the whole weekend." Olivia was practically bouncing out of her chair with excitement.

"That sounds fun. I'll talk to Tim about it and let you know."

"Oh." Olivia widened her eyes. "Tim will be in town?"

I nodded, taking my chopsticks out of their paper casing and breaking them apart. "He'll be here that weekend because of Thanksgiving, so hopefully he'll come with us."

"Gotcha. How are you and Tim doing with the distance? Sometimes I feel like I'm going out of my *mind* missing Matt."

Our server appeared with our soup and edamame. "Thanks," I told the server, then waited for her to walk away. "Honestly, I'm not going 'out of my mind' missing him. Is that bad?"

Olivia swallowed a spoonful of soup and tilted her head speculatively. "No, I mean, I bet it helps that you get to talk to him. That's the thing I hate the most about when Matt's gone. When we say goodbye, I pretty much don't hear from him until the next time I see him. We had letters in boot camp, but it wasn't the same. I miss being able to have 'how was your day' talks with him. Maybe because you get to have those conversations it's not as hard?"

My phone vibrated next to my bowl. I glanced at the display and saw that Tim was calling. "Speak of the devil," I said to Olivia. "Do you mind? I won't be long."

"Of course not! Take your time."

With a smile of thanks, I excused myself from the table and took the call in the hallway leading to the restroom. "Hello?"

"Hey, you," Tim greeted me.

"Hey. I'm glad you called. How were your classes today?" I asked.

"Pretty boring."

I paused, waiting for him to elaborate. He didn't. "Well, hopefully they get better soon."

"They probably won't," Tim chuckled. "They're all introductory classes. I won't get to the good stuff until next year I bet."

"Oh."

"So, what are you up to?" he asked.

"I'm at dinner with Olivia. They opened a new sushi restaurant in the Gaslamp. It's good."

"Cool. Well, I guess I'll let you get back to that. Have fun."

"Wait, I was just talking to her about the three of us taking a trip to Camp Pendleton the weekend of Thanksgiving. You're still coming to town, right? We'll probably go down Friday and stay until Sunday. What do you think?"

"Why Camp Pendleton?" he asked, his voice trailing off. I could hear him typing on his laptop and I wondered what had him so distracted.

I narrowed my eyes though I knew he couldn't see me. "Um… to visit Olivia's fiancé, Matt. And Spencer."

More typing. "Right. How could I forget? Yeah, that's cool."

"Okay." I paused to see if he would say anything more. Again, he didn't. "All right, well, I guess I'll talk to you tomorrow?"

"Maybe, I'm pretty packed tomorrow. I'll call you when I can. Might have a busy weekend coming up though."

"Okay, I'll be here, I guess. Love you."

"Yeah, you too, babe."

I disconnected the call and walked back to the table feeling a little unsettled. I was sure it showed on my face, judging by the look of concern Olivia gave me.

"Everything okay?" she asked.

"Yeah, I guess. That was just kind of an awkward conversation."

Olivia sighed. "Distance sucks."

"Apparently," I stirred my soup and found that it didn't look very appetizing anymore. "I talked to him about the libo weekend, though. He said it sounded cool."

"Oh, good. Not going to lie, I feel like I should have my popcorn ready for this adventure." Olivia said with a laugh.

"What do you mean?"

"Oh, I don't know, you being around Spencer and your boyfriend at the same time."

I narrowed my eyes at her. "That's happened plenty of times, I don't see what would be so exciting about that."

Her mouth quirked into a smile. "You guys are ridiculous."

I scowled at her through a mouthful of edamame. "What?"

"You *really* don't know?" She countered, eyebrows almost reaching her hairline.

"Know what?" I worked another edamame bean out of its shell between my teeth, then threw the empty shell into the bowl between us.

"He's clearly in love with you."

My jaw dropped. "He is *not* in love with me."

Our server reappeared with our main courses and Olivia didn't even pause while she was at our table before continuing. "Like, borderline obsessed, wants to wife you up, in love with you."

I blushed as the sweet older woman giggled. "That's not true. And I have a boyfriend."

"*That* doesn't matter." The server said, a twinkle in her eye. "If he loves you, he'll love you whether you have a boyfriend or not. The rest is up to you."

"See?" Olivia said as the server picked up our empty soup bowls and left the table. "Just because you have a boyfriend doesn't change how he feels. Trust me. Matt told me some interesting stuff in letters back in boot camp. And then when I saw the way you two acted on Family Day, I knew he was right."

My stomach flipped. "What did Matt tell you?"

"He said Spencer tried to make him feel bad for asking me to marry him, but that I shouldn't hold it against him because he was just mad that he couldn't have the girl he wanted. I asked him for more details in my next letter... it was like a soap opera, sorry, not sorry."

"Did he give you more details?" My mind spun with this information. Could it be true? Did Spencer feel that way about me?

She shook her head. "Nope. He said Spencer wouldn't even admit it to himself, let alone to Matt. He just said he knew because of the way Spencer talked about you. Told me I'd see for myself on Family Day. And I did. I can't believe you don't, honestly."

I swallowed a sip of my drink and then took a deep breath. "That night after we went to dinner with you guys... we kind of had a moment."

"Really?" Olivia's eyes widened.

"I don't know how to describe it. We were outside talking, and it really wasn't a big deal. But he gave me this... hug. It was just a hug. But I don't know. It also *wasn't* just a hug. If that makes sense."

"Wow."

"Mm-hmm." I leaned forward and lowered my voice. "I thought he was going to kiss me. Honestly, I had no idea what I was going to do if he did. It freaked me out."

. . .

Olivia rolled her eyes. "Girl. Being around you guys is like watching a chick flick. The way he looks at you and then tries to hide it from you. It's like the hottest thing ever. I'm engaged, not blind. I can't. You guys just need to get it over with and be together."

I shook my head. "Hello? Remember Tim?"

"Right... listen. I know we haven't known each other very long. But I'm just gonna say this. You shouldn't ask yourself if it's bad that you're not losing your mind over missing Tim. You should ask yourself how much you're missing Spencer. Like honestly. I think that will tell you a lot."

I walked through my front door a few hours later, mind racing. I hung my keys on the hook by the door, slipped out of my painfully high heels, and tossed my purse on the first step of the stairs on my right. I couldn't decide if I wanted to go upstairs and shower or just flop into my bed and pass out, pencil skirt and all.

"Ellie?" Mom asked from the living room.

I wandered into the living room and kissed both of my parents on the cheek. "Hey, Mom. Dad."

They were in the middle of their evening routine. After dinner, my mom curls up with a book and a cup of tea and my dad looks over some business papers with two fingers of Scotch. It was moments like this that reminded me what kind of life I wanted to have. I loved the way my parents could spend time together but still do their own thing.

When I used to look at a scene like this, I always thought about how Tim would probably have charts to look over and I would read a book like my mom. This time, a new image crept into my mind. Spencer and I, curled up on the couch together, watching a movie. I shook my head. *What is happening?*

"How was dinner?" Mom patted the seat next to her on the sofa.

"It was great. Olivia and I ate sushi and chatted about her wedding."

Dad grunted from his armchair.

"Oh, Dad, knock it off. They've been together a long time." My father didn't understand why Olivia and Matt needed to get married so young. My parents had been out of college and almost thirty when they'd gotten married and settled down. I was sure he didn't want me getting any crazy ideas. It was a good thing promise rings go on your right hand or I would've gotten a serious ear full from him about that.

"I didn't say anything," he mumbled, without looking up from his papers.

Mom cleared her throat. "Anyway, darling, I'm sure it's wonderful for you to have a friend like Olivia. It must help that you can bond over your boyfriends being away from home."

"*Mom.*" I exhaled sharply. "Spencer is *not* my boyfriend."

Dad looked up from his papers and met Mom's eyes,

then looked at me. "Ellie, I think your mother was referring to *Tim*."

My cheeks flamed in embarrassment, and I blamed Olivia for getting in my head.

"Well," Mom smiled, picking up her book again, "I'm glad you had fun, dear."

## 12

## SPENCER

Lost in thought, I cringed slightly when everyone around me sounded off. I hadn't even heard the command. Mills was at my side, so when we broke from the formation, I nudged him in the arm.

"What'd they say?"

Mills chuckled. "Daydreaming or somethin'?"

"Or somethin'," I confirmed. It was getting harder and harder to keep myself from thinking about Ellie throughout the day. I knew I wasn't right for her, but that didn't change how I felt. I'd been torturing myself wondering what would have happened if I'd kissed her that night on the porch. Maybe she wouldn't have been as opposed to it as I'd thought. I knew it was wrong, but that didn't make it sound any less appealing.

"They told us not to drink, or do drugs, and be back by sixteen hundred hours on Sunday."

I sulked. "There go my plans for the weekend."

Mills laughed, but his step faltered when he looked up. I raised my eyebrow and followed Mills' line of sight, finding Ellie, Olivia, and Tim standing on the sidewalk nearby. Olivia had clearly put more than the usual effort into her appearance, which probably explained why Mills was so dumbstruck. Much to my annoyance, Ellie took my breath away in just jeans and a sweater. She was laughing and running her fingers through her long, blonde hair. I had the sudden urge to run up and lift her off her feet. Tim draped an arm possessively around her shoulders, giving me the urge to punch him in the face instead.

As we got closer, the three of them started toward us. Olivia ran into Mills' waiting arms and I sidestepped to avoid getting smacked with her swinging purse as she ran by. Shaking my head ruefully, I approached Ellie and Tim with a wide smile on my face.

"How's it going, man?" Tim extended his hand for me to shake.

"Can't complain." I shook his hand then held my arms open for Ellie to step into.

"Hey," Ellie said, hugging me briefly. "Good to see you, best friend."

*Thanks for reminding me. I was about to kiss you.* I rubbed my hands together. "It's good to see you guys, too. Are you hungry? I'm starving."

"I am," Tim piped up. "What's around here?"

"There's a Domino's Pizza right over there," Mills said, as he and Olivia joined our group. "There's also Mexican food and a burger place."

Ellie shrugged. "I'm down for whatever. Why don't you

guys pick since I'm sure you don't get to eat at those places much."

"I want pizza," I announced, smiling appreciatively at Ellie.

"Wow," Ellie said from the driver's seat as we drove the twenty minutes from the north side of Camp Pendleton to the south, where our hotel was located. I could see her eyes glance back at me in the rear-view mirror. She looked concerned. "Is it really that bad, Spence?"

Mills and I passed the time by fielding countless questions about MCT. Olivia was hanging on Mills' every word, and I'd rolled my eyes more than once as he tried to make our hikes sound longer and harder than they actually were. In truth, the hikes *were* awful, but Mills was taking it to the extreme to impress his girl.

I glanced at Tim sitting in the passenger seat and noted his left hand resting casually on Ellie's thigh. His thumb was moving back and forth on her jeans. His hands looked almost manicured, and for all I knew, maybe they were. I looked down at my own hands and examined the dirt that had been permanently engrained in the creases.

In the last month, I'd slept in dirt, crawled around in dirt, ate my food in dirt, and washed my hands with just water and more dirt. Even if I'd scrubbed for hours, they'd still look dirty. Mills may be exaggerating about the horrors of combat training, but it was definitely worse than boot camp. I would normally downplay something like that, but there was something about Tim's smug attitude and pretty-boy hands that made me want to play it up, too.

"Yeah, I mean, not everyone could do this," I answered her, staring at the back of Tim's head, hoping he got my message.

Olivia smiled lovingly at her soon-to-be husband. "That's why I'm so proud of you, babe."

I met Ellie's eyes in the mirror again. She smiled when she said, "Yes, it's definitely something to be proud of."

Mills and Olivia headed straight for the dance floor when we reached the popular eighteen and over club. I knew Mills had promised her he would attempt to dance, so I laughed as I watched her try to teach him how to two-step. I looked around at all the girls nearby, scoping out the ones who didn't already have a guy hanging on them. My eyes landed on Ellie and Tim, and I could tell she was trying to get him to dance with her. I frowned as he brushed her off.

*Screw it.* I walked up to them and held out my hand to Ellie. "May I have this dance?"

She grinned and looked at Tim. Before he had a chance to reply, I tugged her by the hand toward the dance floor. We cruised into the throng of dancers, all moving in sync to the upbeat country song. Two-stepping was one of my favorite dances. I loved doing complicated turns with my dance partner, and Ellie was great at following. She kept up with the pace and let me lead her around the floor, nailing the spins. We'd practiced a lot over the years.

I was a lot taller than Ellie in her cowboy boots, so I kept my eyes on the room over her head. I glanced down briefly and saw she was watching her feet. She used to do that when she first learned this dance, but her confidence had grown so much since then that I wondered why she was doing it now.

"Hey," I winked at her when she looked up at me. "If you're looking at your feet, you're not having fun."

She flushed, looking guilty. "Sorry."

"You don't need to apologize, just loosen up. You're doing great."

She didn't look back down at her feet, but I silently wished she would. She was looking at me now, and I couldn't look away. She was beautiful.

"It's good to see you," she said, her eyes not leaving mine. "I've really missed you."

I swallowed and looked away, steering us around another couple who were clearly both beginners. "You, too."

"Spencer, I need to ask you something."

"Shoot," I replied, twirling her to the beat of the song. It wasn't quite a slow song, but it was slow enough for us to chat rather than just speed through the motions. I prayed the song would change to fast one if she started talking about anything having to do with feelings. I wasn't sure if I could keep lying about mine.

She wrinkled her nose like she was trying to figure out the words. "Why did you decide to speak up about Tim?"

My steps faltered and I caught myself right before my boot covered hers. "E, I already apologized to you about that. I shouldn't have said anything. I confused you. I get it."

She narrowed her eyes at me. "I just want to know *why*."

"I told you," I bit out, frustrated that she wanted me to talk about something I was trying really hard to keep to myself. "I just wanted to make sure you were good while I'm gone. If you're good, I'm good. I don't want you to get all mad at me again."

I said the last part with a wink to lighten the mood, but inside I felt a quick flare of anger when I remembered how pissed she'd been on Family Day. She'd seemed so sure that she had a great relationship and the only problem was me butting in where I didn't belong. First of all, who belonged in her business more than her best friend, anyway? Second, I was right. But for whatever reason, she didn't want to admit that, so I'd conceded.

Ultimately, it was good I'd apologized. Her having a boyfriend kept me from acting on my feelings. As much as I hated the guy, if it weren't for him, it would be nearly impossible for me to keep my hands to myself when I was around her. At the end of the day, my life in the Marines wasn't the life she wanted. Why go down that road only to crash and burn somewhere along the way?

She wasn't done. "You said he wanted what I wanted on paper, but that he wasn't good enough for me. You said I deserved better. Why?"

"Because you do."

"And you're just looking out for me? As my best friend?" Her eyes held mine as I led her around the dancefloor. She was challenging me. She was daring me to tell her how I felt. She *knew*. She knew, and I was screwed.

My hand tingled where it rested on her hip, almost as if it had a mind of its own and wanted to move up to graze her cheek. My lips straightened into a hard line as I fought the urge to stop right there in the middle of the dance floor and kiss her. I wanted to answer her question in a way that she would never see coming. I wanted to show her, not tell her, that it wasn't because I was her best friend. It was because I was stupidly, hopelessly, pitifully, in love with her.

The music changed to a faster tempo, breaking the moment and rescuing me from ruining everything. I gratefully picked up the pace and added a complicated move. She couldn't help but laugh as I twisted our hands together over her head and quickly lowered her body to the ground, snapping her back up and switching to the other side. When she was upright again, I looked over her head and saw Tim scowling at us with his arms folded across his chest.

I tossed my head in his direction as we two-stepped along the floor. "He looks pissed."

She raised an eyebrow when she caught sight of his expression. "Looks like it."

"About what?"

She looked at me seriously. "Maybe, it's because he sees the way you're looking at me right now, Spence."

*Okay, that's enough.* It was one thing for me to pine over her in my own messed up way. I didn't need her saying things that made me think she might have feelings for me, too. My eyes shifted above her head again, scanning the room for a single girl. I needed to get Ellie out of my arms as soon as possible. I couldn't believe how out of control this was getting.

A striking brunette wearing daisy dukes and cowboy boots was eyeing me from the edge of the dance floor. I nodded at her and then leaned down to Ellie. "I'm gonna go get that chick. You should go fix things with Tim. Like you said, you're happy with him. I was wrong."

She glared at me and then looked to where I had pointed to the brunette. Her brows lifted in that distinctly female way when they assess one another, and it made me even more eager to let her go. I wheeled her to where Tim was standing and deposited her into his arms. Without looking back, I made a beeline for Daisy Duke.

"Hey, beautiful," I said, resting my hand on the wall next to her head. I felt a little off my game, but it was like riding a bike. "Wanna dance?"

Her red lips parted, revealing a million-dollar smile. "Sure, you seem like you have some skill."

"You have no idea," I purred in her ear as I led her into the crowd.

I kept up with the fast pace of the song and I could tell I impressed her with my moves. She seemed like she knew what she was doing, too. A lot of girls try to be that adorable klutz who needed a teacher when I could tell that they actually didn't. This girl was brimming with confidence and style. She was prattling on about herself as we danced, so I said the usual stuff to make her think I was interested. I couldn't help glancing in Ellie's direction once in a while to make sure she was patching things up with Tim. It was the only thing keeping me from ruining everything.

After a few more circles with the hot brunette, I saw Ellie haul off and slap Tim across the face. I stilled immediately. She shoved through the crowd to the door, with Tim following close behind her. Without a word to the girl in my arms, I took off after them. Mills called to me on the way and I pointed to the front door, giving him the signal that I was going outside.

I reached the parking lot and Tim immediately turned on me. "Stay out of this, Hawkins. Your 'knight-in-shining-armor' services aren't needed right now."

I bristled. "Someone needs to have her back since her own boyfriend never does."

"Oh, is that what you call it? 'Having her back'?" Tim got right up in my face, his eyes on fire. "Are you sure it's not having her *on* her back?"

I pulled my arm back to hit him, when Ellie screamed out, "Spence!"

It only made me hesitate for a moment, but that was long enough for Mills to appear behind me and pull me back. I didn't fight him off, knowing that if it weren't for Mills, Tim would be within an inch of his life in a second.

"Let it go, Hawk." Mills pulled me further away from Tim.

"How could you say that after what you did?" Ellie asked, tears coloring her voice.

I froze, connecting the dots. "You *cheated* on her?"

Tim didn't answer me, but I looked at Ellie and she nodded shakily. Olivia immediately walked past me, stepping carefully around Tim. She put her hand in Ellie's in a show of solidarity. Seeing the hurt on Ellie's face made me take a step toward Tim again, but Mills tightened his grip. I allowed him to pull me back once more. I could get away from Mills if I really wanted to, but I didn't. Ellie looked upset enough already.

"Tim," Ellie took an unsteady breath and waited for him to look at her. "You should go."

He had the nerve to look surprised. "I should *go*?"

"Yes."

"It's your car. I live an hour away," he argued.

I glanced at Mills to let him know I was fine. He didn't stop me when I stepped forward. I tucked a twenty in the front pocket of Tim's dress shirt and smiled cruelly. "There's my contribution to your cab fare."

He sneered at me and turned back to Ellie. "I hope you're happy with this Jarhead."

I turned to Mills for permission, and he nodded. Tim didn't see my swing coming.

After Mills got Tim into a cab, a wad of paper towels pressed against his broken nose, I sat on the curb with Ellie. She was staring straight ahead, worrying her hands. She said nothing, but I could see her wheels spinning a mile a minute. Olivia offered to sit outside with Ellie to talk, but thankfully Mills had suggested they give us a minute alone.

"Ellie," I began, my head in my hands. I couldn't look at her yet.

"It's okay, Spence," she mumbled.

"No, it's not. I'm sorry."

She turned to me then, lifting my head with her hands so I would look at her. "What are you sorry for? Hitting him? He deserved it."

I stared into her eyes as she held my face. "I'm not sorry I hurt him. I'm sorry he hurt *you.*"

She released me and took a deep breath. I watched as she stared out into the dark parking lot with a thoughtful look on her face. "I'm really not that hurt. It was a shock, don't get me wrong, but he only told me he cheated after I broke up with him."

There was nothing she could have said at that moment that would have surprised me more. I didn't know what to say, or if I even knew how to speak English. She broke up with him? He'd told her he cheated after *she* broke up with *him*? Ellie, white-picket-fence-wanting Ellie, broke up with the guy who wanted to give that to her?

"I went to dinner with Olivia a couple of weeks ago, and she asked me if I missed Tim," Ellie continued. "She said sometimes she thought she would lose her mind over missing Matt. I realized I didn't feel that way about Tim at all. I mean, sure, I missed him. But Olivia always looks like she's lit up from the inside when she talks about Matt."

When she stopped speaking, she looked at me. I looked away.

"So, yeah," she went on. "I think he hurt my pride more than anything else. He probably wouldn't have even told me if I hadn't hurt him first. I wonder how long it's been going on... Looks like you were right about him after all."

I put my arm around her and pulled her against me, resting my cheek on the top of her head. "I didn't want to be right, E. I never wanted you to get hurt."

Mills and Olivia came out of the club with all our stuff. "You guys ready to head out? I know we just got here, but I think I'm kinda over it." Olivia said, holding her hand out to help Ellie stand from the curb.

"Definitely. Let's just hang at the room," Ellie answered.

I stared up at her, forgetting to stand up and act like a normal human. She'd just found out her boyfriend of more than a year had cheated on her, and she was holding it together. I, on the other hand, was unraveling.

"What a night." Ellie plopped down on one of the two queen beds in our hotel room. Mills and Olivia had gone down to the gift shop to get some toiletries Olivia had forgotten, leaving Ellie and me alone again.

I sat next to her. "Your boyfriend was a buzz kill."

She laughed softly. "Ex-boyfriend."

"Right." I got up and took the spare blanket off the chair to make my bed on the floor. I wasn't sure what else to say after everything that happened. I wasn't thinking about how it affected my feelings for her, I was just concerned with how she was doing. That should have made me feel *more* comfortable because that was how a best friend was supposed to feel. Instead, I felt like a schizophrenic.

"You don't have to sleep on the floor, you know," Ellie whispered from behind me.

I cringed. That was the last thing I needed to hear right then. I swiped a pillow from the bed and tossed it on top of the blanket, not looking at her. "It's no problem, really. I've been sleeping in dirt holes for the last month. The floor looks great."

"Spencer."

Something in her tone made me turn around. She was standing now, her eyes welling up with tears. She looked so *vulnerable.* I crossed to her in two quick strides, folding her into my arms. She didn't cry. She just sniffled quietly with uneasy breaths. Her fingers curled into my shirt and I smoothed my hands down her back, trying to be comforting. She tilted her head up to look at me.

As I gazed into her eyes, my stomach turned like crazy. It was the same situation from that night by the swings, only my respect for her relationship with Tim had stopped me from kissing her then. Warning bells clattered in my head. She told me what she wanted, and I wasn't it. This wasn't going to happen the way I wanted it to. Was it?

She licked her lips. I swear I stopped breathing at that moment. Just when I thought I couldn't take it anymore, her eyes raked down to my mouth and back up again. *Twice.*

In an instant, I placed a hand on each side of her face and brought her lips to mine. She responded to my kiss immediately. Her hands gripped my shirt, and she stood on her toes, pulling me to her. She was just as greedy for this as I was. Our mouths moved together in a way that was so familiar, it was almost as if we'd practiced it a hundred times.

My fingers tangled in her hair and I brought one hand down to rest on her lower back. I pressed her against my body, not sure how to handle the fire running through my veins. It was more than lust. It was more than anything I'd ever felt. It scared the heck out of me, and I wanted more.

With a silent curse, I steadied myself. I could absolutely devour her, but I also felt the need to savor this moment while it lasted. As if on cue, I felt her palms press flat against my chest and she pushed me back. Regretfully, I broke the kiss and rested my forehead to hers. I didn't take my hands off her though. I couldn't.

"Wait," she whispered, breathing hard.

I closed my eyes, inhaling her scent as I waited for her to tell me to let go. I wasn't sure I'd be able to, but for her, I'd try. After a moment, she didn't pull away. I felt my heartbeat even out with each moment she let me keep holding her.

"Spencer, I'm a mess," she murmured, her breath mingling with mine. "I don't want to ruin things between us. I don't want you to kiss me because you feel bad for me or something."

My eyes snapped open. I pulled my forehead back and stared at her, bewildered. "I'm not."

"I don't want to make a mistake just because of what happened tonight."

I brought my hand to her cheek again and smoothed my thumb over her soft skin. Her lashes fluttered at my touch. She felt perfect in my arms, and for once it wasn't about what I could or couldn't offer her. I just needed to keep feeling this way. As selfish as that was, something changed at that moment that neither one of us could ever take back.

"You can't be my rebound, Spence."

"I'm not."

She glared at me with a touch of humor in her eyes. "Is that all you can say?"

"Tell me this feels wrong."

I watched her face as the seconds ticked by. If she said it was wrong, I would let her go. It would be wrong to expect her to feel something more for me than she did. I couldn't take back my feelings, but I could respect hers. If she said she didn't want me, I'd back off. I wasn't sure what that would mean for our friendship though. Could we go back to being 'just friends' after this?

Ellie shook her head, and that was all I needed. I pulled her to me again, slanting my mouth over hers. She let out a gentle moan that almost brought me to my knees. I grabbed her hips with my hands and lifted her so her legs wrapped around my waist. I carried her to the wall in front of me and we continued to explore this new connection between us. My mind on overdrive, I ran a hand over her soft curves. She was familiar and brand new at the same time.

We heard laughter from down the hall and knew Olivia and Matt were back from the store. Ellie wriggled out of my grasp in an instant. Her boots touched the floor, and she ducked under my arm, adjusting her shirt as she went. I stood, frozen, with my hands braced against the wall for support. Blood pounded in my ears and I needed a moment to get ahold of myself. I wished more than anything they'd gone on a longer errand.

"They'll be here any second," she said from behind me.

I turned around and saw she was bundling up her pajamas and digging through her toiletry bag. I chuckled. "You gonna take a shower?"

"Yeah," she nodded. "A cold one."

I smiled wryly at her.

She sighed and stopped in the doorway of the bathroom, looking flushed and absolutely gorgeous. I brushed her hair back from her face, tucking it behind her ear. The door beeped as Mills used his electronic key to open it, and Ellie disappeared into the bathroom. I quickly flopped into the chair next to the bathroom door and pulled out my phone, trying to look casual. Hopefully they didn't see me as the frantic idiot I felt like in that moment.

"Hey," Mills greeted me, holding the door for his girl.

"Did you get what you needed?" I asked them, working to keep my voice steady and even.

"Yeah," Oliva answered, holding up a small plastic bag. "Where's Ellie?" Olivia asked.

I hooked my thumb at the bathroom door. "Shower."

"You sleeping on the floor, bro?" Mills asked, eyeing my makeshift bed on the ground.

"Clearly," I answered with a short laugh.

"Man, I would've thought you'd bunk with Ellie. Since you're *just friends*, and all."

"Uh, yeah, I don't think that would be a good idea," I answered, looking between Mills and his girl. They both stood there looking at me with knowing smiles. "Okay, I left my bag in the car. I'm gonna go get it. And you guys are acting weird. Chill out."

I got up and grabbed a room key off the table, tucking it into my back pocket. When I reached the door, Olivia laughed softly.

I turned around. "What?"

"I'm just really happy for you guys." Olivia stage whispered, and Mills poked her in the side to shush her.

"*Chill out.*" I motioned with my hand like I was trying to calm a child, palm out and pressing toward the ground. Shaking my head, I stepped out into the hallway and closed the door behind me. Letting out a shaky breath, I leaned against it and stared at the ceiling. No going back now.

# 13

# ELLIE

I woke up with a smile on my face. I was facing Matt and Olivia's bed, but they weren't in it. I peered down over the side of my bed onto the floor, spying Spencer sleeping on his back with one strong arm behind his head, and the other resting on his chest. His full lips were peaceful. I touched my own lips, remembering the kiss from last night. The kiss that ended all kisses. The kiss that I never knew how much I wanted until it happened.

Spencer stirred, so I rolled back onto my pillow, afraid he'd wake up to find me staring down at him like the creeper I was. I waited a beat, then peered over the edge again. "Good morning."

"Good morning," he smiled sleepily.

I didn't know what to say. Was he replaying last night's kiss in his mind like I was? What did he think about it all?

"How did you sleep?" he asked, rubbing his hands over his face.

"Great, thanks."

"Do you regret last night?"

I chuckled. "Wow, getting straight to the point, huh?"

"Might as well."

His face was blank as he waited for my answer. It was like a mask, and it made me uneasy. My confusion must have shown on my face because he frowned.

"Do you feel like I took advantage of you?"

I shook my head, my chin resting on my arm as I looked down at him. "No, I don't. Though, I doubt it would have happened if I hadn't been such a mess. But that's not your fault."

He quirked his brow. "You only kissed me because you were a mess?"

"Not exactly... I just know my feelings were all over the place when it happened."

"So, how are you feeling right now?"

"I feel like I probably *should* feel worse than I do. I had a dramatic and public break up, complete with a slap and a broken nose for the guy, and then I made out with my best friend. I should definitely feel worse."

Spencer stared at me for a long moment. "I think you summed it up just fine in the parking lot afterward. He hurt your pride. You're not as upset now because you know you weren't supposed to be with him. Which brings me to my next question..."

I pursed my lips, waiting.

"When you said you broke up with him because you

realized you didn't miss him enough, was that it? You ended your relationship, promise ring and all, because you didn't think you missed him the way Olivia missed Matt?"

I paused for a long time, not sure if I should be honest in my answer. Where was this going between us? Why had he kissed me, and what did it mean for our friendship?

"I see your wheels turning," he said. He sat up, resting his back on the side of Matt and Olivia's bed, facing me.

I smiled at his impatience. "I was just thinking about what you said."

"Well?"

"Well..." I shrugged, trying to seem nonchalant. "I didn't miss him the way I missed *you*."

"Come here." He crooked a finger at me.

I hopped down off the bed and sat next to him, resting my back on the side of the bed and hugging my knees to my chest. I held my breath as he trailed his fingers up my arm, then my shoulder. I watched his hand until it curled into my hair. Sighing, I looked into his bright blue eyes. I couldn't believe the emotion I saw there, and I wondered if there was any way I could get him to talk about his feelings without ruining this moment. I had never noticed how stunning his eyes were. But... maybe it was just the way he was looking at me.

"Let me just clarify something," he started, his face serious. "Last night, you were an emotional wreck, and you think that's the only reason we kissed."

I nodded, my face resting in the palm of his hand.

"This morning, after a good night's sleep, you feel better."

I nodded again.

"Good."

Slowly, he shifted closer and brought my face to his, lightly touching his lips to mine. He was much gentler than he'd been last night. I had time to register the softness of his lips, and the way he held my face like I was breakable. He pulled my bottom lip between his and sucked lightly. The sigh that escaped from my open mouth prompted him to deepen the kiss. Just when I was about to lose my senses, he kissed me once more and pulled back to look at me. His eyes looked as fierce as they had last night even though this kiss had the complete opposite vibe. Slow and soft versus fast and hard. Both were amazing.

"Well?" he asked again.

My brows pulled together. "Well, what?"

"Did you need to be a mess for that to feel right?"

I stifled a laugh. I was a mess, all right. "No, it felt just as right as the first time."

"I agree."

Just as he was about to move in for another kiss, we heard the electronic beep of a key being used on the door. We sprang apart and tried to act natural, just two friends hanging out on the floor, as Matt and Olivia came in. They were carrying bags from the bagel shop just outside of the base.

"We brought coffee!" Olivia announced cheerfully. She set the drink container she was holding on the coffee table and removed a paper cup. "I wasn't about to drink the crap they have here."

Matt rolled his eyes and laughed. "Yes, even though there is a free continental breakfast and tons of coffee in the lobby, my girl here needed to run off base."

"Hope you don't mind we took your car, Ellie." Olivia brought me a cup from the drink holder, and I waved a hand in dismissal.

Spencer rose from the floor and stretched. He'd slept in a tightly fitted olive-green shirt and basketball shorts. I knew from the years we'd been friends he usually liked to sleep in nothing but his boxers, but I was glad he'd avoided doing that last night. Not that he would with Olivia in the room, I hoped. He thanked Matt for the food and dug through the bags, leaning across the table to reach for his own cup of coffee.

"Here." Spencer came back over to me with a coffee stirrer, a handful of sugar packets, and plenty of creamer pods.

"Thanks." I blushed. Why did I suddenly feel so shy?

I made my coffee while Spencer practically inhaled his food and then announced he wanted to take a shower. I uncharacteristically wished I could follow him into the bathroom and finish what we'd started. How had I not noticed how hot he was? I mean, logically, I knew. But I don't think I really *knew* until last night.

"Ellie?"

"What?" I cringed. "Sorry."

Matt laughed. "We were just saying we wanted to go to the beach today if you guys are down."

Olivia stared at me suspiciously. Leave it to another girl to recognize when there was something juicy to talk about. "Yeah, that sounds great. It's gonna be freezing in the water though."

"A few of the guys from our platoon are going there to play football. It'll be sunny out, no big deal."

"I just want to tan, anyway," Olivia agreed.

I frowned. "I didn't bring a suit."

"I brought two," Olivia offered with a wide, problem-solving, smile. When Matt and I both looked at her curiously, she laughed. "What? I'm an over-packer."

"You forgot a toothbrush, but you brought two swimsuits?" Matt asked.

Olivia shrugged. "I didn't say I was good at it."

I stared out at the ocean as I rubbed tanning lotion on my legs. Matt was chasing Olivia, trying to get her to go in the water by force. She dodged him as he made a grab for her and I grinned when he tripped and fell into the surf. They were laughing and kicking the frigid water at one another. I couldn't help but smile. It was so obvious they were in love.

My eyes traveled to Spencer. He was tossing a football around with the other guys from his platoon. They all had their shirts off, their chests literally glistening in the sun. The scene reminded me of Baywatch or something. Eye-roll worthy, gratuitous hotness, on display. Were they running in slow motion, or was it just me?

"Hey, hot stuff," Olivia greeted me as she sat down on the towel next to mine. "I think that leg has enough lotion."

I flushed. "Oops."

"Yeah, oops. Too busy staring at the shirtless Marines playing football?"

"Pretty objectifying, I know."

Olivia patted my arm. "I'm sure they don't mind. Hey, are you doing okay? We haven't had a chance to talk alone after all the drama last night."

I wondered if Olivia would judge me if I told her about kissing Spencer. She knew I'd been with Tim for more than a year. Would that make me seem callous in her eyes? It was bad enough I wasn't upset about our breakup, let alone moving on with another guy so quickly.

I cleared my throat. "Ugh, safe space?"

"Of course," she assured me, holding up the universally known hand signal of the Girl Scouts. "Scout's honor."

"I'm totally okay with what happened with Tim."

"I thought you might be."

I rose my brow. "Really?"

Olivia sighed heavily and made a face like she was searching for the right words. "I hate it when a girl breaks up with a guy and her friends are like, 'I knew there was something wrong with him,' or 'I didn't think you guys would last, anyway.' It seems so fake and unhelpful. But, there was something about the way you and Tim acted around each other... it kinda made me want you to break up. I don't know... maybe you weren't as happy as you could be."

Frowning, I looked down at my hands. In all the commotion, I'd totally forgotten to take the promise ring off last night. I pulled it off and played with it in my hands.

"I'm sorry if I'm overstepping." Olivia put a hand on my knee. "I know we haven't been friends for very long, so this might be inappropriate for me to say."

If I'd really loved Tim, Olivia's words likely would've offended me. But she was right. "No, it's okay. I had a similar talk with Spencer about how I think I'm okay because some part of me knew it wouldn't last with Tim. It's weird you got that impression just from watching us together."

"Don't beat yourself up. This stuff is confusing. If it were easy, there wouldn't be any truly great love stories." Olivia smiled at me and then laid back on her towel. "Oh, and whenever you want to tell me what happened between you and Spencer, feel free."

I swung my head around to look at her. "You *know*?"

"I'm not stupid. You guys have been acting like total weirdos around each other. Spill!"

"I don't know what it means yet... But we kissed."

Olivia propped herself up on her elbows. "Shut *up*. Did he kiss you or the other way around?"

"He kissed me. Last night. You guys were at the gift shop. And then again this morning before you got back."

"Was it amazing? I bet he's a great kisser." She wiggled her eyebrows.

I glanced over at Spencer and couldn't help the grin

that spread over my face. I'd never talked about stuff like this before... probably because I'd never had a first kiss worth gushing over. I'm sure having a guy for a best friend had something to do with it, too. I filled Olivia in on as many of the juicy details as I dared, laughing and blushing all the while. It felt good to be excited about a guy. I'd been kidding myself with Tim for far too long.

"The only problem is, I'm worried I'm treating him like a rebound. I was with Tim for a long time. Spencer and I definitely have chemistry, but that could be just because we know each other so well."

Olivia cocked her head as she considered. "I see what you mean. But I don't think this is a rebound. If you didn't want this so bad I doubt you would have risked your friendship for it, would you?"

"No," I confirmed. "That's the last thing I want to do. I tried to think about it rationally, but every time he looks at me, I get butterflies."

Olivia made a face like she was going to throw up and we both laughed. "Seriously though, he kissed you when we weren't around. Is this like a secret thing? Or are you guys together now?"

Before I could respond, Olivia let out a small squeal. She ducked her head between her knees and shielded herself with her arms. I turned just in time to see Spencer diving through the air, trying to catch the football that was careening toward my head. One of his long arms snaked out just far enough to catch it before skidding through the sand and colliding with me. His rough landing had tossed sand all over us. I tried to brush it off, but the tanning lotion acted as an adhesive on my skin.

The impressive catch had Spencer panting. He abruptly rolled to the balls of his feet and crouched over me. Before I could say a word, he grabbed me by the back of the neck and crushed my mouth to his. It was as brief as it was surprising, and in the blink of an eye, he was gone. I watched, stunned, as he jogged back to his laughing friends. Matt's face was absolutely dumbfounded by what he had just seen, and Spencer just slapped him on the shoulder as he ran by.

"Well," Olivia chuckled, brushing sand off her arms and chest. "Guess he's not planning on keeping anything a secret."

I touched my fingers to my lips as I stared after him. "I guess not."

## 14

## SPENCER

"See you lovebirds in a few hours," Ellie called, shutting the door to our hotel room and joining me in the hallway.

Thank God Mills and his girl wanted alone time. I felt like a zoo-exhibit with how much they watched me interact with Ellie. It was nice to get out and hang with her alone.

"Dinner was good," Ellie commented as I took her hand. She stared down at it for a moment with a bewildered look on her face and then brought her gaze up to meet mine.

"Yeah, it was." I hoped my smile was reassuring. To be honest, I was just as surprised about the ease of this as she was. I hadn't even thought about taking her hand. It just happened. Easy as breathing.

We made our way into the stairwell that led to the

grounds below. Outside, the air was chilly, and Ellie shivered beside me. I put my arm around her. The sun had kept us warm on the beach that day, but the temperature had dropped since then. I peered down at her. She was wearing the Marine Corps hoodie she had purchased at my graduation. She looked adorable in it. I almost sighed, and then caught myself. Too much.

"So, where are we going?" Ellie asked.

I shrugged. "I figured we could walk around for a bit, maybe head over to the Starbucks over there."

"That sounds good. But I think I might get hot chocolate so I'm not up all night."

"Who knows, we might need to be up all night. Mills was pretty eager to get some time alone with Olivia."

"Well, it's only been a few weeks since they've seen each other."

That made me laugh. "Yeah, well, it's been weeks since any of us have even seen an attractive female."

"There are no girls in combat training?"

"Not here; they go to the east coast."

"Oh." She smiled ruefully. "You must be going through withdrawals with no girls to hit on."

I pulled her to a stop and swung her into my arms. Pressing my mouth to hers, I couldn't help but feel a tightening in my stomach as she gave herself over to me. I wanted her so much. Again, easy as breathing. Why hadn't we done this sooner? *Oh, right, because there are a ton of reasons we shouldn't do it at all.*

I felt her smile against my lips and all negative

thoughts left my head. I wasn't sure how long we stood there kissing on the sidewalk. I barely registered the cars whizzing by on the street, feet away. One thing about military bases, a young couple kissing in random places was a common sight.

I broke the kiss and smiled down at her. "Well, I *was* going through withdrawals. But as long as we keep doing that, I think I'll survive."

We laughed and continued walking, hand in hand.

"This is nice," Ellie said. "I wish I could stay until Tuesday like Olivia instead of leaving tomorrow night."

I squeezed her hand. "Me, too. You sure you can't call in?"

"I already tried, my dad said we have a big filing on Monday, and he needs me there to help. I'll come back again on Tuesday to pick up Olivia though, so at least I'll see you then."

"How's the job going?" I asked.

"It's going well..."

I noticed the hesitation in her voice. "But?"

"But, my dad isn't letting up on me about becoming a lawyer. Honestly, the more time I spend in that environment, the more I realize that I wouldn't like to have his job."

"Have you tried explaining that to him?"

"Yes, and no," she shrugged. "I've told him I'm still not sure it's the right career for me. Before I took the job, I had no problem telling him I didn't want to be a lawyer. But now I'm supposed to be learning about the field and giving it a chance, so I try not to be so critical."

Ellie was so smart. She was always thinking about the many sides of a situation, not just the one that was most relevant to her. I admired it. But at some point, she needed to stand up for herself. If it was possible to be considerate to a fault, Ellie definitely was.

"Just do me a favour." I started, staring straight ahead. "Don't let your dad - or anyone - talk you into doing something you don't want to do. You have so much going for you. I know whatever you do, it will be great. You don't have to be a lawyer."

She smiled and squeezed my hand. "Thanks, Spence."

"So, how's the new guy? Fat and bald?"

"Eric? Not quite." She chuckled. "But he's nice. He doesn't treat me like a five-year-old like some of them do."

"That's good."

We didn't talk for a while, but it wasn't an awkward silence. Sometimes we didn't feel the need to fill up the empty air with random words. It was comfortable just to be together. That was one of the best parts of our friendship, and I was glad it wasn't changing now.

We reached the Starbucks, and I held the door for her as she walked in. Since it was a libo weekend, there were couples everywhere. We weren't the only ones on a late-night coffee run. Then again, there wasn't much to do on base, so it made sense people would chill there.

As we approached the counter, I had a moment of panic. Ellie and I always bought our own food or drinks whenever we were together. But now, I realized if she were anyone else, I wouldn't even hesitate to buy her coffee.

Would she think it was weird, or was she expecting it? Was this a date?

"Can I help you?" The clerk behind the counter had a sullen expression. He was obviously ready to go home for the night.

I turned to Ellie and gestured for her to order ahead of me. She asked the guy for a hot chocolate with whipped cream, and I asked for a black coffee. When he gave us the total, we both reached for our money.

"I have cash. I think mine was like three dollars." She was already unzipping her wallet and pulling out the bills.

"No, it's fine." I put a hand over hers on the wallet. "I got it."

The cashier rolled his eyes and thrust his hand out further for my money. I glared at him as I handed over the cash for our drinks, deciding not to tip him. He needed to get laid. We stepped over to the end of the counter to wait.

"Thanks, Spence. I'll get the next round," Ellie offered with a smile.

I wondered if that meant she didn't think this was a date. When we got our drinks, we took a seat at a table on the patio since it was less crowded out there.

"So, this is crazy," she blurted out.

I had just taken a sip of my coffee and it scalded my mouth. "What's crazy?"

"Oh, you know. Us, acting like a couple."

Not sure what to say, I just watched her. Ever since my feelings for Ellie first changed, I'd been convincing myself it would never work between us. Now, I was trying not to think about any of that. It felt so good to be with her like this. I didn't want to dwell on all the reasons it was a bad idea. Still, they leaked in. What happened when I left and she was alone again? What happened when she realized this military life wasn't for her? What if I'm just a rebound? I'd really stepped in it this time.

"Anyway, since you're obviously not in the mood to talk about this, how do you like being a Marine so far?" Her tone was joking, but I mentally told myself to relax and stop being a baby.

"I like it. Combat training was pretty rough, but I'm about to graduate and start actually learning about my job. I'm looking forward to that."

She sighed. "Where are you off to next?"

"After this, I go to Florida for A School."

Ellie fidgeted with the cardboard sleeve on her to-go cup. "And after that?"

Shaking my head, I let out a breath. "I won't know until the end of A School. I know it'll be another school. I just don't know where."

Saying this out loud didn't help my mood. My future was so uncertain. Before I left for boot camp, this was an adventure I couldn't wait to get started on. Now, I felt like I was somehow disappointing Ellie by being on the move all the time. I didn't like that feeling. This was my dream. Now I was conflicted over something I'd been so excited about only a short time ago. One thing was for sure, for this to work at all, I needed to figure out a way to balance both the Marine Corps and the girl of my dreams.

"And what happens after that school?" She didn't meet my eyes.

"I don't know. It'll be months before I know where I'm stationed."

Ellie looked up at me and tried to smile. "Have you thought about where you want to end up? I bet there are a lot of really cool places you could go."

"Ellie." I held my hand out to her and when she took it, I gently tugged her from her seat and onto my lap. I put my finger under her chin to make sure she was looking at me. "You've always been there for me. I want... I *need* you to know, no matter where I am, or what we are to each other, I'll always be there for you, too. No matter where they send me, I'll always come back to you."

The look in her eyes made my chest hurt, but I held her gaze as I waited for her response.

Ellie leaned down and kissed me softly. "I know, Spence."

When she pulled back, I noticed a lone eyelash on her cheek. I touched it with the tip of my finger and then held it out to her. She grinned and pressed the tip of her finger to mine, with the eyelash in the middle. She closed her eyes, and I watched as she made a wish. This was a tradition we'd started a long time ago. I wasn't sure how it started, but it was always the same. It was like a wishbone. We would make a wish, and whoever had the eyelash on their finger when we pulled our hands apart would get their wish.

We separated our fingers, and she pouted when she saw the eyelash on my finger.

"Don't worry, you'll still get your wish," I told her.

She looked up at me, surprised. "How?"

"I wished that your wish would come true."

"Hey guys!" Olivia greeted us warmly when we returned to the room.

Mills' text had come a lot sooner than I'd expected, and I was pretty annoyed to have my time with Ellie cut short. He'd called us back to the room after only an hour.

The two of them looked almost giddy as they stood together, holding hands. I could tell they were on the verge of telling us some pretty big news, and I immediately worried Olivia was pregnant. Talk about rushing into adulthood.

"Olivia and I are getting married."

I nodded slowly at Mills. "Yeah... we know. We were there when you proposed."

"No, man, I mean we're getting married *tomorrow*. And we want you guys to be our witnesses."

Mills was practically jumping out of his skin with excitement. All I could do was stare at him. Was he serious? I was just barely getting used to an eighteen-year-old proposing marriage, let alone actually following through with it. Of course, I knew they would eventually get married. I just didn't think it would be on a libo weekend with Ellie and me as the only guests.

"Slow down, Mills. Where are you planning to do this?" I scratched my head as I tried to think about logistics.

"Vegas."

Everything moved in slow motion and I found myself wondering if I was on a reality TV show about to get *Punk'd.* I continued to stare blankly at my friend. He had this hopeful expression in his eyes. Olivia and Ellie were already prattling away about what she should wear and how she should do her hair. I gawked at them, bewildered, as they dug through Olivia's suitcase and pulled things out. This was getting out of hand.

"But what about the big wedding you were planning? We spent all that time talking about colors and flowers," Ellie laughed.

Olivia waved her hand. "Sweetie, in the military, a wedding like that is a luxury."

"Really?" Ellie bit her bottom lip. "I feel like I've been planning my dream wedding since I was five. And you seemed so excited to be planning yours. Are you sure you want to do this?"

"Yeah, a lot of military couples get married in the courthouse first and then eventually have a big wedding later. My parents never did though. My mom got pregnant with my brother, so they put it off, and then my dad had a deployment, and when I came along... life just went on. I'm fine either way, as long as I get to spend my life with this handsome guy."

Mills crossed the room and kissed her on the forehead. "If you want a big wedding, I'll make it happen someday."

I watched Ellie while she looked wistfully at them. I could see Olivia's description of military weddings didn't sit well with her. Being the best friend for so many years, I had first-hand knowledge of the silly little things she wanted at her fancy wedding. She wanted red roses, a chocolate fountain, and a huge dress. Most of all, she wanted to get married on Valentine's day, because it was her grandmother's birthday and she thought it would be romantic.

I wondered how many Valentine's Days would go by before my schedule allowed me to make that happen? It's not like I'd be able to take leave whenever I wanted if I was in training or deployed. Looks like I'd found another dream of Ellie's that I wouldn't be able to make happen for her. I shook my head. This wasn't about me and Ellie, this was about my lovesick friend and his hairbrained ideas.

"Okay, I know you guys are excited," I began, holding out my hands, "but your plan needs a little work. We are absolutely, positively, not allowed to leave the state. Heck, we're only allowed to go as far as the beach. The Marine Corps will take one look at that marriage certificate when you turn in your paperwork and find out you went out of bounds on a libo weekend. You'll be screwed. We'll *both* be screwed."

I watched as one by one, the other three faces in the room fell. I couldn't believe Mills hadn't already thought of this scenario. They looked totally crushed and I simultaneously hated myself for bringing them down and hated them for getting carried away and putting me in that position. It was a stupid idea.

"We thought about doing it here, but we don't have a

marriage license." Olivia crossed to her bed and plopped down with a sigh.

"Sorry, but no matter how fast Vegas does marriage licenses, they probably won't do it tomorrow. It's a Sunday. Not even Vegas has county clerks at work on a Sunday." I felt like a jerk for adding another layer of disappointment, but this plan was ludicrous.

Mills sat down by Olivia and took her hand. "It's okay, babe. I'm sorry. I got a little carried away and didn't think it through. We'll do it next time I come home, okay?"

Olivia squeezed his hand. "Okay."

"We'll leave you guys alone again." Ellie, who had been silently standing by the window during this whole exchange, walked out the door. She shot me a dirty look as she passed, and I could feel the ice radiating off of her. I followed her into the hallway with a sigh. She didn't turn when I approached, so I let her lead me in silence down the hall and out into the night. Finally, when we were a good distance away, she rounded on me.

"What is *wrong* with you?" she asked, hands on her hips.

I lifted a brow. "What's wrong with *you?*"

"Me? I'm not the one who barged in there hell-bent on bursting bubbles."

"Bursting bubbles?" I frowned at her, not understanding why she was mad at me for explaining the flaws in their plan. If it weren't for me, we'd be halfway to Vegas by now on a fool's errand.

"Look," she let her hands drop with an exasperated noise. "I know you aren't a big fan of marriage, but you didn't have to ruin that for them. They were really excited. And here you come ready to rain on their parade."

"You're laying it pretty thick with the analogies, don't you think?" I tried to smile crookedly at her, but she only scowled. I stuck my hands in my pockets and shrugged. "Ellie, Las Vegas is four hours away. I'm not sorry I 'rained on their parade.' We can't just sneak off to Vegas so these kids can get married."

"Okay, I admit, they didn't put much thought into it, but you didn't have to seem so happy about shooting it down. You were so insensitive. They're not *kids*. It was a romantic plan and they got carried away."

I groaned. "Look, the last thing I need is to get caught going out of bounds for my buddy's quickie wedding. This is my career. It's important. I can't let 'romantic plans' ruin that."

She stared at me, apparently out of things to say.

Why were we having this argument? We never did this bickering crap. I must have been wrong earlier about the easiness of our friendship remaining unchanged. We were acting like a couple, and not in a good way. This was the kinda thing I'd always avoided.

"Ellie," I sighed. "I don't want to fight with you. I'm sorry if you think I was insensitive. It's none of my business what they do, but this time it affected me. Selfish or not, it wouldn't have worked out anyway without a marriage license. Now can we stop acting like this? This is why I don't date."

It was quick, so quick I almost missed it, but that last comment did *not* go over well. I could see it all over her face. I wasn't sure what to say, though, because it was true. I didn't date because I didn't want to deal with all these feelings mixing together and coming out in a fight. I didn't date because then I only had to be responsible for my own feelings. Reason number 647 that we shouldn't even be together. I'm not good at relationships.

After a moment, she closed her eyes and stepped into my arms. "Yeah, we can stop. I get it... Just... don't be a butt."

I kissed the top of her head and then rested my chin there, staring out into the night. "Don't be a pain in one."

"That was some weekend," Mills said, throwing himself on his bunk. Our squad bay at MCT was slightly nicer than the one in boot camp, even if it was only because there were no drill instructors around to wreck our day for no reason.

I sat on the footlocker at the end of his rack and leaned back against the cold metal bars. In a lot of ways, it had been one of the best weekends of my life. Definitely up there with some of the vacations I used to take with my mom, since just like in those times, reality had been far away. We were tucked into the safety of the base, no real-world nonsense to cloud our fun. We'd laughed, kissed, hung out at the beach... and then just as quickly as it started, it ended.

"You okay?" Mills asked from behind me.

"Yeah."

I heard him shift into a seated position and move closer to where I sat. "You look weird."

I shrugged. "I'm good."

Two guys slammed through the door, adrenaline radiating off of them. Allen, the taller of the two Marines, slammed the side of his fist against his rack.

His buddy flinched. "She's not worth it man, you gotta chill."

Mills and I glanced at each other with matching looks of confusion. Allen had been in our platoon in boot camp but we'd only met Thomas when MCT started. I assessed them both, trying to figure out if they were having problems with each other and we'd have to break up a fight, or if Allen was throwing a fit about an outside issue and Thomas was handling it.

"I haven't even been gone that long," Allen lamented, throwing his hands out in frustration. "She didn't even give it a chance."

Ah, it was over a girl. And I couldn't be sure, but it looked like Allen was drunk. That wouldn't go over well if our instructors found out. Showing up to the barracks, drunk? Big no-no. Allen stumbled around the wide space between our racks, looking at the ground and rubbing his hands over his head. The rest of the Marines in the room were paying attention now, some pretending not to, others moving towards the middle of the room to blatantly watch.

"I know, man, but you gotta just let it go. She's just not that into you, or she would stick it out." Thomas tried to help his friend, but Mills and I just looked at each other as if to say, "awkward."

Allen kicked his footlocker and then turned on his friend. "We've been together for two years, Thomas. She *was* into me. I never should have come here. It ruined everything."

Something in me recoiled from the pain in his voice. The bigger part of me was embarrassed for him. He was drunk, causing a scene in the squad bay in front of all these dudes. But a small part seemed to connect with him on a level that I didn't like. He had a girl. He thought they were solid. Then, one day she leaves him because she didn't want to stick it out.

I glanced at Mills. His face was relaxed and disinterested. He had a girl, too. He thought their relationship was solid. Was he going down a rabbit hole like I was? Did he worry this could happen to him and Olivia? Based on his expression, I would say not. Which made me feel like I was alone on an island of suck. Well, maybe not completely alone, since life sucked for Allen right now, too.

"Man, don't say that," Thomas said, rolling his eyes. "You haven't even gotten started in the Marines yet. Don't do something you'll regret over some girl. This is way more important. If she can't stand by you, screw her."

Before Allen even moved, I knew he would. I sprang to my feet and caught his arm before his fist connected with Thomas' nose. He didn't need this scene to get worse or he'd definitely get busted. Like an idiot, Thomas held his hands up and defended what he said, refusing to back down. Allen squirmed in my grasp yelling at him to shut his mouth. The few Marines who'd been loosely standing in the center of the room all stepped forward and picked a side, getting between the two guys and separating them further. The scene was getting out of control now, with a dozen Marines in a mob of yelling for each other to shut up, back off, and calm down.

The door to the squad bay slammed open and everyone sprang apart. One of our instructors blasted into the room. He looked around the mob, but there was no clear source of the scuffle, no two Marines who looked like they'd started it. We were all in a group with no obvious sides.

"What's going on?" Sergeant Nichols asked no one in particular. "Huh?"

Allen stood to my left, and while the rest of us were still, he swayed slightly. Slowly, I angled my body so that it mostly blocked him from the instructor's view. I took pity on the guy. He may have started this whole scene, but he was still just an eighteen-year-old kid who'd gotten dumped because his girl didn't want to be in a long-distance relationship. He didn't need to get held back from graduation over this.

"Maybe you didn't hear me," Sergeant Nichols said, eyeballing each of us. "What's going on?"

Again, no one spoke. No one moved. No one outed Allen and Thomas. We may be new to the Marine Corps, but we already understood the importance of having each other's backs. Even when it wasn't a life or death situation. I stood a little straighter. He couldn't hold us all back. The next cycle was ready to start, and the machine had to keep moving, churning us all out to our next schools and locations.

"Okay, must have been a team building exercise," Sergeant Nichols said, hands on his hips. "Am I right?"

Several of us nodded, and a few said, "Yes, Sergeant."

"Rah," our instructor said, shaking his head and going back out the way he came in. It was the shortened form of "oorah," the familiar battle cry of the Marine Corps. We'd shouted it a lot in boot camp, but so far in MCT we'd heard it shortened and used as if to say, "good to go" or "understood."

We took a collective breath when the door slammed shut behind him. No one spoke about it, just ambled back to their racks and carried on with whatever they were doing before Allen and Thomas came in. Mills had moved to the end of his rack to watch, and he sat back down when I came over.

I blew out a breath as I sat next to him.

"That was close," Mills said, referring to the instructor almost busting us.

"I'm just glad that didn't happen at MCRD. I highly doubt our DIs would be as chill as Nichols."

"Agreed. How did you know he was gonna hit him?"

"It's what I would have done if I was in the same situation."

"Yeah, me too, I guess. Allen's an idiot though. Who shows up drunk after a libo weekend?"

I bristled. "A dude who got dumped just for being a Marine."

Mills eyed me carefully. "Mm-hmm."

"What?"

"You're overthinking this."

I shook my head. "No, I'm not."

"Just because Allen got dumped," Mills started, looking around and lowering his voice, "doesn't mean *you're* going to. You guys just got together. She's not going to dump you."

"Maybe not yet, but two years from now, maybe I'll be showing up drunk and pissed off for the same reason. He clearly didn't see it coming either." I hooked my thumb over my shoulder at Allen, who was on his rack with his pillow over his head. I shuddered, not wanting to be him.

"Bro, seriously, take a break from being broody and lovesick. Just be happy."

I glared at him. "Mills, she never wanted this. It may not be tomorrow, it may not be next month, but someday, she's going to wake up and realize she's not down with all this. Who is?"

Mills cocked his head at me and blinked slowly.

"Okay," I amended. "Some people are, *Olivia* is. But Ellie isn't. And if we're going to crash and burn anyway, I'd rather keep her as my best friend than try this and lose her completely."

"You're jumping the gun, Hawk."

"I don't think so. I never should have started things with her in the first place. I really don't want to end up like Allen, over there. What if it happens during a deployment? I'm better off alone."

Mills shook his head and stood, looking down at me

with an expression that could only be described as pity. "You're making a mistake."

I stood from Mills' rack, ready to head back to my own and get some sleep. "No, Mills, I already made the mistake. Now I have to fix it."

## 15

## ELLIE

The ride back to base to pick up Olivia was a long and frustrating one. I was so excited to see Spencer again, but I also had this odd feeling of foreboding. The weekend had been amazing. I couldn't believe how right it felt to be in Spencer's arms. After being friends for so long, we just seemed to fit. But no matter how right everything felt at the time, there was something eating away at me now.

I approached the gate and saw Spencer, Matt, and Olivia waiting for me. Pulling over and parking near them, I saw that Olivia was grinning widely, while Matt just looked uncomfortable. My eyes met Spencer's through the windshield and that feeling of doubt spread. Something was wrong. I just knew it. I hadn't spoken to him since I left on Sunday, but I knew he wouldn't have access to his phone once libo ended. Had something changed between then and now?

I pressed the button on my door to unlock the car so Olivia could put her bags in the back. Spencer was at my window, and I rolled it down. He narrowed his eyes at me with a slight smile. "You're not getting out?"

Without replying, I unbuckled my seatbelt and opened the door, taking a deep breath. I wasn't sure what I was bracing myself for. "Hey."

"Hey, yourself."

"How was graduation?"

"Boring."

I tilted my head. "Sorry I missed it."

Without another word, he closed the distance between us. His arms held me tight against him and he buried his face in my hair. He inhaled deeply, one hand just above my waistline and the other cupping the back of my neck. This hug wasn't just a hug. He was saying goodbye.

He pulled back to look at me, eyes searching my face. "Can we take a walk?"

My heart sank. He took my hand in his and led me away from Olivia and Matt. I could feel her eyes on me as we passed them. Did she know what was going on?

"Ellie," Spencer brought me to a halt when we were a safe enough distance from our friends. Not much of a walk, it seemed.

"Are you ending this?" I asked, cutting to the chase.

He nodded. "Yeah, I think it was a mistake."

Though I'd seen it coming, his words felt like a punch to the gut, knocking the wind right out of me. He was holding my hands between us, and he tightened his grip when I took an involuntary step backward. The sparks were still there, and they were huge and unmistakable. Why was he ignoring them? His eyes were scalding as they searched my face, and I felt like there were a thousand things we were both trying to say without speaking. At that moment, I don't think I could have spoken if I'd tried.

"Ellie? Did you hear me?" His voice was rough and sounded like gravel in my ears.

I narrowed my eyes at him in response, still at a loss for words. I hoped my silence would make him say more. Because he wasn't saying enough and all I could feel was *anger*. Raw and raging anger.

"It's just... I'm leaving. You're staying. You have your job with your dad, you're still trying to figure out what you want to do. I already know. This, being a Marine, *leaving* San Diego, has always been my dream. We had a fun weekend, but now it's time to get back to reality."

"Reality?" I parroted. "You want to just go back to being friends?"

"I just think it would be better to do that now, before we get in too deep." He swallowed hard and looked away. "It's what's best for both of us."

I shook my head. "Don't speak for me. If you're ending this, it's because it's what's best for you."

"Okay. Then it's what's best for me." He dropped my hands and stepped back, looking over at Mills. "You ready?"

"Really?" I asked, staring daggers into him. "That's it?"

He smiled slightly. "We gave it a shot, but I just don't think it's going to work with the distance and everything."

"Fine." I turned on my heel and walked back to my car. I was proud of myself for walking smoothly and not stomping like I wanted to. He was out of his mind for starting all this crap with me and then ending it after a weekend.

Olivia had already finished saying goodbye to Matt, so she got in the passenger side of my car and put her seat-belt on without a word. Spencer was still standing about twenty feet in front of me, wearing his woodland cammies, arms crossed in front of him. He looked every bit of the Marine he'd always wanted to be. I couldn't decide if I wanted to put the pedal to the metal and run him over or get out and launch myself into his arms. I settled for neither, pulling the car onto the road and turning back towards home.

"Ellie, are you going to tell me what's going on?" Olivia asked quietly.

I snorted. "You're telling me you don't already know?"

"I mean, I could tell he ended things."

"Yep."

She frowned. "I just don't get it."

"Me neither." My tone was clipped. *I shouldn't take this out on Olivia.* Rolling my shoulders, I tried to relax. I pulled onto the highway towards downtown San Diego and checked my mirrors for oncoming traffic. California was famous for traffic, but it was like playing high-speed Tetris. You had to pay attention because even though it was bumper-to-bumper, the entire mass of cars traveled at seventy miles per hour.

"Are you okay?"

"I guess."

She adjusted in her seat, clearly uncomfortable. "He was acting strangely after you left on Sunday. Extra broody. Matt kept asking him what was wrong, but I could tell he didn't want to talk about it in front of me. I figured it was because he missed you. I didn't see him yesterday, but after the graduation today he still didn't seem like himself."

"What could have happened to change his mind? I thought we were fine. We had a weird fight—if you can even call it that—on Saturday night. It was dumb, I was mad at him for shooting down your idea and being so insensitive. He said he didn't want to fight and this kinda thing was why he didn't date."

"Ouch," Olivia whistled.

"You know what? Oh, well. I think I just mixed up some signals at some point. I want stability and he wants adventure. I don't even know why we started this in the first place. Let's just drop it. How are you doing with all of this? Matt leaving for a few months, that is."

Olivia looked out her window and sighed. "I'm fine. At least while he's in school he'll get to use his phone. As long as I can hear his voice, I don't think it'll be as hard as it's been for the last few months."

"Christmas break will be here before you know it." I reached over and patted her knee. The schools closed over the holidays so Spencer and Matt would be home for two weeks. My stomach knotted up again thinking about seeing Spencer after what we'd just gone through. I wasn't sure I'd be able to be around him after this. It was three weeks away... maybe that was enough time for me to get over one ill-advised *mistake* of a weekend.

"Good morning, Elizabeth."

I smiled at Eric as he leaned casually on my ledge. "Good morning."

"How are you today?"

"Fine, thanks. You have some calls from yesterday." I reached for the stack of messages I had set aside for him and handed them over. He didn't leave my desk as he read the messages. Not sure of what else I should do, I turned back to my computer and continued checking my email.

After a few moments, I could feel his eyes on me. I glanced over at him. "Is there anything else you need?"

He smiled. "No."

"Okay, then why are you still leaning on my ledge?" I laughed.

He abruptly straightened, raising his hands palms out. "Forgive me. I'll keep my hands off the sacred ledge. You okay?"

I stiffened. I hadn't slept well the night before. After dropping Olivia off, I hadn't gotten home until almost midnight. Then, more obsessing over the Spencer thing had kept me tossing and turning until almost dawn. I truly hoped I didn't look as crappy as I felt.

"Like I said, I'm fine." I lied. He scrutinized me for a long moment, and I knew if I didn't change the subject he would press further. "So, how do you like working for my dad?"

The handsome attorney narrowed his eyes at me with mock suspicion. "Are you going to tell him whatever I tell you?"

"Yes, he hired me to find out what his team really thinks of him."

"In that case, I hate it. He's a tyrant. If there aren't better snacks in the lounge and Kool-Aid in the drinking fountains by Monday, I'm out of here. In fact, I want Mondays off. No one should have to work on Mondays. It's cruel and unusual."

"I'll pass that along." I couldn't help but laugh at his serious expression.

He leaned farther over the ledge and whispered conspiratorially, his eyes twinkling. "You didn't hear it from me, but the rest of the guys are planning a coup to take the old man down."

I snickered, feeling the tension I'd been carrying that morning lift a little. It was nice to joke around with Eric. The rest of the lawyers at the firm were always so serious. They scrutinized my every move as if waiting for me to make a mistake and prove that I had no business being there. I understood the pressure they were under to meet deadlines in big cases, so I didn't take it personally. But it still sucked.

"Seriously, though, I enjoy working here. Your dad is really something. I could learn a lot from him," Eric said.

"Yeah, he's great. That's why I'm here, you know. To learn from him."

"I figured as much. My dad had me filing for him in the summers to get me used to the environment. It helped a lot when I was pre-law, and later in law school. It's never too early to learn the legal jargon."

I gaped at him. "Your dad is a lawyer who groomed you to be a lawyer?"

"Well, when you put it that way it sounds a lot less appealing than 'joining the family business' or 'following in my old man's footsteps.' I take it you're resistant to doing the same?"

"You could say that."

He waved a hand. "I wasn't. I knew from a young age I wanted to be a lawyer like my dad. It wasn't just because I wanted to do what he did. I knew that it was the right choice for me. So I don't feel *groomed.*"

"How did you know it was right for you?" I asked.

Eric cocked his head, thinking about his answer. "Well, as far back as I can remember, I loved going to work with my dad. I would sit in a chair in his office with a pad and pen, saying I was doing depositions just like him. I would go to interview the other lawyers in his practice and steal supplies for my 'office' he let me set up at the corner of his desk. When I got older, I always asked him about his cases, and he challenged me to find other cases he could use as precedents. It was just what we did. I loved it. Still do, in fact."

"Wow."

"Your resistance to the whole thing is probably because deep down you know that you don't want to be a lawyer. You can't let someone else dictate where your heart is."

My heart pinched, thinking of how Spencer had said something similar the other night at Starbucks. "No, I guess I can't."

Eric folded his arms on the ledge again. "So, what *do* you want to do?"

"Honestly, I have no idea. I think it's making him nervous that I don't have a passion for anything. That's probably why he pushes this field on me so hard. It stresses me out." Again, it made me sad remembering Spencer had given me that advice right before he'd left for boot camp. I wished with all my heart we'd never crossed the line. I missed my friend. He knew me so well.

Eric chuckled. "Elizabeth, you'll know what you want to do as soon as you know. It's no more or less profound than that."

I couldn't help but notice the twinkle in his eye again. It was like he knew so much more than I did, and I wanted him to tell me everything he knew. He was like a hot version of Yoda. I blinked and looked away, embarrassed.

He rapped his knuckles against the desk and walked away, and I let out a breath I hadn't realized I was holding. Before I had a chance to process any of that, he was suddenly in front of me again.

"Yes?" I blinked up at him, startled by his sudden reappearance.

He tilted his head, studying me. "Go to dinner with me."

My jaw dropped. "Excuse me?"

"You heard me."

"I'm not deaf."

"I know it's kind of against the rules, asking out the boss's daughter and all, but I figured you weren't really the type to always play by the rules."

His good mood was infectious, and I couldn't help the smile that spread over my face. Just as abruptly, Spencer popped into my head and I closed my eyes. If Spencer was right, and our weekend together really was a mistake, then clearly, I had no good instincts when it came to my love life. I'd been faithful to a cheater, I'd crossed the line with my best friend, and now my dad's employee was asking me out. I didn't trust my own judgment anymore.

"I can't."

"Really? Guess I was wrong, then." He looked genuinely disappointed.

"No, it's just that... I'm kind of prone to making mistakes right now. I can't handle another one."

He nodded in understanding. "How much do you know about law school?"

The sudden change of subject baffled me. "I know it's hard."

"That it is. And to get through it, you have to have a lot of persistence and patience. I have a good feeling about you and me."

This time, when he walked away, it was with a wink.

## 16

## SPENCER

"Hey," Mills nodded at me as I came through the door of our shared room. It was Friday, and we'd just finished a long week of classes. The rooms looked a lot like dorm rooms, from what I'd seen while hanging out with college girls, anyway. I was exhausted from the long day, but since my days were all long now, it didn't really matter. I flung my bag onto the twin bed on the left side of the room and plopped down after it.

"You feel like going out tonight?" he asked.

"Why do you want to go out?" I asked, unlacing my boots. When Mills didn't answer right away, I looked up at him expectantly. "What?"

He cocked his head. "It's Friday. No reason."

"Is everything okay with Olivia?"

"Of course."

"So, why do you want to go out?"

Mills sat opposite me on his bed and rested his elbows on his knees. I could tell he wanted to say something, but he was hesitating for some reason. After a few more breaths he met my gaze. "Because we've been here for two weeks, are about to leave for Christmas break, and we haven't gone out once. That's fine for me, I have a fiancée. But... you need to move on or something, man. This isn't healthy, moping around like this."

I glared up at him. "Are you serious?"

"Not as serious as you. You're just not yourself, Hawk. And you won't talk about it so I can't even help you. It's depressing."

"It's not that I won't talk about it. It's that I don't know what good it'll do. I broke it off with Ellie. Never should have started something between us in the first place. It was stupid. We're better as friends." Before Mills could reply, I grabbed some jeans and a nice shirt out of my closet. "You wanna go out? Let's go out."

I slammed my way into the bathroom to take a shower. With no one to face but my own reflection in the mirror, I hung my head. The only reason I'd lashed out at Mills was because he was right. But just because he was right, didn't mean that I needed him trying to get inside my head like a shrink. It was none of his business. Or was it? I shook my head in frustration and got in the shower.

The hot water did nothing for clarity like I'd hoped it would. I stood there, letting it fall over me, wishing I knew what I was supposed to do. Move on? Snap out of it? I didn't know where to start. That weekend with Ellie had been just as good as I imagined. But as soon as she'd left the base, it all came crashing down. Being able to hold her and kiss her had been just enough to show me how much I loved her. Which led to showing me how bad it would suck to lose her.

It wasn't a matter of *if* I would lose her. It was a matter of *when*. There were so many things that could naturally go wrong with military relationships—or any relationship. How long could I keep her from being with her 'white-picket-fence-guy'? The thought of her being with anyone else made me sick, but what else was I supposed to do? I'm not that guy.

I didn't have a choice that day... I'd had to let her go. Wasn't that a thing? If you love someone, let them go? She'd waste valuable time waiting for me while I was in training, and then when I got stationed in some foreign country, was she supposed to drop everything and come with me? That'd mean we'd have to get married. I shuddered. The other option was for her to put her life on hold and keep waiting for me.

There were too many questions I didn't like the answer to. Not to mention the thought of telling her I couldn't have kids with her. Not that I couldn't, but that I *wouldn't*. There was no way I would have kids and then leave them all the time like my dad did, forcing Ellie to be a single mom whenever I was gone. It wasn't right. I felt like the biggest jerk in the world for letting it get this far with nowhere to go.

My phone, signaling I had a text, brought me back to the present. I hurried up with the rest of my shower and vowed to put it out of my head for just one night. In fact, maybe it would be best if I did what I was so good at and turned everything off for the night like I used to. Maybe it would be better if I were true to who I really was, so Ellie could find a guy who deserved her. I sure as heck didn't.

"I'll be right back." I crushed the rest of my soda and tossed the can in the trash on my way to the counter.

"What about our game?" Mills called after me, gesturing to the pool table.

I ignored him. We were losing anyway, and the hot blonde I'd seen leaning against the counter waiting to order was hard to resist. Apparently, I had a type. She wore cowboy boots and jeans, the tight denim hugging her curves. She had her hair down and curled, like Ellie's. I shook my head. It was a popular style, and the pickings were slim. I wasn't just into her because she looked like Ellie. That'd be weird.

The rec room was expansive, and as one would expect a military base, there were more guys than girls hanging out there. We hadn't known of anything better going on that night, so this was the best option for us to have a little fun. I still didn't understand why Mills was so bent on me going out tonight, anyway. Did he want me to find another girl to bring me out of my funk? The idea seemed a little less like the sappy Mills I knew, and a little more like something I would try to do if the situation were reversed. Whatever. He'd gotten me here, and I'd found a girl. Mission accomplished.

"Hey," she said, reaching for the can of Coke the bartender had sat in front of her.

I smiled, even as my stomach turned. "Hey."

"I'm Claire." She held out her small hand for me to shake and I caught sight of a tattoo of an anchor on her wrist.

"Spencer." I shook her hand. "Where are you from?"

"Miami. I'm stationed here now, though."

"Are you a Marine?"

She twirled her hair with a slow smile. "Navy."

"Ah, gotcha." I had no game, whatsoever. No clue what to say next, no clue how to act normal. I glanced toward Mills playing two against one in the billiards area. Maybe I should just order another Coke and head back to finish the game. I craned my neck, looking for the bartender, to stall.

"Want to get out of here?"

I almost choked. The one time I didn't have any game, it turned out I wouldn't need it. Almost as if on autopilot, I nodded and let her take me by the hand and lead me away from the bar area. Some guys were watching basketball on one of the rec room's large TVs and didn't even look up at us as we passed. I wondered who her friends were, or who she was here with. It didn't look like she was planning to let them know she was leaving with someone. We passed a few tables where guys were playing card games, ducked around the Marines throwing darts in competition with some sailors, and stepped over what appeared to be a push up contest. I looked back at the pool tables. Mills was just staring at me with his head cocked to the side in question. Without responding, I turned back to watch where I was going as I followed the blonde out the door.

I listened with half an ear as she talked about her job in the Navy. I couldn't hear her well over the music and the sound of my own... conscience? Is that what that was? I looked her up and down as she led me through the rec room and toward the door. She was Ellie's exact body type, and with her long hair falling in waves down her back, I almost—*almost*—let myself imagine it was her leading me home.

The alarm blaring next to my face sent me shooting up straight, panicking. What time was it? Was I late for class? I frantically grabbed at my phone to silence the incessant beeping, my head pounding. When my mental fog cleared, I dared a look around the sunlit room. Mills rolled his eyes at me from his bed. He closed the lid down on his laptop and set it aside. With a shake of his head, he stood and reached for the water and pain reliever on my nightstand.

"Thanks," I said, taking the offering. I was parched.

He sat back down on his bed. "What happened to you last night?"

Keeping my eyes closed against the bright room, I swallowed the pain reliever and wracked my brain for memories. Images flashed by and I tried to sort through them, putting them in order. Things clicked into place. I may have stayed out until after dawn, but I hadn't had anything to drink, so I wasn't hungover.

"Bro, I wanted you to blow off some steam," Mills said. "But then you left with that girl and stayed out all night."

"It's not what you think," I answered, flopping back on the bed, exhausted.

"It seems pretty obvious. One minute we were playing pool, the next you disappeared and told me to finish without you. Next thing I knew, you were following her out the door to get lucky."

"I wish."

He looked confused. "What do you mean, 'you wish'? What happened with the girl?"

"Nothing."

"Okay," he snorted.

"No, really. I couldn't do it," I admitted. "Well, not that I couldn't, like literally *couldn't*. I just... didn't want to. It was awkward, man. She was so mad. Like, never been so offended in her entire life, mad. Definitely never been in that situation before."

Mills whistled, his brows nearly reaching his hairline.

I couldn't believe what I was about to admit to him, but I was sick of not talking. I used to talk to Ellie about everything, but we hadn't talked since I'd ended things with her. I sighed. "We walked to her barracks room, and I remember thinking she looked like Ellie. It was weird. Like I almost wanted to be with her because of that... but then I got freaked out about it and made up an excuse to leave. It all just felt too weird, like I was using her, or like I was cheating on Ellie, even though I'd broken up with Ellie. It was a nightmare."

"Seriously?"

"Yeah."

Mills went back to his own bed and sat down, looking a little shell shocked by my admission. "You really just left?"

I nodded. "Yeah."

"Man, I'm actually kind of proud of you. I mean, I wanted you to get out and loosen up a little, but I'm not going to lie, I was pretty bummed out that you left with her."

"I wondered if that's what you wanted me to do..."

He shook his head. "Nah, I mean, maybe if you could hang out and have some fun to take your mind of things, sure. But I wasn't trying to get you to go home with someone."

"Well, I didn't plan it. But I'm glad it didn't wind up happening."

Mills frowned. "Wait, if you didn't sleep over at that girl's house, where were you all night?"

"At the beach," I answered, taking another drink of water. Going on about an hour of sleep had me feeling like a zombie as I recalled where I'd been the night before. "I walked down the boardwalk for a while, then stopped and just sat there, listening to the waves. It was cool. But I guess I fell asleep for a bit because the sun woke me up."

"You're a mess, Hawk." Mills chuckled.

I took my pillow out from under my head and pulled it over my face. "Don't I know it."

## 17

## ELLIE

The last thing I wanted to do was leave the warmth of my bed to go answer the door. I threw back the covers with a huff, knowing Olivia would just keep bugging me until I let her in. I padded down the hall, tightening my floral robe as I went. I passed the mirror in the hallway and caught sight of my reflection. Wincing, I paused to re-do my much-too-messy bun and gently patted the bags under my eyes.

I took a deep breath and continued to the door. I opened it slowly, stifling the urge to hiss at the bright sunlight like a vampire. Olivia's encouraging smile was almost equally blinding, but I let her in. She walked straight to the kitchen and deposited the bagels and coffee she'd brought over. If she'd asked me first, I'd have told her not to bother. But now, I followed the delicious aroma wafting like a yellow brick road to the kitchen.

"How've you been?" she asked sweetly, handing me a cup of the caffeinated lifeline.

My lips moved into a tight line. "Fine."

"You don't look fine."

I scowled at her. "Well, how would you be if you thought the love of your life was right under your nose and then he just wants to go back to being friends? I feel like an idiot."

Olivia hung her head. "I'm sorry he hurt you, Ellie. I was really rooting for you guys. Which makes me want to tell you the story Matt told me this morning that makes me think he's still in love with you, but I also don't want to get your hopes up just in case."

My brows shot up. "Hello. Tell me. No question."

"Okay, but you have to promise you won't ever bring it up to Spencer. He'll know Matt told me."

"Fine. Tell me."

Olivia sighed, and got ready for her story. I could already tell by her demeanor that it was going to be really juicy. "Okay. I guess he was in bad shape this morning. He had a rough night."

"What kind of rough night?"

She sat down on one of the three barstools at our kitchen counter. "Well, first, there was this girl."

"Ugh. I don't think I want to hear this story, after all." My stomach churned and I felt like I was going to be sick. If I had known how hard it would be to move on after kissing that boy, I never would have done it. Well, maybe I would've. It was great. It was great, which is why this is hard. Such a vicious cycle.

Olivia put a hand on my arm. "Trust me, you do."

I nodded for her to continue, holding my coffee like the warmth and comfort of it would somehow protect me from whatever I was about to hear.

"Okay, so they went to the rec room to play pool and stuff, because Matt said Spencer has been super mopey lately. Matt thought it would be good for him to go out and have some fun."

My eyes widened, heart beating a little faster. "I'm not mad at the mopey thing."

Olivia snorted. "Why? Because you've been equally mopey?"

I stuck my tongue out at her.

"Anyway," Olivia waved a hand and then dug into the bag of bagels, pulling out a plain one. "They were playing pool and everything was fine, until Spencer suddenly took off to go talk to a blonde girl. At first Matt didn't think it was a big deal, since you know, *guys*. Until Spencer left with her."

I cringed. "Are you sure I want to hear this?"

"And, he didn't come home until after dawn."

"*Olivia*."

She laughed, put her bagel down, and sat up straight in her chair, ready to spill the proverbial tea.. "Hang in there, this is good. So Matt was ready to kind of tell him off for going home with someone when he was obviously still hung up on you, but then Spencer told him he couldn't even go through with it."

I balked. "He couldn't?"

She shook her head, taking a bite of bagel. She looked totally giddy over her news, but I was in turmoil.

"Did Matt tell you anything else? Like about why he couldn't?"

"It's pretty clear you're the reason, don't you think?"

I picked at the edges of my bagel. "If that were true, why did he end things then? It could have been so good."

Olivia worried her lip. "I'm not sure."

"Where was he all night if he wasn't with her?"

"I guess he just walked the beach and fell asleep out there. But he was definitely alone with his broody thoughts and not with the Ellie-lookalike, as Matt called her."

I swallowed a bite of bagel and sighed. "It's so weird not talking to him. He's got his phone on him all the time now and I still haven't heard from him since he was here. Now with all of this... I feel like we should talk. Should I call him?" I asked.

"Maybe you should just wait. If there's any hope of you guys working this out, maybe you should give him some space until you guys are face-to-face on Christmas break. It's only a week away."

She was probably right. Spencer wasn't much for words. He had a hard enough time communicating his deepest feelings in person, let alone on the phone. Christmas wasn't too far away, so it wouldn't kill me to wait to get my answers until then.

~

I couldn't wait. I stared at the phone in my hand and felt like a chump. Yes, I could. I could wait. My fingers, as if they had a mind of their own, navigated through the phone to his name in my contacts list. My thumb hovered over the little phone icon that when pressed, would make my name show up on Spencer's screen. I had to decide if I was ready for this *before* I pushed that little button, since caller I.D. would give me away even if I hung up before he answered.

There was no sense in dragging it out. I'd just obsess over it between now and Christmas. Besides, if he still had feelings for me, we could both stop being upset about it and pick up right where we left off. Long-distance, of course. But happier, anyway.

Pressing the button, I took a deep breath and brought the phone to my ear. With each ring, my heart pumped faster. By the fourth, I thought I would pass out. Needing something to focus on, I stared through the sliding glass door of my house and into the kitchen. It was almost dinner time, and from my view on the swings, I could see my mom at the stove.

"Hey," he said when he picked up, making me jump.

"Hi."

Silence.

More silence.

"I'm sorry, I shouldn't have," I started, ready to hang up.

"No, I'm glad you did," he assured me. "It's been a while."

I breathed a little easier. "Yeah, it has."

"How've you been?"

"Great," I lied.

"Me too."

Somehow, even though I'd lied about being great, it bugged me to hear him say the same thing. I straightened up on the swing. "Really?"

He chuckled. "Well, have you?"

"No."

"Okay. Same page then."

I let out a noise of frustration. "Why are we doing this? This is not who we are."

"You're right. And I want nothing more than for us to go back to how we were before."

"Before... as in, before you ended things between us?"

He paused. "No. Before I left for boot camp. When we were just friends. I want that back."

Even though he'd already dumped me once in person, hearing him confirm that he still felt that way was like a second punch in the gut. Except this time, I'd allowed the story of his rough night to give me hope that his feelings for me ran deeper than friendship.

"Are you still there?" he asked.

"Yeah. I just..."

"What?"

I took a shaky breath, deciding to go out on a limb. "Why did you kiss me?"

"I don't have a good answer for you, E. I messed up. You were there... you know... and you're gorgeous. I shouldn't have taken advantage of the situation like that. You deserve better."

"Are you kidding me right now? You're gonna play it off like you kissed me because I was 'there?' That I could have been any girl with a pulse? *That's* what you're going with?"

Spencer sighed heavily. "I don't know what to say."

I stood from the swing and resisted the urge to throw my phone. "Okay, message received. I'm gonna go now. Goodbye, Spencer."

I didn't bother waiting for him to reply before I disconnected the call. What a complete moron. I didn't know if he was lying to himself or to me, but he definitely didn't kiss me just because I happened to be available to him. I'd seen it in his eyes that night in the hotel room. And even though he didn't know it, I knew he wasn't able to follow through with another girl the night before.

It didn't matter. Whatever his reasons, he was clearly done with the romantic part of our relationship. Maybe he lied about why, but he'd had every opportunity to fix things just now and he didn't. If I were being honest, it was for the best. The short time we were a couple only showed me how amazing it could be. If it'd gone any further, I would have gotten my heart broken. Who knows, maybe I already had.

~

"Good morning, Elizabeth."

I jumped, startled by the smooth voice coming from above my desk. I flushed when I saw Eric casually posed with his arms crossed on my ledge, like he'd been there a while. "How long have you been standing there?"

He tilted his head with a crooked smile. "Long enough to see you brooding into that deposition you're supposed to be reading."

"I was distracted."

"I have that effect."

I looked back up in time to see him wink, causing me to flush a deeper shade of red and laugh at his confidence.

"So, what were you thinking about that had you all distracted?" His words were flirtatious, but I could tell he asked because he genuinely cared. It made me brave.

"Remember when you asked me out?"

He slowly straightened from his relaxed posture against my desk, lifting his chin. "Ah, yes. The heartbreak I suffered at your refusal has barely given me peace."

I rolled my eyes, flattered. "Does the offer still stand?"

"I'll pick you up at 8 o'clock on Friday." He tapped a hand once on the ledge and then turned to walk away.

"Wait, you're going to pick me up?"

He turned, confused. "Why wouldn't I pick you up? I do have a car, you know."

I laughed. "I figured."

He cocked an eyebrow at me in question, so I lowered my voice and looked around to make sure none of the other lawyers were around. "What about my dad?"

He smiled a quick, easy smile, tucking his hands in the pockets of his well-tailored suit. "What *about* your dad?"

This time, it was my turn to look confused.

"Elizabeth, are you a grownup?"

I nodded.

"So am I."

Friday night at dinner, I marveled at the ease with which Eric kept the conversation flowing. There was never a dull moment. He had so many stories and interesting opinions. What was even more impressive was that he listened to my stories as if they were just as interesting. Fascinating, even. He sure knew how to make a girl feel wanted. Over dessert, I was having fragmented everything-happens-for-a-reason thoughts.

When he'd picked me up from my house, I was shocked to find that he'd already talked to my dad about our date ahead of time. Or, I figured he must have, judging by the lack of surprise on my father's face when he saw Eric in his foyer. They'd shaken hands in greeting and he waved politely at my mom, saying it was nice to see her again. With that, they told us to have a good time, and we'd left. It was spookily casual.

"Figure out what makes you tick," Eric said, referring to my future career plans—or lack thereof. "Are you into numbers? Do you love to write? Are you a dreamer or more practical? Have you ever taken one of those aptitude tests?"

I took a bite of the vanilla ice-cream on the dessert between us. "Actually, I'm really good at numbers. I love making spreadsheets and using them to stay organized and on budget."

He chuckled. "You're a special kind of person. I hate numbers with a passion."

"Maybe I could be an accountant." I wiggled my eyebrows like it was super exciting.

"That, or a personal finance advisor. That could be a lucrative career, depending on who your clients are. They don't have classes about managing money in school like they should, so most people don't know what to do with it once they have it. Including myself. I use the same guy my dad always has."

"That actually doesn't sound bad at all. I've always admired entrepreneurs and wanted to be one, but I never knew what kind of business I'd start. Maybe I can help someone who owns their own business to manage their finances, instead."

"True," he said, "But if you're working independently to do that, it sounds like you'd be a business owner, too."

I looked up from our shared dessert and smiled. "Yeah, I guess so. I can almost picture the cute little business cards I could make. Ellie Burton - Personal Finance Advisor. I like it."

Eric smiled back at me and crossed his arms on the table in front of him. "Next step, the accounting degree."

"Ugh, yeah. *Details*."

"So, are you going to tell me what happened?" he asked, changing the subject.

"What do you mean?"

"The whole 'prone to making mistakes' thing. I'm curious."

He looked so genuinely interested in my answer, it made me want to be honest. I would be vague, but honest, nonetheless. "We were best friends for years. Last month we attempted to make it more than that. It didn't work."

He nodded as if he'd been there. For all I knew, maybe he had. I waited to see if he would ask for more details, but he seemed to be waiting for me to elaborate.

Finally, I cracked. "See, he doesn't really do the whole 'relationship' thing. I guess I just thought I'd be an exception."

He nodded again.

Maybe I hadn't been that close to falling in love with Spencer after all. If I had, would it be this easy to go on a date with another guy and have such an amazing time? Maybe Eric was the guy I should focus on. He seemed like he had all the qualities I was looking for, and besides, my dad obviously approved.

"Ellie?" He was smiling, but the corners of his mouth didn't quite turn up the way they had before.

"Yes?"

"I think you might need some closure with your friend before we see each other again."

The rejection in his words hit me like a slap. When it sunk in, it hurt worse knowing he was being just as kind and perceptive as he always was. I knew I wanted closure, but he picked that information right out of my head as if he knew me inside and out. This guy really was something.

"Before you misunderstand, let me tell you where I'm coming from with this." He reached across the table and took my hand, his thumb brushing lightly over the back. "My ex had an unresolved thing with her last boyfriend. She never got her closure, and it wasn't until I was completely in love with her that she left me to work things out with him. I'm just trying not to go down that road again. Fool me once, and all that."

I couldn't help but smile at him. "I understand."

"I want to make sure you know how I feel about you, though. I spend a large part of my day at the office trying to come up with reasons to come see you at the front desk. You're the only thing that makes me look forward to Mondays."

"My dad would probably love to hear what he pays you for."

He shook his head with a laugh. "I doubt that very much."

"So, after I get my closure?"

He brought my hand to his lips in an old-fashioned gesture. "I'll be waiting."

## 18

## SPENCER

I reached up to release the tray table in front of me and unwrapped the sub sandwich I hadn't had time to finish before the flight.

"So, what's your plan?" Mills elbowed me in the arm as I raised the sandwich to my lips. "Are you going to go see her?"

I took a huge bite of the sub to stall him. It had been three weeks since I'd seen Ellie in California and one week since our awkward phone call. It had almost made me sick to lie to her that night. Telling her I'd only kissed her because she was there. And 'gorgeous.' I felt queasy just thinking about it. Not that she wasn't gorgeous. She was. But that wasn't why I'd kissed her. And it sounded like she knew it, too. Finally, I swallowed the last bit of bread and cheese and realized I had to answer his question. My mouth felt dry, so I peered up and down the aisle for any sign of the drink cart.

"Well?" Mills prompted.

"I don't know yet."

He raised his eyebrows. "That's the best you can do? You've been stuck in your head every minute since we left California, and you *still* haven't made a plan?"

I shrugged, taking another bite.

"Okay," Mills said, putting his earbuds in and opening the music app on his phone. I hoped that meant the conversation was over, but he pulled the earbuds back out with a huff. "Are you going to see her? Tell her you lied to her?"

"I don't think that's a good idea. For anyone."

He rolled his eyes. "You're doing this to yourself. If she knew how you actually felt about her..."

"If she knew how I *actually* felt about her, she'd have to forget the life she's always wanted and trade it for this one. And before you get all mad at me, I know Olivia is cool with the military life. But you don't know Ellie like I do. I know what she wants. This isn't it."

"I don't think you should make that call for her."

I took another bite of my sandwich and spoke with a full mouth. "You're my friend, so I say this with love. *Butt out.*"

He chuckled. "Fine. But I'm gonna say one more thing."

"Of course you are."

"You need to go see her."

I shook my head. "No way."

"We're gonna be there for two weeks. She was your best friend. If nothing else... fix that part."

Mills put his earbuds in again, so I focused on finishing my sandwich without throwing up at the idea of seeing Ellie again.

We grabbed our olive-green sea bags from the conveyor belt and slung them onto our backs. They, along with our camo-printed duffel bags, were easy to spot as they came around the corner of the baggage carousel. Scanning the crowd at San Diego International Airport, I waited while Mills gathered everything he needed. It felt good to be home and out of class for a couple of weeks.

When we got to the curb of waiting cars, Mills and I scanned the area for any sight of Olivia. After a few minutes, she pulled into a vacant spot and got out. She immediately flung herself into Mills' arms. With the giant seabag on his back, it was all he could do to remain upright. I hesitantly edged toward her car. A big part of me knew Ellie wouldn't be there, but I casually peered through the tinted glass of the car. It was empty.

I heard the happy couple coming up behind me, so I abruptly straightened. I didn't want them to see how much I wished Ellie's small frame had been sitting in one of those seats. Olivia popped the trunk and Mills threw in his bags. She stood with one hand on her hip and one hand on the lid of the trunk. When it was my turn to put my bags in, I half expected her to slam it on my head, judging by her facial expression.

"Cat got your tongue, Olivia?" I asked, as I tried to fit my bags into the small trunk.

She smiled, but it wasn't a friendly look by any means. "Sorry that Ellie couldn't make it to pick you up, Spence. She was busy. I'm sure there once was a time when nothing could have stopped her from being here, though."

"Wow," I chuckled. "You and Ellie must be really good friends now. I'd recognize that protective tone of voice anywhere. Well done."

Her hand was still on the lid of the open trunk even though my bags were all loaded, so I closed it for her. She put her hands on her hips and had what was hopefully a flicker of appreciation in her eyes. I rounded the car and slipped into the back seat, pulling out my headphones.

I was oddly grateful for the attitude Olivia had given me. It meant she truly cared about Ellie. I was the bad guy for hurting her and she was only being loyal to her friend by being rude to me. That made me respect Olivia, since I would have acted the same way. In fact, the way she acted made me want to fix things with Ellie. On the friendship level, that is. As cool as she was, I couldn't have Olivia completely replacing me in Ellie's life.

I ripped the earbuds from my ears with a snap. "Olivia, turn right."

She quickly flicked on her blinker and made a sharp right.

"Where are we going? This isn't the way to your house." Mills scanned the buildings we passed, looking for a clue.

I glanced up at the rear-view mirror and Olivia met my

eyes. She realized where the change of direction would eventually lead. "I'm turning around."

"No, don't." I put my hand on her shoulder. I hoped that my eyes conveyed my intentions when she flicked her gaze back to mine in the mirror. "I just need to apologize."

Olivia sighed deeply and her grip got tighter on the steering wheel. She didn't say anything, but she didn't turn around either. The closer we got to Ellie's, the louder my pulse drummed in my ears. I had never been nervous about seeing a girl before. It was obnoxious.

"Can I just say something?" Olivia asked.

I sighed.

Mills held up a hand. "I'm not responsible for whatever she's about to say."

Olivia swatted him in the arm. "Hush, *you*. I'm being nice. Spencer, seriously. You guys were so happy that weekend. What happened?"

I rubbed my hands nervously on the tops of my thighs, not sure how to respond without offending her. I'd done plenty of that while talking to Mills about it. Besides, could I even be honest? She'd probably just repeat whatever I said back to Ellie, anyway.

"Look, that weekend was fun. But I shouldn't have started something with Ellie. I think what you and Mills have is great... for you. I don't want that kind of thing. And neither does Ellie. Trust me, she wants a nice civilian husband and kids and all that. That's not me."

Olivia started to reply, but Mills put a hand on her thigh. "Let it go, babe. I've tried."

"Fine." She rolled her eyes. "But you're being an idiot, and everyone knows it but you."

I chuckled. "Noted."

We pulled up to Ellie's house and Mills got out to help me get my bags. We tossed my stuff on the sidewalk and then Mills stood there with his hands in his pockets, shifting his weight. "You should just be honest with her."

"Butt out, Mills." I grabbed my bags and patted his shoulder as I passed.

I stopped about halfway up the driveway. The sound of Mills calling out a goodbye and getting back in the car barely registered with me as I stared at the familiar house in front of me. They drove away, and I was alone.

What the heck was I doing here? I wanted to apologize for hurting her. I shouldn't have kissed her. And then I shouldn't have lied to her about why I kissed her. But it didn't change anything. I still didn't want to be with her. It would be too much. Too hard on both of us. Too far from the life she'd always wanted.

I realized I was standing in their driveway like a moron, so I adjusted my grip on my bags and headed to the door. Before I could even knock, the door flew open to reveal a smiling face. Ellie's mom beckoned me inside with a warm and affectionate tone.

"How have you been? It's been too long, Spencer, honey." She turned her back to me briefly as she called up the stairs. "Ellie, Tom, we have a visitor!"

Carol was just as warm as ever, so I put together pretty quickly that Ellie hadn't told her anything about us. To Carol, I was still her daughter's best friend. I hadn't crossed any lines. I hadn't made any mistakes. I hadn't started something huge and then ended it, all in the same weekend. I wished more than anything I deserved the way Carol treated me. But I had crossed those lines and made those mistakes, and the huge thing I'd started would probably haunt me forever.

Tom lit up with a grin when he saw me from the top of the stairs. He looked nothing like a man about to punch some jerk in the face for hurting his daughter. So, clearly, Ellie hadn't confided in him, either.

My social skills finally kicked in again when Tom made it to the bottom of the stairs and offered to help me with my bags. We brought them into the living room and Carol wrapped me into a tight hug. She'd been so much of a mother to me after mine died that a hug from her was like a security blanket. I hadn't realized how much I'd missed it.

"Let me look at you," Carol said as she pulled back and put a hand on either side of my face. I had been taller than her for many years. Her arms were completely straight as she reached up, looking into my eyes. "You seem older, Spencer."

"I think I am."

"Oh, leave the boy alone, Carrie." Tom waved a hand at his wife. "How was your flight?"

I shrugged. "Not too bad, thanks. I slept through most of it."

"Oh, I could never sleep on airplanes. Not unless there was a lot of turbulence." Carol took a seat on the couch, so Tom and I followed suit.

"You can only sleep if there's turbulence?" I asked.

She nodded. "That's right. After college, I had a job downtown with early hours. I used to catch a little more sleep on the bus on the way in, and it was a very bumpy ride. Now, if I'm on a plane and there's turbulence, it's soothing."

I snickered. "You're probably the only one who thinks turbulence is soothing."

Just as I got comfortable, I heard Ellie's feet padding down the stairs. I stood and turned to face the stairway. My heart stopped. It had been too long since I'd last seen her or touched her, and my hands instinctively twitched with the need to reach for her. But then I read the flash of hurt and confusion that played across her face before she covered it up with a blinding smile, and I stuffed my hands in my pockets.

"Spencer!" She took the last few stairs and crossed the room, feigning excitement.

Her steps faltered slightly when she got within arm's reach, and I could tell she was deciding if she wanted to hug me. If she wanted to put on a show for her parents, I wanted to reap the benefits. I pulled her into my arms, lifting her feet off the ground. It probably looked like a normal hug for us, to the outsider. At least, I'd hoped it did. I inhaled deeply, knowing that much too soon I'd have to release her.

After just long enough to torture me, she jumped down and gave a fake laugh. "What are you doing here?"

Carol tilted her head, oblivious. "You didn't know he was coming home for the holidays?"

Tom raised his eyebrows with a conspirator's smile. "Must have been a surprise then, huh?"

I nodded, not taking my eyes from Ellie. I was trying hard to keep my face relaxed and normal, but I had no idea if I was pulling it off or not. Obviously, Ellie had known I was coming home for the holidays. She was asking why I was there, at her house, when she clearly did not want to see me. I needed to get her alone to talk, but I also wanted to stay around her parents and let her keep pretending she didn't hate me.

"Oh, you two are just adorable." Carol beamed. "It's great to see you together again, like old times."

Ellie made a small 'humph' sound, and I cringed.

Unaware of our quickly crumbling facade, Carol squeezed her husband's hand and rose from the couch. "All right, I guess we'll let you guys get caught up. Spencer, will you be staying for dinner?"

I smiled at Carol and glanced hopefully at Ellie.

"No, mom. I'm sure Spencer has plans to see his dad."

Ouch. I nodded to confirm Ellie's lie. "Yeah, thank you anyway, Carol. I'll have to take a rain check."

Carol nodded good-naturedly. "Just as well, if you give me more notice, I can make your favorite meat sauce and spaghetti. See you kids later."

I saw Ellie roll her eyes as her parents gave me more quick hugs and then left the room. Too bad Tom and Carol hadn't hung around longer. I wasn't ready for whatever was coming.

"Let's go outside." She didn't wait for a response before turning toward the back door.

I followed her onto the patio and then out to the swings. Part of me didn't want to talk there, because if the conversation went badly it would ruin every good memory we'd ever made hanging out on those swings. I glanced over to the flowerpot on the porch and wondered if it still hid the half-empty pack of cigarettes I'd stashed there. I hadn't smoked in forever, but I felt like I was about to go on the chopping block, so why not?

"Say what you came here to say, Spence." Her words were cold as ice.

"I came here to apologize," I said through the lump in my throat. "I don't want to lose you, E. You're my family."

Her features softened slightly, but she crossed her arms across her body. She looked like she was trying to protect herself. I resisted the urge to reach for her by crossing over to the slide and leaning against it. She took a seat on a swing. I watched her sway back and forth. She was beautiful.

I could fully admit to myself that I was in love with her. There was no denying my feelings. Being this close to her set my blood on fire and all I wanted to do was tell her that. But my reservations about not being able to give her what she wanted were still there. How long before she got sick of waiting for me and just bailed? Then what?

"I'm glad you didn't tell your mom about us," I said when she didn't say anything.

She scoffed. "Tell her *what*? That you kissed me, convinced me we felt 'right,' and then randomly ended things, all in the same weekend?"

Each word was like a separate dagger to my chest and

hearing her cheapen what happened between us was awful. She deserved an explanation. But the same sarcastic voice that just came out of her, was now in my head. *I'm sorry I freaked out about how much I love you and ruined it. I just knew that it would end in some terrible way eventually, so I figured I'd speed up the process. That way no one would get hurt.* It was the most pathetic thing I'd ever heard, if I said so myself.

"I'm sorry." It was all I had to give. At this point, I'd sound dumb no matter what I said.

Ellie blew out a long breath and finally met my gaze. "I didn't tell my mom because I know how much she means to you. After everything with your mom, and the way your dad is, I just didn't want you to lose my parents. They don't need to know things are messed up between us."

Even though it was painful to hear, I felt a tiny hint of hope. If she didn't want me to lose her parents, then she obviously still cared about me at least a little. She was willing to lie to her parents, hug me when she obviously didn't want to, and maybe even sit through a family meal with me sometime soon, just so I wouldn't lose what little family I had left.

I stared at her profile. She would sacrifice what she wanted to make me happy. I recognized it because I was doing the same thing for her. If I admitted we couldn't be together because I didn't want her to give up her white-picket-fence dreams, she'd probably try to convince me she didn't want it that bad. She would try to compromise. She might even say she was okay with not having kids. I would never let her go through with any of that, so it was pointless to start down that road only to get stopped later. She deserved all those things, and more, with someone who could be there for her whenever she needed him. Not halfway around the world on deployment.

"Ellie," I crouched down in front of her and took her hand. The charge that shot through my fingers was a painful reminder of the connection we shared. "Can we be friends, please?"

She squeezed my hand. "Friends don't lie to each other, and I think you're lying to me."

I swallowed. "About what?"

"I feel this. I know you do, too."

"Okay, but I don't want it. I want my friend back. Can we please just try to go back to the way things were?"

She let out a harsh laugh. "Sure. Is that where we talk to each other about our separate love lives?"

I let go of her hand and stood up. "Yeah, I mean, I guess."

"Okay, cool. I had a date the other night. It went really well." She tilted her head, watching my face. "His name is Eric, and he's the new lawyer at my dad's practice. I think I'm going to go out with him again. He's a few years older, but it's kind of nice that he's got so much of his life figured out. Knows what he wants, and stuff."

My face was a hard mask. No emotion leaked through. I imagined myself standing in formation, eyes on the back of Mills' head. Total control. Inside, I felt rage coursing through me in waves. She'd already found a nice guy to give her what she wanted. This was exactly what I wanted, and I was furious. I should be happy. Why couldn't I just be happy for her?

"Anyway," she continued, rising from the swing and coming to stand a foot away from me, "he wanted me to get closure with you before we went out again. I guess we have that now, right?"

I swallowed hard, deeply disturbed by the charge in the air between us. "Yeah, I guess so."

"Great. So, as long as we're back to that kind of friendship again, I'll let you know how it goes."

I peered down at her. Her eyes dared me to speak up. She was brimming with confidence, almost as if she knew exactly what she was doing to my insides by telling me about this guy. She wasn't playing games to be cruel, she was putting the ball in my court, asking me to do something with it. But I knew I was right. She didn't get it yet, but it was the right thing to do. Maybe this guy deserved her. Maybe this guy would give her a good life. In the end, that was all I wanted.

I gave her a crooked smile. "Sounds good. Can't wait."

# 19

# ELLIE

"Yes, Elizabeth?" Eric's pleasant voice came through the receiver, and I could tell by the slight echo he'd answered the call with the speaker button. I wasn't sure who might be in his office, so I tried to play the part of the detached receptionist as best as I could.

"You have a package waiting up here and it's marked urgent."

I could hear the smile in his voice when he replied. "Are you seriously calling me up to the front desk by saying I have a *package?*"

Hearing the way it sounded when he repeated it back to me, I clapped my hand over my mouth. Instead of responding, I put the receiver back on the cradle and buried my face in my hands. I'd called him up to the front desk using a sexual innuendo. And now I was blushing like a fool.

I heard him clear his throat, and I snapped my head up, sure that the color on my cheeks matched my crimson dress perfectly. His eyes twinkled with humor, but I was still mortified.

"I would ask for the *package* in a very serious voice, but this whole thing seems like a really cheesy porno."

I fidgeted nervously. "If it was, wouldn't *I* be the one asking for the package?"

His mouth popped open slightly before he collected himself. Sometimes I used humor to cover up extreme emotions, embarrassment being one of them. I also tended to ramble when I was nervous. I kept my jaws clamped shut, just in case.

"Anyway," Eric adjusted his deep blue tie, "what did you call me up here for?"

"Honestly, if I tell you now, it'll seem pretty ridiculous."

He smiled. "Why's that?"

"Because my attempt to seem professional just in case you had someone in your office backfired and turned into this big, awkward porn thing!" When he didn't say anything, just stood there and smiled at me, I continued. "I was going to ask you to dinner."

The look of shock reappeared on his face. "Elizabeth, that's the second time you've surprised me in the last five minutes."

I put my hands up and shrugged in a 'what can I say?' gesture.

"Did you figure everything out between you and your friend?"

"Yes, a few days ago. He's in town for the holidays and we talked everything out in person. I think it'll probably take some time before our friendship is back to normal... but anything more than that just isn't smart for us."

Eric nodded contemplatively. "Okay."

"Yeah. So, I guess I just figured I'd see if you wanted to go out again, since I got my closure."

He was leaning against the ledge, arms crossed casually in front of him. "No."

It was my turn to be shocked. "No?"

"No. Thank you for the offer, though." With no further explanation, he rapped his knuckles once on the top of the ledge and headed back down the hall.

I sat there silently for a moment, trying to figure out what had just happened. When I'd asked him out last time, he'd seemed flattered, so I knew he was at least mildly interested. Then, our date had gone well until he told me I needed to get closure with Spencer before we would go out again. Ever since that night, we'd been flirting non-stop at work, so I thought he was probably still interested. Maybe he didn't think I'd ever get closure with Spencer so he just told me that as an easy way to let me down? Was he worried I would dump him like that other girl did and get back with my ex?

Before I got too far down the rabbit hole, he came strolling back up to the front. He looked casual as ever, even taking it so far as to whistle.

"Elizabeth," he said cheerily, resuming his signature position against the ledge. "Have you worked out your issues with the friend?"

I nodded slowly. He was the most confusing man on the planet. Had I dreamed the last five minutes? That might be a good thing, considering the embarrassing way it had all started.

"Good. Would you like to have dinner on Friday night?"

I nodded again, still baffled.

"I couldn't let you ask me out twice in a row. It was my turn." And with a wink, he was gone.

"He sounds like a character in a romantic comedy, Ells." Olivia laughed after I told her about the day's events. We were on our way to pick up Matt and Spencer for a movie. "But he was right, you really couldn't come up with anything better to say than he had a *package* waiting?"

I felt my face flush again and playfully swatted her arm. "I know, I know. It was the stupidest thing I could have come up with. It's just that with Eric, one minute I feel classy and mature around him, and the next I'm like a bumbling idiot!"

Olivia shook her head wryly. "Well, I have to say, you haven't seemed this happy since before the disaster with Spencer."

I swallowed over a sudden lump that appeared out of nowhere. I wasn't sure what to say to that, so I nodded and looked out the window.

"You're sure you're okay with Spencer coming

tonight?" Olivia asked, cautiously. "Matt said he felt bad not inviting him once he found out we were going."

"Of course." I smiled at her. "We need to do normal things like this, or else we'll never get back to the way we were. And normal for us means I have a boyfriend, and Spencer is my friend. Not that Eric is my boyfriend, but you get the picture."

I couldn't tell if she wanted me to hear it or not, but Olivia mumbled, "I can't with you two."

"Hey. He made his choice. It's over. I still call bull on his reasons, but that doesn't change the fact that he doesn't want to be more than friends. He told me three times. I just want to move on and forget this whole thing ever happened."

She sighed. "Look, we both know how you felt about Spencer. I don't know if you still feel that way or not, but I think this thing with Eric could be great for you. If Spencer doesn't want to be with you, it's his loss. Whatever the reason."

I knew she was right. The problem was, I didn't want to think about my feelings for Spencer. When we were together that weekend, I couldn't have been happier. Being with him felt like coming home. But it was way too easy for him to drop me and then lie about the reasons why. I loved him as a friend, but how could I ever trust him again?

"Hey! You should invite Eric to join us tonight."

I cocked an eyebrow at her. "You don't think that would be weird?"

"I think it will definitely be weird." Olivia laughed.

"But I also think Spencer needs to see that you've moved on. I'm sure it will do wonders for your friendship if he can see that you're with the right kind of guy. Besides, this is normal for you guys, right?"

I shook my head when I caught sight of the wicked grin plastered on Olivia's lips. "I'm in."

"Okay, there's a showing in about ten minutes, and another one an hour after that," Matt reported as he rejoined our group. "The lady at the ticket counter said this one is almost sold out but the next one isn't too full."

"I'm fine with waiting, babe. We can go over to that coffee shop and chat for a bit." Olivia smiled that devilish smile again, and I couldn't help but think she was only saying that because she wanted to watch Spencer and Eric interact.

Seeing the two of them standing next to one another gave me conflicting feelings. Even though Spencer and I had put our fling in the past, it was still hard not to notice how attractive he was. Now that I knew what it was like to kiss his lips, they seemed fuller and more appealing than before. And now that I knew just how hard his chest was under my fingertips, the more I wanted to reach out and touch him. I noticed he was wearing his favorite jeans. He'd also worn them the night he'd pressed me against the wall of that hotel room.

I shook my head, feeling a blush rise to my cheeks. On the other hand, Eric was equally attractive in his own way.

Where Spencer had on jeans and a navy-blue polo shirt, Eric was wearing a black blazer over a maroon V-neck tee and fancy Italian shoes, with his jeans. There was a level of class in how he carried himself that I found to be sexy beyond belief. It was completely different, but just as tempting. He seemed like the type who would wine and dine you and actually know a thing or two about the wine or the food. And while I had no idea what it was like to kiss his lips, I definitely wouldn't mind finding out.

"Ellie?" Spencer's voice broke through my lust-filled daydreaming.

"What? Sorry."

"Are you cool with getting coffee until the next showing?" he repeated.

"Yeah, that's fine."

Apparently, I was the only one who'd yet to agree to this plan because as soon as I'd said yes, we all made our way to the coffee shop. Eric and Spencer had an awkward standoff at the door over who would hold it open and who would go through it. One of my dad's biggest interests was business psychology. The guys were doing a subconscious dance over who was more dominant. The theory went that if you held the door for everyone and were the last one inside, you were the most powerful person in the group. My dad always said these things are funny to watch because people were usually unaware of what they were doing. Since I knew perfectly well what the little show meant, I turned away before I could see which one of them 'won' and got to be the last one inside.

I didn't need to think about who was more dominant out of the two of them.

After we all got our coffee and sat on the plush armchairs by the fireplace, I watched contentedly as Eric entertained my friends. He told story after story and seemed to make quite an impression. I'd known people in the past who thought they needed to embellish their stories to be impressive, and everyone knew it, but that wasn't the case with Eric. They all seemed genuinely interested in what he was saying. Not only that, but I could tell they all really liked him. Including Spencer, to my surprise.

## 20

## SPENCER

I couldn't concentrate on the movie. After the way Eric had carried on like his entire mission in life was to get us to like him, I was feeling sick to my stomach. You would think it was because I didn't like the guy. Unfortunately, it was because I did. I found myself genuinely amused by a lot of his stories. Eric was the guy who could fit in with any crowd. You wanted to hate him because he seemed to have it all going for him, but you couldn't help but like him. He was just that cool.

It pissed me off like nobody's business.

I snuck a glance to my left. Ellie was sitting cross-legged in the seat like she always did, face relaxed as she watched the movie. Eric had his arm on the armrest between them, palm slightly open. It looked like he was keeping his hand in the perfect position in case she decided to put hers in it. I hoped to God she wouldn't. I faced forward again, feeling tense and helpless. This was such a bad idea.

I risked a glance to my right. Mills had flipped up the armrest between him and Olivia, so she was snuggled up against him. At least they weren't making out. That would be just too much. No sooner than I turned back to the screen, I heard the sound of sweet nothings being whispered to both the left *and* the right of me.

Okay, enough was enough. Whose bright idea was it for me to sit in the middle of two pairs of lovebirds? I had to get out of there. Just because I said I wanted my friendship with Ellie back, didn't mean I wanted to be the third wheel (or in this case, the fifth wheel) on her dates with other guys anymore. Things would never be that way again. You can't un-ring the bell.

I stood, and with as much grace as I could manage in the dark, I headed for the exit. I guessed my friends would probably assume I was going to the bathroom. They wouldn't know I'd gone home for at least a few minutes. Not having a car didn't bother me at all as I strolled out of the theater and into the lobby. I'd call an Uber if need be. I could even walk. The distance from the theater to my house was probably shorter than some of our hikes in MCT. I only knew I couldn't sit there for a moment longer.

On my way out the door, I made a pit stop to the men's room. It must not have been a time when a movie was letting out, because the expansive bathroom was empty. I walked up to a urinal and did my business. I straightened when I heard the door open behind me. The squeaking of the hinges was loud in the severe silence of the tiled room.

As I zipped up my fly, it occurred to me that whoever entered the bathroom hadn't approached the urinals. I turned slowly. Eric was standing at the sink, leaning nonchalantly against it with his arms crossed. He didn't seem aggressive, but I narrowed my eyes at him, anyway. Who approached another dude in an empty bathroom?

"What's up?" I asked, trying for a casual tone as I headed to the sink.

"I just wanted to check in."

I furrowed my brow. "Check in?"

"Yeah," he nodded, shifting his weight. "You seemed uncomfortable in there."

I had no clue where he was going with this, so I stayed quiet, washing my hands. Had I misjudged this clown? Was he trying to start something with me now that we were alone?

"Look, Spencer, I know this thing with you and Ellie is fresh."

I dried my clean hands on a paper towel and then threw it in the trash under the sink. I turned to face him, looking him square in the eyes. Was he going to ask me about my feelings? I didn't see a campfire or hear 'kumbaya' in this bathroom. I crossed my arms over my chest. He was only an inch or two shorter than me, but didn't look like he could fight. His hands were pretty like Tim's had been. He probably wouldn't want to hurt them.

"You seem like the type of guy who would kill anyone who hurt someone you cared about," Eric continued. "So, I wanted to offer my intentions now, and let you know I'm fully aware of what will happen if I hurt her."

The surprise didn't show on my face, I was getting good at keeping my bearing. This guy blew my mind. Here he was, approaching me in the men's room of all places, telling me his *intentions* towards Ellie? What was I supposed to do with that information? Besides, the way he said the part about hurting her almost seemed like he wanted to finish with, "like you did." That might have been my guilty conscience talking, but it infuriated me either way.

I stood a little straighter, arms still crossed, fully aware of the unspoken language of posture. He frowned slightly, like I'd disappointed him. What a piece of work. I knew I should say something. I just couldn't figure out what.

Before I could get a word out, Eric sighed and shook his head slightly. I watched stonily as he walked back out the way he came without another word. What was he so disappointed about? Did he expect me to stand here and give him my blessing to date her? I wasn't sure if I was ready to be that self-sacrificing. Baby steps were important in a lot of situations. This was definitely one of them. Heck, I was about to sneak away from this little play date without telling anyone. I wasn't exactly the mature gentleman this lawyer was looking for. Was twenty-four really that different from nineteen?

I turned the key in my front door and stepped inside, grateful for the familiar sounds of baseball coming from the living room. I wasn't sure why, but someone else being in the house was a comfort to me right then. When I rounded the corner from the foyer, my dad called out. He was sitting in his recliner, beer in hand.

"Want a beer?" My old man asked.

I raised a brow. "I've never had a beer with you before."

He chuckled. "You're a trained killing machine. Have a beer."

"I don't think I'd go that far, Dad. I'm a private." I walked into the kitchen and grabbed a bottle of beer from the fridge, popping it open and taking a long pull.

"Yeah, I know. You don't know squat about anything, yet. But I've always agreed with that whole 'old enough to die for your country, old enough for a beer' rule."

I couldn't help but smile slightly at that. My dad hadn't been this conversational in years, so I plopped down on the couch and set my eyes on the game. I was interested to see if our relationship was somehow magically fixed now that I was a Marine. If so, that was pretty messed up. But I was cool with it.

"Where were you?" he asked. His tone wasn't accusatory, more like curious. He had an interest in my social life now? What a strange night this turned out to be.

"I went to a movie with some friends."

He swallowed the gulp of beer he had just taken. "Ellie, I'm assuming."

"Yeah."

"What movie was it?"

I paused. They'd picked out the movie ahead of time,

and Mills had bought my ticket because he owed me money. Apparently, Eric was right. I must have spent a decent amount of time distracted by the lovebirds if I couldn't even name the movie.

My dad glanced over at me. "You know, I was just askin'. If you weren't at the movies, it's not like I'm gonna ground you or something."

"No," I shook my head and leaned forward on the couch, resting my elbows on my knees. "I was at the movies. But I didn't stay for the whole thing."

I could tell he wanted to ask why, but wasn't sure if it would be too nosey. He must have figured it didn't matter, because he asked anyway. "Was it that bad?"

"No, I just couldn't sit in there as the fifth wheel. I sat in the middle of two couples, like an idiot. It got on my nerves."

Dad whistled and got up from the recliner. "Need another beer?"

I shook my head and took another drink from my still half-full bottle. It didn't feel as awkward as I would have thought talking to my dad about this stuff. Maybe having common ground made us closer. The old me would have resented that and taken some beer upstairs to be alone. It seemed the new me was sick of running away from people I used to be close with.

"I've never liked that kid that Ellie's dating," Dad said as he sat back down with his fresh beer.

I frowned. He must mean Tim. "I broke Tim's nose during MCT. They haven't been together since then."

Dad raised his eyebrows in approval. "Good for you."

"Thanks."

"She was out with someone else tonight?"

I nodded.

"Does it bother you?"

I rolled my shoulders. "What?"

"That she's always got a boyfriend."

"Why would it?" I finished the rest of my beer as I awaited his answer. He was much more perceptive than I gave him credit for.

"Well, it'd bother me if somebody I felt so strongly about was always with someone else."

There it was. He might have seemed like an absentee father, but I always thought there was something in his eyes that told me he knew a lot more than he let on. All this time, as I was resenting him for not caring about me, he was paying enough attention to have seen my feelings for Ellie. He might have even recognized it before I did. I used to think it had started around the time I left for boot camp, but lately, I'd been thinking maybe there was never a time I didn't love Ellie. It just took me a while to admit it to myself. Or maybe it took leaving to realize I didn't want to leave.

"Son?"

I blinked. "Yeah?"

"Struck a nerve, there?"

"Guess so." I got up and tossed my empty bottle in the recycle bin before getting a new beer from the fridge. "We dated, or something, for a minute."

"I would have thought it would have lasted longer than a minute once you two finally got together."

I let out a short laugh. "What's that supposed to mean?"

"Your mother told me once, right before she died, that you and Ellie were made for each other. I laughed at the time; told her she couldn't possibly know that. But there was a part of me that always wondered if she was right."

This had me reeling. My mom thought we were made for each other? Are you freaking kidding me? *No pressure or anything, Mom.* I gulped down more of my beer while I processed that. It shocked me to hear what my mom thought about Ellie and me, but hearing my dad mention her was a big deal. He hadn't so much as said her name in years, let alone tell a story involving her. It was a strange night, indeed.

"So, what happened?" he asked.

"I messed it up."

He laughed out loud. "Of course you did."

I felt an angry heat rise in my cheeks. "Thanks."

"You're a teenage boy. That's what you do."

"I guess. It was when she and Tim split up. Then, when I was about to leave for Florida, I just couldn't deal. It was too much. So, I ended things."

Dad nodded contemplatively. "So, it really *was* a minute."

"Yeah."

"So, why'd you end it?"

I sat back on the couch with a huff. "I guess I just

started to feel like she deserved better. I didn't want the pressure or something. It was too big."

"Spencer, I'm not the best at this stuff. You'll have to explain to me why she deserved better. She already knows everything about you... I always figured when you two got together it'd be easy as breathing."

I sighed at his phrasing. He was right; it had been. Until I'd thought about it more. "The answer to that will be kind of touchy."

He waited, silently.

"I'm going to make a career out of the military. Ellie's always wanted a stable life. A life that includes her dream wedding, and a nice house by the beach with a white-picket fence, and a husband who has a good job like her dad does. This new guy, Eric, is a lawyer at her dad's law firm. Can't hate on that."

"You don't think being a Marine is a good enough career for her?" He raised a brow.

"It's not that. She just doesn't want this life. Most importantly, she wants kids. I don't. So, I don't see the point in us starting something now only to end it, eventually."

Dad shook his head. "I must have really messed you up, boy."

"What?"

"Was your childhood that awful?"

"No, it wasn't." I shifted in my seat. "I loved my life growing up. But now I'm older, and I think about how Mom had to be a single parent and sacrifice so much for you. I don't want to do that to Ellie."

He stiffened. "Are you saying being with your mom was wrong of me? Or that making a career out of the Marine Corps was wrong?"

"I mean, maybe it's just not for everybody. I remember nights when I could hear her crying because she missed you."

He sat up straight and slammed his fist on the arm of his recliner. "Of course she missed me. I missed her, too. And I missed *you*. And I think she would be about ready to kick you if she heard you talking about her life like this. Your mother was the strongest and most amazing woman I will ever know. When other women couldn't handle it if their husbands left for a weeklong business trip, she was raising her son, working, and staying as positive as ever. Even when I was gone for almost a year at a time. She never complained about our life. She made the best of it. Are you under the impression that all military families are miserable? What kind of sense does that make?"

"What about the crying then? That doesn't sound like she made the best of it."

"She was human, Spencer," he all but shouted at me. "She was allowed to have feelings. That doesn't mean that she would trade our life for anything. One of the last things she said to me was not to be sad about the time we missed, because she wouldn't have traded it for the world."

I swiped at the lone tear that had made its way from my eye. Hearing all of this, hearing so much about Mom in general, was like bringing her death right back to the present instead of safely tucked away in my past. I hadn't ever stopped to think about Mom's strength, and whether she might have taken pride in being so tough. I'd only ever blamed dad for trying to balance a family and the Marine Corps when it was so obvious to me you couldn't... or shouldn't.

"I'm sorry. I just didn't want to think about Ellie crying in the dark while I was gone like Mom did. And I didn't want kids because I didn't want them to think about stuff like this."

His expression softened. "Look, your mom supported my dream to be a Marine. She married me when I was a private. She knew what she was getting herself into. Her dreams in life became my dreams too, and vice versa. I did my best to give her everything she wanted whenever I could. She wasn't lacking, son. She was happy. Even to her last breath."

I swiped at another tear and swallowed hard, not trusting my voice to respond.

"This whole thing was a cop out on your part. You acted like a child because you didn't want to grow up and have real feelings. You made a decision that wasn't yours to make. If she knew about your concerns, she could have decided if she wanted this life or not. You sure stepped in it this time."

I smiled bitterly. "Well, I guess it doesn't matter now."

"Why's that?"

"Because she's dating Eric. I think he might be exactly what she wants. It's hard to hate him, which makes me hate him even more. You know what he did tonight? He told me he had good intentions towards Ellie, and he knew I'd hurt him if he hurt her. How do I hate a guy like that?"

Dad laughed again. "You don't have to hate him, Spence. But you don't have to lie down and let him take your girl, either."

## 21

## ELLIE

I stared out at the water, enjoying the feel of the wind as we glided over the Pacific. Eric had been nice enough to have us all out for a day on his dad's forty-foot yacht. I was definitely more than a little hesitant to ask my friends if they wanted to come. Not because I didn't want them to, but because it felt strange to say, "Hey, guys, want to spend the day on a yacht with me?"

One summer, my dad had joined a yacht club, allowing us to rent boats for the day for a monthly fee. It was fun for that summer and had seemed pretty extravagant at the time. Owning a million-dollar yacht, on the other hand, was way beyond what my family could afford.

"Hey gorgeous," Eric said, coming up behind me. I was leaning on the rail at the back of the sleek, white boat. He put his hands on the rail on either side of me and rested his chin on my shoulder. We stood there for a few minutes, just watching the waves we left in our wake.

Even though we wore sweatshirts, and the air had a bit of a bite to it, I loved that living in San Diego meant we could go boating at Christmas-time. There was just something about the year-round sunshine and ocean breeze that spoke to my soul. I couldn't imagine ever leaving. Spencer getting cross-country orders flashed through my mind, but I blinked the thought away. Not like I'd go with him.

"Where is everybody?" I asked.

"I think they're inside, but I'm not sure. I was up top and came right down when I saw how good you looked back here with the wind in your hair." He punctuated his words by running his hands through my blonde hair as it whipped in the wind.

I blushed, smiling over my shoulder at him. "Thanks for inviting us. It's been an amazing day so far."

"I'm glad. It seemed like a good way for your friends to spend the day before their wedding. I have champagne in the cabin for a sunset toast."

I was impressed, which was probably his plan, but I didn't care. It felt nice to have a guy pull out all the stops for me. The last few days since we all went to the movies had been great. My friends genuinely seemed to like him, and he seemed to like them, too.

"So, your dad lets you take this bad boy out whenever you want?" I asked, referring to the yacht.

Eric laughed. "This is only the second time I've gone out without him."

"I see, so this isn't the way you normally spend your Sunday afternoons?"

He shook his head. "Hate to burst your bubble, but I'm usually just playing *Call of Duty* at my apartment on a Sunday afternoon."

"Well," I said, turning to face him, my back against the rail, "I don't think we're going to work out, then. I was under the impression your life was always this glamorous. If not..."

"Hey, the captain is cool though, I'd like to come out more often and have him teach me how to drive. Would that be impressive enough?"

I smiled as he brought his forehead down to mine. We hadn't kissed yet, and I couldn't help but notice it would be the perfect time for that to happen. I heard the not-so-subtle sound of someone clearing his throat behind Eric. I peered over his shoulder, seeing Matt coming through the doorway of the cabin. Eric stepped away from me, looking unperturbed by the interruption. Matt, Olivia, and Spencer came out of the living area and onto the deck, waving at us as they headed up the stairs to the lounge area at the front of the boat.

When they were gone, Eric turned back to me. "So..."

"So," I parroted, suddenly a little nervous. "I don't know much about you, you know."

"I could say the same thing about you."

I frowned. He may know about my history with Spencer, and my resistance to my dad's life plans for me, but not much else. Honestly, there wasn't much else to tell. What was I supposed to tell him about, my high school adventures? It didn't happen often, but insecurities about our age difference had a way of sneaking up on me.

"I'll start," Eric said, taking a seat on a nearby bench. "I was born in San Francisco. My dad's law firm opened another branch in San Diego, so we moved here about ten years ago. Like I told you before, I've always known I wanted to be a lawyer like my dad, so I focused my high school days on getting straight A's and getting into a good college. Then, college was all about keeping that 4.0 record to get into a good law school. I didn't have much of a social life in college, other than what Jordan got me to do here and there."

"Was Jordan the one who went back to her ex?"

His eyes flashed a hint of residual anger and he nodded. "That's her. Hindsight is twenty-twenty, but I can't help but think maybe if I hadn't spent so much time focused on my grades and more time focused on her, things would have been different. I have this rule now, not to put school or work before a woman again."

"Did you think she was 'the one'?" I asked, pensively.

"At the time, yes. But I guess she wasn't. I haven't seen or heard anything about her since before law school. Sometimes I wonder if she wound up marrying the guy."

"Have you Facebook stalked her?" I asked.

He rolled his eyes. "Nah. Not sure I want to know."

I didn't know what to say, so I let the silence drag on. We stared out at the ocean for a while until Olivia's excited voice from the side of the yacht broke the silence.

"Hey, you two. Come join us!"

We made our way along the boat to the lounge area, holding hands. I was glad I got to know a little more about Eric, but thoughts about our age difference kind of put a damper on it. I was worried about only having the high school stuff to talk about, and he'd had college and law school experiences. At twenty-four, he seemed way closer to marriage and kids than I was. Considering I was only nineteen, the thought was intimidating. Was that something he wanted right now? Because I didn't think I could go there yet. There was a lot I wanted to do before I had kids. Would he want to wait until I was his age? That would make him thirty. I was shocked by how old that sounded.

"E?" Spencer's voice broke through my silent worrying.

"What?"

"I asked if you wanted a Coke."

I nodded and thanked him as he handed me the can from the cooler at his feet. I sat on the bench along the side of the lounge area, popping the top and taking a long drink. There was something about an ice-cold Coca-Cola.

"You look like you're in a commercial," Spencer said, grinning.

I eyed him suspiciously. "What do you mean?"

"I don't know, your red sweater, sitting on a fancy yacht, drinking a can of Coke with a smile on your face. It's like a commercial, or a magazine, or something."

I blushed and made a face at him.

"So," Olivia piped up, probably trying to smooth out the silence that followed Spencer's observation, "we decided where we wanted to go to dinner tomorrow night."

"Dinner?" Eric asked.

Matt nodded. "Yeah, we figured since we'll have the real wedding later, we'd just celebrate with dinner after the courthouse."

"Babe!" Olivia hit Matt's knee. "Don't say the 'real' wedding, say the 'big' wedding. This wedding is real, too, you know."

Matt groaned and playfully rolled his eyes at his fiancée. "Sorry. The 'big' wedding will have the reception and everything, so dinner is fine for now."

"Where did you pick?" I asked.

Olivia clapped her hands together in excitement. "We're going to that Italian restaurant I love. We went there for my last birthday and it's amazing."

"What's the dress code, Mills?" Spencer asked.

"Blues."

I cringed inwardly. It would not be easy seeing Spencer in dress blues. There was just something about that uniform that made Marines super-hot. I scolded myself. It was a horrible thing to think about while sitting on Eric's yacht, enjoying a Coke from the cooler he'd provided, just because I'd mentioned *once* it was my favorite soft drink. I told myself to focus on the obvious choice.

"Ellie, I'm so excited for you to wear that dress we picked out the other day. That blue is stunning on you." Olivia complimented me.

"Thank you, but you're the one with the special dress! It's just perfect."

Matt put his hands over his ears. "I'm not listening."

"It sounds like you guys have a great day planned for

tomorrow, congratulations, again," Eric said, raising his own Coke in salute to the happy couple. It occurred to me that he could drink beer if he wanted to, but he wasn't. I wondered if that was out of respect for us, so as not to highlight that we were all underage.

"Sorry you won't be there, Eric." Spencer's tone was slightly combative, and it had me glaring daggers at him. He'd been making little comments here and there that were less than polite. As if he wasn't enjoying a day on the open ocean courtesy of Eric.

Eric laughed good-naturedly. "Oh, it's fine. Ellie and I have brunch plans tomorrow. But I'm sure you guys will have a fun evening."

"Brunch?" Spencer mouthed the word silently to me as if to say, *really?*

"Spencer," Eric said, his tone conversational, "I actually have a cousin who's a Marine."

"That's cool." Spencer leaned against the back of the seat stretching his arms across the top. "You didn't want to join with him? They have a buddy program, you know."

Eric laughed. "Uh, no. I knew my path. He's the one who was a little lost after high school and the Marines helped him find his way. He's stationed here now so we hang out as much as his job allows."

"He's stationed here?" I asked. "What does he do?"

"He's a recruiter," Eric answered.

I blinked at Spencer. "Eric *Moore.* As in, Sergeant Moore?"

Spencer leaned forward on his elbows. "Sergeant Moore is your cousin? Your cousin was my recruiter?"

Eric raised his brows. “Wow. Small world.”

“Clearly. Well... he’s a good dude. I liked him,” Spencer bit out, almost begrudgingly, like he was mad his recruiter was related to Eric.

Fed up with the tension, I excused myself to use the restroom. I made my way to the back of the boat and into the spacious cabin. It was full of rich mahogany and plush, white leather. I flipped off my sandals as I stepped onto the pristine white carpet, the softness of which was cloud-like as I walked down the small hallway to the bathroom. The carpeting and leather couches didn’t seem very practical for wet feet or swimsuits, but practicality wasn’t a priority for the super-rich. The small bathroom was just as luxurious as the rest of the cabin, and I felt the need to wipe the water droplets off the edge of the sink after I washed my hands.

I opened the tiny door and stepped into the hallway, then I jumped when I saw Spencer leaning against the wall. My hand went up to my chest automatically, and I could feel my heart pounding beneath my skin. I wasn’t sure if it was because he’d startled me, or because he was standing there looking at me like he was burning up on the inside. His large frame took up the entire width of the hallway. There was no way to get past him.

For a moment, we just stood there, staring at each other. I took a step back, just to put some distance between us. Unfortunately, that put me in the bedroom area of the cabin. The backs of my legs touched the soft duvet of the bed behind me, and I froze.

"You okay?" He eyed me, a wicked smile playing at the corners of his lips.

I swallowed, not sure what to say. The knowing glint in his gorgeous blue eyes made me want to kick him.

He seemed to deliberate about something, and I would bet this yacht I knew what it was. I hoped he made the right choice and just went into the bathroom and let me pass. I wasn't sure what I would do if he went with the other option. There were still sparks between us. You could practically see them flying around in the cramped space between us. It scared me to death, knowing how I'd react if he put his hands on me right now.

Thankfully, he shook his head and ducked into the bathroom, locking the door behind him. I let out an audible breath, flopping down on the bed behind me. Just as soon as I did, I realized that he wouldn't stay in there forever. I jumped up and scrambled out of the gorgeous cabin. The ocean breeze felt like a lifeline when I emerged from below. I stood there on the deck, drinking it in, and tried to collect myself before I had to face Eric. I felt like a tramp.

"Elizabeth?" Eric made his way to the back of the boat and reached for me.

"Hey," I replied, forcing a smile as I took his hand.

"I just came back to check on you. You look pale, are you seasick?"

I closed my eyes, feeling guilty. "Maybe a little."

"Can I get you anything?" The concern was clear in his eyes, making me feel even worse.

"No, I'm fine. It passed." I pulled him over to the

railing and leaned my back against his chest like we had earlier. I knew I was being sneaky, positioning Eric so his back was to the cabin door for when Spencer came out.

"There's something we need to talk about," Eric began, whispering in my ear. "I don't think Spencer just wants to be your friend. I think he wants more."

I blinked, not responding for a moment. There was no way he had seen what just happened, right? No, he couldn't have. "What makes you say that?"

"The way he looks at you. The way he looks at me. I'd be an idiot not to see it."

I took a deep breath, and just like before, I turned in his arms to face him. "He was the one who ended things. He doesn't want to be with me like that. We're better as friends. If he felt that way about me, why would he have done what he did?"

Eric shrugged, staring over my head. "I wouldn't know. But it looks like he regrets it now."

I put my hand on his cheek, bringing his eyes back to mine, trying again to focus on the obvious choice. "Even if that's true, it's too late now."

Eric smiled down at me, his arms leaving the rail on either side of my waist and wrapping around me. He leaned down, slowly, and brought his lips to mine. He smelled like the ocean, and his soft lips were cold after spending all day in the winter wind. It gave me a chill, and not in a bad way. I brought my other hand up and around his neck, pulling him closer. His touch was gentle and sweet, a slow burn, as our mouths moved together. He gave my lips one last peck, and then pulled back, bending his head to nuzzle my neck.

I gasped when I saw Spencer in the cabin's doorway. The hurt was plain on his face, his eyes huge and full of betrayal. There was only one thing more shocking than the emotions splayed out across the deck in front of me, and that was just how much the force of his pain hurt me, too.

# 22

## SPENCER

"Whatever you're about to say better be encouraging, bro." Mills was already shaving when I entered the bathroom of our hotel suite to do the same. "I don't need any of your lectures about how marriage and the military don't mix. Not today."

I scoffed. "It's your wedding day. I'm a better friend than that."

"Yeah, sure."

"Besides, I don't feel that way anymore."

Mills paused with the razor halfway to his shaving cream-covered face and gaped at me in the mirror. "Since when?

"Since that night we all went to the movies."

"Is that why you bailed halfway through?"

I put a mountain of shaving cream on my hand to lather up my face. "Yeah. Sorry. I was just over it."

"I don't blame you, Hawk. No one wants to be the fifth wheel. When I invited you I didn't know Eric was coming."

I glided my razor over my face, pausing our conversation while maneuvering around my Adam's apple. "I had a beer with my dad when I got home. It was good. We talked about all this. He said some stuff that actually helped."

"Like what?"

"Like personal stuff about my mom and how she felt about being a military wife. He was pretty offended by my opinion on the whole thing."

"Can't imagine that." Mills smiled as he rinsed off his razor.

"Shut up," I chuckled. "He also said I was choosing what was right for Ellie when it was her choice to make."

"Also sounds familiar. Your dad's a smart guy. All jokes aside, you haven't had a decent conversation with your old man in years. That had to be weird talking to him about all this."

"Tell me about it. Of all things, I can't believe a heart-to-heart with my dad changed the way I feel about this thing with Ellie... but it did."

"So, what are you going to do?"

I'd finished shaving, so I bent my head to rinse my face while I thought about my answer. "Honestly, I have no clue."

"You want my advice?" Mills asked, drying his face.

"Let's hear it, Romeo."

"Be honest with her. Tell her exactly why you ended things in the first place and admit you were taking the choice away from her. Then let her pick."

"Sounds so simple, and yet, could go so terribly wrong."

Mills shrugged and put his shaving kit back in his hygiene bag. "I don't know what else to tell you, man. Olivia and I have had some rough conversations before, but it always just kind of worked out. I think that's because we're always honest with each other."

I stared at my reflection in the mirror, wondering if I had the balls to lay it all out there to Ellie. "I guess I've got nothing to lose at this point."

"Good attitude. Now get your blues on."

I followed him into the bedroom of the suite where the various pieces of our dress blue alpha uniforms covered each of the two queen beds. I pulled on the royal blue pants, fastening them around my white undershirt, and stepped into my black dress shoes. The only piece left was the iconic black, red, and gold coat that finished the look. I held it up and examined it closely before putting it on, making sure that there were no loose threads that needed cutting. I brushed the chest of the coat with my hand, straightened my medal, and picked a tiny piece of lint off the shoulder. Satisfied, I pulled the coat on. I worked my way through the line of gold buttons down the middle and then fastened the gold buckle at my waist. I grabbed my hat, known to us as a 'cover,' and turned it upside down on the bed. I put my white gloves next to it and turned to examine my reflection in the long mirror on the wall.

It was hard not to swell up with pride. The rest of the Marine Corps may only know me as an inexperienced 'boot,' but only a small percentage of the military earned the right to wear this uniform. Boot or not, I was proud to be in that group. I'd worked hard for it, and I wore it well.

"I'm a little nervous." Mills sat on the edge of his bed. He was fidgeting with his white cotton gloves, twisting them in his hands and then trying to straighten out any wrinkles.

"I can tell."

He didn't look up at me. "So, distract me."

I sighed. I hadn't planned to tell Mills about what happened on the boat the day before, but he obviously needed something to take his mind off things. I knew it wasn't cold feet, just stage fright. If it were anything more than that I would try to help him through it. This couple was solid as a rock, though. Anyone would be nervous on their wedding day.

"Well... Something happened between Ellie and me on the boat yesterday," I said, sitting opposite him on my bed.

He looked up. "Really?"

"Not much, but when I went downstairs to use the head, she was just coming out, and it was just really intense. Nothing happened, but I could tell we both wanted it to. I thought it meant something, you know? But then I felt like an idiot when I came upstairs and saw her kissing Eric."

Mills cringed. "Ouch."

"Yeah, tell me about it." I stood and paced, feeling tense. "That's why I'm nervous about telling her to make her choice. She might not pick me. This thing with Eric could seriously get in my way."

"Not if you can get between them before they get too close." Mills had put aside the gloves, so I could tell I'd distracted him with my personal drama.

"I guess I'll just have to lay everything out like you said. What's the worst that could happen?"

Mills frowned. "I'm not sure you want to tempt fate on that one, man."

"Speaking of fate," I stood, putting my cover securely under my arm, "let's go get you married."

Mills and Olivia each repeated their wedding vows with million-watt smiles on their faces. It would have been sickening if I weren't so happy for them. I gave Mills a hard time in the beginning about getting married so young, but things had changed since then. Ever since I saw how great they were together, there was no denying these two were role models for how love was supposed to be. Not that I would ever say that out loud, of course.

The ceremony itself was brief. The parents of the bride and groom were very emotional, and I couldn't help but get a little sad thinking about how my mom would never witness this day for me. Other than the two sets of parents, Ellie and I were the only other guests. We were the best man and maid of honor, so we had front-row seats to the action.

I wish I'd paid more attention to my best friend's wedding, but Ellie in that sapphire blue cocktail dress held way too much of my focus. Her eyes sparkled when she looked at me, all welled up with girly wedding tears. She'd swept her long blonde hair up into a messy style I knew had probably taken her an hour to do. Girls put a lot of effort into things that were supposed to look effortless. I could just picture her with her phone on the counter so she could watch someone teach her how to do it on YouTube.

Thoughts like that occupied me so much during the ceremony that Mills had to elbow me when it was time to hand over the rings. I tried not to be too obvious. It was their day. But every time I tried to focus elsewhere, my eyes inevitably traveled back to Ellie's long, tan legs under that short, blue dress. Or the way she smiled encouragingly at her friend, giddy to be so close to so much love.

Before I knew it, it was time for Mills to kiss his brand-new wife, and everyone cheered. We took their pictures while they signed their marriage certificate and shook hands with the judge. Olivia even tossed her tiny grouping of three red roses in Ellie's face, playing on the bouquet toss at a traditional wedding. My stomach turned when her eyes met mine, and I scolded myself for taking the tradition too seriously. She was the only single girl in the room who could have caught it.

Outside, Mills gave the parents the directions to the restaurant and they got in their cars. Then, he swept up his new bride and carried her to the car he'd borrowed from his dad for the occasion. It was all decked out in 'just married' writing and cans hanging off the back tied to fishing line. I was sure it was Ellie's handiwork. She was definitely sappy enough to want a movie-like exit for her friends on their big day. I loved that about her.

I glanced at Ellie.

"Well, I guess you're riding with me, then. Ready?" she asked, fidgeting with the small bouquet she still held.

I nodded and walked to her car, opening the passenger door for her. She glanced at me strangely and crossed to the driver's side, getting in behind the wheel. I stood there like an idiot for a moment. Before we'd hooked up, I always drove. That it was her car didn't matter; it was just what we did. I let out a bitter laugh and got in the car.

She said nothing the whole way to the restaurant. I was still annoyed about the driving thing, even though it was extremely petty and childish. What was she trying to tell me by switching up our routine? Was she trying to say we would never go back to the way things were? Or maybe I was just being a total girl about it and should just let it go. I rolled my neck and pulled at the tight collar of my blues. It still annoyed me.

When she parked the car and started to get out, I grabbed for her arm. "Wait."

She hesitated and then looked at me warily. "What?"

"I need to tell you something."

"Now?"

I nodded. "Yeah, Mills already knows I wanted to talk

to you. Besides, they can have time with their families without us for a minute."

She settled back into her seat with a sigh, apparently waiting for me to begin.

"I made a huge mistake."

She snorted. "Spencer, we already made amends that day on the swings. It's fine."

Before I could respond, she grabbed her clutch and got out of the car.

"Wait, let me finish," I called, having jumped out to catch her before she walked away. "Wait, hang on."

I ducked back into the car and grabbed my cover. We had to wear a cover whenever we were outside in uniform, so I popped it on my head and crossed back over to her.

She wrapped her arms tightly around her middle to fight the December chill. "I'm just not sure why you need to do this right now. I think it's obvious I'm moving on. I *need* to move on."

"That's exactly *why* I need to do this. You can't move on without hearing me out. And I have a lot to say. Probably too much. So just... stay here and let me say it."

Ellie threw her hands out in frustration. "This is what *you* wanted. You told me repeatedly that you wanted to go back to the way things were before. Here you go. We're friends, and I have a boyfriend. Ta-da."

I chuckled bitterly. "This is *nothing* like the way things were before."

She let her arms fall to her side, almost in defeat.

"I'm taking my shot," I continued. "I ended things with you because it scared me. That weekend at Pendleton was amazing. It was like living in a fantasy world for a couple of days."

She moved to the side of her car and leaned against it, so I leaned against the adjacent car to face her.

"After you left that weekend, it hit me how much I missed you already. And then I realized I'd probably miss you all the time if we were together. Deployments and stuff would suck. Not to mention how it would be for you. I know what you want for your future. And it doesn't include moving around every three years, raising a family without your husband for months at a time, or always worrying about things that could happen to me. Besides, I wasn't even sure if I wanted to have kids if they would grow up without me around."

She gaped at me. "That's kind of intense after one weekend, Spence. You went from a totally out-of-left-field kiss to marriage and kids."

I tilted my head at her. "Was it really out of left field, though? Honestly? You've never thought about kissing me?"

She blushed and looked away. "Is that why you got weird about Tim before you left for boot camp? You felt that way about me back then?"

I hadn't planned on admitting how long I'd battled these feelings. Mills had said to be honest. "That's when it started, I guess. I'd never looked at you like that before, I swear. You were my best friend. You had Tim, and I had no one... in a good way. But when I was getting ready to leave... something changed. It hit me that I would miss you. I mean, I knew I'd miss you. But it felt different."

"Why didn't you say something then?" she asked quietly.

"A lot of reasons. All the stuff I said about keeping you from your dream life with a stable guy. Not wanting kids to go through what I went through, but knowing you wanted a family someday. Plus, you were with Tim. I didn't want you to be with him because I thought you deserved better... but then I was glad you were with him because it kept me from telling you how I felt."

"Until the night Tim and I broke up." She crossed her arms again.

"I had to... I just couldn't keep it all bottled up anymore."

Ellie seemed to wrestle with this for a moment. "So, you ended things with me because military relationships seemed too hard?"

"It sounds dumb when you put it like that. I didn't want to put someone I loved in the position my mom was in. You know, waiting and worrying and doing everything alone."

I watched her as she thought about what I'd said. She was staring right at me. She wasn't looking around or appearing uncomfortable. She was focused on this conversation and I couldn't have been happier about that. It made me think I had a chance.

"Are you done?" she asked after a moment.

I shifted. "I guess."

"I don't even know where to start, Spence. There is so much wrong with what you just said, that I literally don't know where to start. You made so many choices you had no right to make. And you have no right to pretend you were doing any of it for me. You were just being a selfish, scared little boy."

"I know that now. I talked to my dad about it. He helped me to realize I was being an idiot."

Her eyes widened. "You talked to your dad about this?"

"I guess I was desperate."

"Spencer, you can't just push me away because you think you know what I want from life. Everything I thought I wanted got turned upside down after that week-end. You were my best friend. I would have..."

When she trailed off, I stood from the car I was leaning on and took a step closer to her. "You would have what?"

"It doesn't matter now. You hurt me before I had the chance."

I squeezed my eyes shut. "I'm sorry."

"I know."

"You would have *what*, E?"

She buried her face in her hands and breathed deeply for a moment. "Being with you would have changed everything. I would have put everything into making it work with you, Spence. I believed in us. For that short time, I believed that we could last forever."

Her words were jagged rays of hope shining down on this messed up situation. I grabbed for them like a lifeline. "Then give me another chance."

"No." Her eyes welled up, and I could tell she was desperately trying to control her emotions.

I stepped closer again and put my hand on her cheek. A tear spilled over, so I used my thumb to wipe it away. "Why not?"

"Because I can't trust you now. I can't trust you won't pull something like that again and get freaked out the first time we're separated and push me away. I can't risk everything for you."

"But you can risk everything for *Eric*?"

"You were the one who said I needed someone stable. Maybe 'stable' just means someone who won't run when it gets scary."

I couldn't argue. That's exactly what I'd done. Funny thing was, I only broke up with her because I figured she'd eventually end it with me once she realized I couldn't give her what she wanted. It was immature, I knew. I couldn't imagine Eric doing that. But I couldn't let her walk away that easily. The next few minutes would show me a lot about how I should proceed.

"Ellie, about that kiss between you and Eric on the boat..."

She swallowed guiltily. "Yeah, sorry you had to see that."

"Oh, me too, trust me. But how did it stack up to that night we kissed? Because if you tell me you felt more for him than for me, I'll drop this whole thing."

Ellie scowled at me. "I am absolutely *not* going to compare."

"Why not?" I got closer again, our bodies touching now. "You should be able to admit who affected you more. Which one felt right, and which one was just a kiss?"

She shook her head, her brows pulled tightly together. Through her indignation, I could tell I was getting to her. She licked her lips and then looked at mine. *Bingo.*

"I think you need a reminder," I whispered against her lips.

## 23

## ELLIE

My entire body went rigid when his lips closed over mine. I felt his fingertips press into my hips as he pulled me closer, and I couldn't help but melt into him. It was like nothing had changed between us and we were back at Camp Pendleton, exploring this new connection. I hadn't realized just how much I'd missed him until I was back in his arms. He wanted me to compare this feeling to that kiss with Eric? There was no comparison.

*Eric.*

I pulled away, and without taking the time to think, I slapped him. The look of shock on his face was instantaneous, and I brought my hand up to cover my mouth. "I'm sorry!"

Spencer wiggled he jaw. "Did you just slap me?"

"You kissed me."

"So, you slapped me? What is this, *The Notebook?*"

I giggled, somewhat unwillingly. "I said I was sorry." He reached for me again, but I ducked under his arm. "Oh, no, you don't. Just stay back. Two feet, at least."

"Are you serious?"

"Yes!" I threw my hands in the air. "You can't just kiss me, Spencer! I'm with Eric now, and you and I need to just forget what happened between us."

Spencer looked confused. "That's not what your lips were saying a minute ago..."

"Read them now. I'm not doing this again." I emphasized each word, drawing them out so my lips made exaggerated motions.

"What about everything I just said? I laid it all out for you. Let's fix it."

I took a step toward him and put a hand on his shoulder. "Thank you for opening up to me like that. It's nice to hear how you feel, for a change. But I still can't trust you not to do it again."

Spencer shrugged my hand off his shoulder and came closer, towering over me in the stupid hot uniform. "You can't deny what's happening between us. I can't force you to be with me, but I know one thing. If you choose Eric, one day, maybe years from now, you'll wonder what it would have been like if you'd chosen me instead."

I took a deep breath, shocked by the intensity of his gaze as he stared directly into my eyes. It was like a new fire was lit under him after that kiss. Before, he looked so vulnerable. Now, he looked determined. There was a steady confidence about him I had never seen before. I tried to speak, but he held up his hand. I wasn't sure what I would have said, anyway.

"Maybe you'll be sitting in your perfect house, drinking coffee and reading the news with your perfect husband, and I'll cross your mind. And you'll wonder how different your life would be if you hadn't taken the easy way out."

I raised my chin defiantly. "Or, maybe I'll be safe and happy, and not heartbroken because I chose the guy who had the power to crush me."

"Maybe." He smiled sardonically. "But the fact that you think I have the power to crush you means you know what we have is real."

I shook my head at him, maintaining my ground.

"Fine," he said through clenched teeth. He took my face in both of his hands. "But just so you know, I'll always be here if you change your mind. There is no one else for me. I'm going to spend the rest of my life proving we're supposed to be together. It's you, or no one. Understand?"

The lump in my throat prevented me from speaking. Never in a million years did I expect him to pour his heart out like this. I should have fallen into his arms. Or maybe I should have run away. Instead, I stood there, frozen.

He pressed his lips hard against my forehead before walking toward the restaurant without me.

~

Sitting in the fancy café with Eric for lunch the next day, I found myself hopelessly distracted by the events of the weekend. First, there was that weird moment between Spencer and me on the boat. Then, there was the first kiss with Eric. And finally, last night's post-wedding confession and kiss from Spencer. I felt like a total mess. Not to mention a total hussy.

"Are you okay?" Eric furrowed his brow in concern.

I shrugged slightly. "Not really."

"Something I might help with?"

"I don't think so."

"Does it have anything to do with Spencer?"

I blinked at him.

Eric chuckled. "Just a hunch. So, what's up?"

I took a deep breath. It was best to just be honest with him. If he got mad and decided not to see me anymore, so be it. But I wouldn't continue this relationship between us with lies hanging over my head. In my book, omitting that another guy had kissed me the night before was definitely a lie.

"Spencer kissed me after the wedding last night." I watched warily for anger or jealousy to appear on Eric's attractive face, but it never came. He just smiled slightly and took a drink from his iced tea. "Well?"

"Well, what?" he asked. "How do you feel about that?"

"I honestly don't know."

"Elizabeth, listen, I really like spending time with you. I think you're a great girl, and I think we could have a lot of fun together. You're smart, funny, and you're absolutely gorgeous. But this is why I told you to figure things out with Spencer before we started dating. Do you have feelings for him?"

I looked down. "It's really complicated."

"Love is always complicated."

Again, I blinked up at him in surprise. What was I supposed to say to that?

"Look, I'm not one for impeding two people who want to be together. What's holding you back from being with him?"

"Well," I started, feeling strange about having this conversation with him like we were nothing more than friends, "he really hurt me. I don't want to go there with him, just in case he does it again."

Eric pursed his lips. "That's not what I would have expected from you. You seemed like the girl who would take a risk if it made her happy."

"We also have very different ideas of how we want our lives to turn out. I'm not sure it's a good idea to force them together."

"Compromise is key to any relationship."

I shook my head. "Why are you doing this?"

"Doing what?"

"This," I gestured between the two of us. "It's like you're trying to convince me to be with him instead of you."

Eric chuckled again. "I think it's quite clear, to me anyway, that you feel more for Spencer than you do for me. Like I said, I think you're a great girl and we've had a lot of fun, but we've only been out a few times. I'm not going to get in the way of an old friendship that's turning into something more. Call me a romantic, but I know when I've lost."

I stared at him, wide-eyed. "So, what, you think I should give him another chance?"

He leaned forward and took my hand across the table. "I think you should do what feels right for you. If you don't take the risk, you won't get the reward. But you're not going to settle for me just because you're scared to be with him. That's not fair for either of us, is it?"

I slumped in my chair, knowing he was right. This guy was seriously perfect. He just wasn't perfect for me. I sincerely hoped whoever ended up with him, deserved him.

I heard my mom calling me from the bottom of the stairs, so I shut the lid of my laptop and headed down the hall. I paused when I saw Spencer standing in the foyer. I hadn't seen him since the night of the wedding, and I had no idea what to do now that I wasn't seeing Eric anymore. I wasn't even sure if I wanted to tell him that yet. I still needed time to figure everything out. There were so many thoughts bouncing around in my mind at any given second that I was only confusing myself. No need to drag him down the rabbit hole with me until I was sure about what I wanted.

"Are you just going to stand there?" My mom asked with a laugh, jerking me back to reality.

I jogged down the steps and gave Spencer a one-armed hug. "Hey."

"Hi." Spencer smiled at me awkwardly and then looked back at my mom. "It was good to see you, Carol."

"You too, honey. Have a safe flight." My mom moved in to hug him, and he closed his eyes as he hugged her back. It made my chest hurt to see just how much he cared about my mom. "All right, I'll let you two say your goodbyes."

I waited until my mom was back in the kitchen before gesturing for Spencer to go out back. "Swings?"

He shook his head. "I've got all my bags on the porch and Olivia and Mills are just getting gas to give us time to talk. Wanna go out front?"

I followed him silently out the door, closing it behind me. "That was a fast two-week break."

"Yeah, no kidding. It was good to be home, though."

Not sure what to say next, I shuffled my feet.

"E, look at me." His words were soft, and he brought his finger up to lift my chin. "What's wrong?"

"I don't know, Spencer. This is just... a lot."

He leaned back against the support beam on my porch. I thought he might have sensed I needed some space. "I know. But look, I won't apologize for the other night. I had to get it out and be honest with you."

"I really can't jump back into things with you, okay? I need time."

Spencer rolled his eyes. "It just kills me that you wouldn't even be with this Eric guy if it weren't for what I did. We'd be together and you wouldn't need time to figure anything out."

I almost told him right then that Eric and I had parted ways, but I knew it would just open a can of worms. He saw Eric as the only thing standing between us being together again, and that simply wasn't true. There were so many things I needed to think about before falling back into his arms. And as much as I hated to think about it right then, I couldn't help but notice just how tempting those arms looked as his biceps strained against the sleeves of his shirt.

Olivia's car pulled up, and I let out a sigh of relief at the same time that Spencer let out a sigh of frustration. He looked back at me, a sad smile playing on his lips. "I guess this is goodbye – for now."

It surprised me at how much those words left a hollow feeling in the pit of my stomach. He stooped to gather his sea bag and heft it onto his back, so I picked up the smaller duffel bag. We made our way down to the waiting car. I noticed that they weren't getting out, so I figured that they were trying to give us some privacy. How much could we resolve in the next thirty seconds? Definitely not enough, that was for sure.

We finished loading his bags into the trunk of the car, so all that was left was goodbye. "Spencer..."

"Yeah?"

"I just want you to know, that I'll always love you. I just need to figure out what kind of love it is, and where this is going."

A new spark of hope appeared in his eye. “I can live with that.”

“Good.”

He pulled me in for a hug and rested his cheek on the top of my head. “I wish I didn’t have to leave.”

“Me too.”

“I’ll always come back to you, Ellie. Whatever you decide.”

Eric was right. If I were to be with anyone but Spencer, I’d only be settling. I knew that the tears would flow if I tried to speak, so instead, I just let him hold me until Mills beeped the horn, signaling it was time for him to go. He got in the car without another word.

# 24

# SPENCER

"I don't know, man. I honestly don't care where they send me," Mills said as we left our classroom.

I frowned. "Why not?"

"Because now that Olivia and I are married, she's coming with me wherever I get stationed. So, I don't need to be in San Diego anymore."

I knew one of the main reasons they got married was so she could go wherever he did, but now that it was becoming a reality, I was jealous. Mills and his girl would move into a new place somewhere and he was going to go to work and come home to a woman who loved him. I, on the other hand, would be rooming with some random dude in the barracks, surrounded by other Marines day and night. Which was what I'd always wanted, so it bugged me that Mills' life sounded like the better scenario now.

"What's up? You look weird."

"I'm just thinking," I answered.

"Like I said, weird."

I glared at him. "Funny."

"Seriously, what's up?"

"I think I need to get stationed in San Diego. If I don't, I have absolutely no chance of making things work with Ellie."

Mills took some time to think about that for a moment. "Look, we worked hard in these classes so we'd have the best chance of getting the orders we want. Hopefully it works out for you."

Mills was right, the guys at the top of the class had the best chance of getting what they wanted, but there was still no guarantee. From everything we'd heard from our friends in class, the needs of the Marine Corps trumped everything else.

"What about those guys who said their whole class wound up with East Coast orders?" I argued.

Mills shook his head and clapped me on the shoulder. "You need to relax, Hawk. Just roll with whatever happens. If you wind up getting East Coast, it'll only be for a few years and then maybe you can transfer or something."

I narrowed my eyes at him in response.

"Okay," he allowed, "not the best thing to make you feel better. But you can't control it, so stop stressing."

My phone buzzed in the pocket of my cammies. "Hold up."

Mills stopped walking and waited for me to fish out my phone.

"It's Ellie." I held the phone up to him and nodded

when he motioned that he'd meet me at the chow hall. "Hey. How's it going?"

"Good, you?"

"Good, just heading to chow."

She laughed. "Does that mean you're frozen in place while you take this call since you're in uniform?"

"Yes," I allowed, looking down at my boots and smiling at her relaxed tone. "Is that why you called?"

"No, but it's a good perk. Should I drag the call out, so you're stuck there for a while?"

I looked around, checking to see if anyone was in earshot of my cheesy answer. "I'd stand here forever if it meant I could keep talking to you."

"Oh *wow.*" She laughed hysterically. "That was really bad."

"You liked it," I teased.

"*Anyway*, I called to tell you I signed up for college. It's a degree in finance."

I whistled. "That sounds terribly boring."

"Shut up. I'm really excited. The end goal is to be an accountant or a personal finance advisor. Eric gave me the idea and I've been looking into it ever since. I think it's going to be really cool."

I took my cover off briefly so I could scratch my head. "Eric gave you the idea, huh?"

"Yeah," she said, her tone casual. "He helped me narrow down some careers that match up with my interests."

"You are really into numbers," I allowed, shuffling my feet. "I can see you being an accountant."

"Thanks. I'm excited."

I wanted to flirt with her again. Maybe say something about how she'd make a really hot accountant, but the mention of her boyfriend kinda brought me back down to Earth. I could have probably helped her figure this out, too, if she'd asked me. I knew she loved numbers. She'd always liked making spreadsheets for things. And she was the one who helped me with my statistics homework in high school. I probably could've suggested she be an accountant. Not a "personal finance advisor" though, because I had no freaking clue what that was.

"Well, as much as I'd love to stand here and chat all day, I should probably get to chow before I miss my chance to eat."

She chuckled. "Fine. I'll allow it. I just had to tell you. Now I need to break it to my dad."

"Eh, I think it'll go okay. He'll lay off about you being a lawyer when you tell him you have another plan."

"Thanks."

I could tell she was smiling by her tone of voice, and I wished more than anything I could see it in person. "Well, have a good day."

"You, too."

We disconnected the call, and even though I was free to keep walking, I still stood there for a minute. Eric really was good for her. He'd helped her find her calling, and it was a good idea. I shook my head. It didn't matter. Maybe he was mature and knew what a "personal finance advisor" was, but he wasn't me. And Ellie knew it.

"You've got to be freaking kidding me." I breathed, staring down at the printout of my orders. "MCAS Miramar, San Diego. What did you get?"

Mills grinned and turned his paper around. "Same."

"Seriously? What unit?"

He glanced down at the paper. "VMFA 303, the Red Snakes."

I looked at my own orders and frowned. "Mine says it's a training squadron. VMFAT 111."

Mills shrugged. "At least you won't have to deploy."

"Where's the fun in that?"

"Quit your whining, Hawk. We're both stationed in San Diego. Life is good." Mills gave me a lopsided grin. "I'm going to call Olivia and tell her the good news. You should call Ellie."

I nodded. "I'll see you later."

I watched as Mills walked toward the smoke pit to call his girl. I wasn't sure if I wanted to call Ellie. It sounded like she and Eric were pretty close... If there was even the slightest hint of disappointment in her voice when she found out I was getting stationed in San Diego, I didn't want to hear it. Besides, Olivia would probably call her as soon as she got off the phone with Mills anyway, so it's not like she wouldn't find out.

Later that night, I felt my cell phone buzz in my pocket just as I was about to fall asleep. I pulled it out, not bothering to check the caller I.D. "Hello?"

"Are you kidding me?" Ellie's greeting was less than pleasant.

I sat up and rubbed my eyes. "What time is it?"

She paused. "Oops. I forgot about the time difference. It's like midnight your time."

I glanced over at Mills. He was sleeping soundly. "What's wrong?"

"I talked to Olivia," she answered with a huff.

If this conversation were happening in person, I could picture how she'd look. She'd be standing in front of me and tapping her foot, with one hand on her hip and one finger pointed at my chest. God, I missed her.

"Okay."

"Okay? She told me you found out you were getting stationed here."

"Okay."

"You found out you were getting stationed here and you didn't call me."

I sighed. "Okay."

"*Spencer,*" she all but yelled.

"Well, you found out, didn't you?"

Ellie made an exasperated noise, and I could picture her throwing her hands up in frustration. "It would have been nice to hear it from you."

If I had any shot of being with her, I needed to get back into the habit of blunt honesty. We'd built our friendship on it, and it had kind of gotten lost in all these other feelings. "I was kind of avoiding your reaction."

"What do you mean?" She sounded genuinely confused.

"I don't know." I scrubbed a hand over my face to wake myself up a bit. "Eric helped you figure out your life plan... you guys sound like you're getting pretty close. I'm not giving up... but I wasn't sure how you'd feel about me coming back there so I was worried about telling you."

She said nothing for a long moment. Finally, she sniffed. "Spence, I'm glad you're coming back. Like you promised you would."

Now it was my turn to be speechless for a moment. "I always will, E."

"I'll let you get back to sleep. We'll talk soon." I could hear the smile in her voice, and it made me smile as I hung up the phone.

I lay there awake for a few minutes, staring at the ceiling. There was something about that conversation that had me hopeful for the future. Now the only thing I had to figure out was how to get her away from her boyfriend.

Mills stirred on his side of the room, then propped himself up on one elbow. "Were you on the phone?"

I nodded in the dark, but then remembered that he couldn't see me. "Yeah, Ellie forgot about the time difference."

"It was probably a call you wanted to take anyway, huh? I'm sure you're pretty stoked about her and Eric breaking up."

I jerked back up into a seated position and turned on the light at my bedside. "What did you say?"

Mills cringed away from the light and pulled his blanket over his face. He started to mumble out a reply, but I bent to pick up my shower shoe and threw it at him. "I can't understand you!"

He removed the covers from his face. "Olivia told me earlier. You were already sleeping, so I didn't tell you. I figured that's what Ellie was calling about."

I shook my head. "She didn't mention it."

"Dude, they haven't been together since the day after my wedding."

My jaw dropped. "What?"

"Yeah," Mills yawned. "Olivia let it slip tonight, though. I figured Ellie might have called to tell you since she knows I know. Girls are weird."

I shut the light and flopped back down on my pillow. If Ellie and Eric were over, why wouldn't she tell me? Wasn't he the only thing that was standing between us getting together? Apparently, there was more in the way than I'd thought. *Look at her being all mad at me for not telling her about my orders, when she was keeping a secret of her own.* I heard Mills snoring again, and for the second time in one day, I was jealous of him. There was no way I'd be getting any sleep tonight.

## 25

## ELLIE

"Dad?" I poked my head into his office. "Do you have a minute?"

Paper covered my dad's rich mahogany desk. Stacks, loose sheets, folders, and files. It looked like a tornado has swept through, but he called it organized chaos. I'd once offered to organize it for him, but he said he knew exactly where everything was and not to touch anything. My brain did not function like that. I must have gotten that from my neat and tidy mom.

"Come on in, sweetheart." He motioned for me to enter the room, turning away from his computer. I loved that no matter how busy he was, he always had a way of making me feel like I was important, too.

"I did a thing."

He raised an eyebrow. "A thing?"

"I signed up for school."

"You did?" He leaned back in his plush desk chair and folded his hands in his lap.

"It's online, so don't worry, I'm not quitting. And it's a bachelor's program... in finance."

"Finance?" He leaned forward on the desk. "Not a bad route. Are you thinking of specializing in transactional law?"

I cautiously lowered myself into one of the two chairs across the desk from his. "Not exactly. I'm actually going to open my own accounting business. Maybe I can be a personal finance advisor for small businesses or something."

My dad narrowed his eyes at me. "No law school?"

I shook my head, sitting straighter in the chair to show I was serious. "No law school."

"Humph." He drummed his fingers on the desk, as he often did when he was deep in thought. "We'll have to do more research on starting your own accounting business... Make sure you'll be qualified to do that right after you get your bachelor's. It may be better for you to work at an actual accounting firm until you have more experience."

I blinked. "Oh, okay. Thanks."

"Accounting, huh?"

I nodded.

"I think you'll be great at that, Ellie. I'm happy for you. Who's paying for school?"

"Well, I used my savings for the first semester, and then I guess I'll just keep saving up what I make here, and I should have enough for next semester by the time it's due."

He smiled. "Tell you what. I'll go halfsies with you."

"Halfsies?" I burst out laughing.

"Yeah, halfsies. Make fun of me and I'll make it quarter-sies." He winked.

"Halfsies is good." I stood from the chair and crossed over to his side of the desk, wrapping my arms around him. "Thank you, Dad. I really appreciate your help."

"You're welcome. Now go back to the desk before your boss fires you and you have to drop out of school."

I made a face at him and left the room. Looks like Spencer had been right after all. My dad just wanted me to have a plan. I couldn't wait to get started.

After a long day at work, I was eager to get home and take off my horribly uncomfortable but fabulous heels. One of the best parts about working for my dad was the awesome wardrobe I'd purchased, but by the end of the day I cursed my impractical choices. Plus, if I was being honest, wanting to look classy—yet sexy—for Eric had once strongly influenced my purchasing habits.

As I made the final turn of my drive, my eyes almost bulged out of my head when my house came into view. A Marine in his olive-green Service Alphas was sitting on my porch holding a sizable arrangement of sunflowers. My heart hammered against my chest as I pulled into my driveway. For a long moment, Spencer just stood there on the porch and stared at me through the windshield. I didn't move to get out of the car. I just stared back. When you can pinpoint the exact reasons why you like someone, it's a crush. But when the very sight of them after time apart has you frozen in place with a muddled mind, I guessed that's how you know it's more.

He cracked a sideways smile and tilted his head. I realized he was questioning why I was still sitting in the car, so I took a deep breath and got out. I smoothed my hands down my gray pencil skirt and buttoned my matching blazer. My legs felt unsteady in the heels as I crossed the driveway to meet him.

"Hi," he said.

I took the hand he extended from the top of the porch steps. "Hi."

"These are for you."

The bouquet smelled wonderful as he passed them over and I took a long whiff. Leave it to my oldest friend to buy me my favorite flowers.

"Thank you." I smiled up at him, suddenly nervous. "When did you get in?"

"Late last night. I spent the day on base checking in with my new command."

I gestured to his uniform. "Is that why you're all dressed up?"

"Yeah, it definitely makes it obvious that I'm the new guy since everyone else is walking around in cammies and I'm all suited up." He adjusted the tie at his neck.

I laughed. "Oh, stop. It looks good."

He swallowed and I could tell he was glad for the compliment. I gestured to the steps. We sat, both staring out into the street in front of us. Neither one of us were sure where to start. The cat was out of the bag about Eric. Olivia had already apologized about letting it slip to Matt, and he'd blabbed to Spencer. I wasn't keeping it from him for any malicious reason; it was just that I needed to figure out how I felt before Spencer knew I was single. He'd said nothing about it yet, but I knew it was coming.

"So," I stalled, "are you sad your days of rooming with Matt are over?"

He chuckled. "That lucky bastard. He has a townhouse with his woman off base and isn't surrounded by stinky dudes all the time. At least he said I can crash there whenever I want."

"Well, there you go. The bromance isn't dead after all."

He bumped my shoulder with a grin.

"I've been helping Olivia set everything up. She wanted it to look nice for the first time Matt saw it. I'm so happy for them."

"Yeah, me too. You know, they have a great relationship. They tell each other *everything*."

I closed my eyes.

"In fact," he continued, "Olivia told Mills about a little secret you've been keeping."

"And Mills told you, because of your bromance."

He nodded. "Yeah, Mills and I have a great relationship, too."

"Looks like we're the only ones who have trouble being honest with each other, huh?" I said, a touch of humor in my tone. "Didn't see that one coming."

"Why didn't you tell me when I came to say goodbye?"

I sighed. "Because I needed time to figure everything

out. I wasn't ready for you to just be like, 'Oh, you're not with Eric anymore, let's try again!'"

He scoffed at my terrible impression of him. "Seriously? I have more game than that and you know it."

"That's my point. I wanted you and your *game* to just take a chill pill for a little bit while I figured things out."

"So, you were playing your own game then? By letting me think you were still with Eric, you were playing a game, too."

I had no response for him. He was right. I had been playing a game. It wasn't fair of me to let him believe that I was still with Eric when I wasn't. What was that old saying about a lie by omission still being a lie? Guilty, party of one.

"Look, I'm not bringing it up to make you feel bad."

"Well, I do. I'm sorry I didn't tell you."

"Don't forget about where we were before all this other stuff started. We don't keep secrets."

I smiled and did a silly version of a salute. "Yes, sir."

Spencer rolled his eyes. "Just so you know, in the Marine Corps I wouldn't be a 'sir.' I'm on the Enlisted side. We call officers 'sir.'"

Rolling my eyes, I did my salute again. "Yes, Private."

"You're a dork."

"That's what you love about me." As soon as I said the words, I realized we were past the point of joking about love. The heaviness of the word hung in the air between us.

"Listen, while we're asking the hard questions," I began quietly, "why did you kiss me after the wedding when you knew I was with Eric? You've always said you wouldn't put the moves on another guy's girl, no matter what."

Spencer stared at his shoes and said nothing for a long moment. "Honestly, I kept thinking about how the last time I'd kissed you at Camp Pendleton was just a short peck. If we wouldn't have another chance, I couldn't let that be our last kiss. So, I kissed you again. And I made sure it would be a memorable kiss, just in case."

I flushed. I wasn't sure what I'd expected him to say, but the sweetness of his reply had completely blown me away.

"You said you needed to figure things out... Did you figure it out?"

I nodded, not meeting his eyes.

"All right, then." Abruptly, he kissed me on the cheek and stood.

"Where are you going?" I jumped up and stood two steps above him, so we were eye-to-eye.

He grinned mischievously. "You'll see. Dinner Saturday night?"

I nodded again, feeling like a bobble head.

With a wink and one last smile, he turned and walked toward his dad's.

"What's wrong with roses?" Olivia scowled playfully. "Matt always gets me roses."

"Well, if you genuinely love roses and that's what Matt

buys you, then that's a good thing! But if you don't even like roses and a guy just buys them because it's what you're supposed to buy for a girl, that's just dumb."

She chuckled. "I guess you're right. It's cute he bought your favorite flowers. Where do you think he's taking you on Saturday?"

"I have no idea."

Olivia stood from the barstool at her kitchen counter and helped herself to more lemonade from the pitcher in the fridge. "All I know is, when Matt left the house this morning in those Service Alphas I about died."

I giggled as she wagged her eyebrows. "I had the same reaction when I saw Spence. I'm sure he could have easily changed at the barracks before he came over. He was *trying* to kill me."

"He's tricky all right. How could you turn down dinner with him looking like that?"

"Anyway, he didn't seem too pissed I didn't tell him about Eric. But, I definitely know it wasn't the most mature way to handle it."

Olivia looked at me as if to say, *duh.*

I narrowed my eyes at her. "Yeah, yeah, yeah. You were right. But when we go out on Saturday, I'm going to tell him exactly how I feel. He didn't even give me a chance earlier. He asked if I'd figured it out and then boom! See ya later."

"I'm sure he just has big plans. I'm glad you're going to be honest with him. Ever since they left after Christmas you've been like a lovesick puppy. And according to Matt,

Spencer's been the same way. You guys just need to stop fighting your feelings already."

"Yeah, I guess we do." I fidgeted. It was kind of amazing just how dramatic and confusing the last ten months had been. Once we stopped playing games and lying about our feelings, I hoped Spencer and I would be able to have a normal relationship. And I hoped it would feel as good as the small glimpse I'd gotten that weekend at Pendleton.

"Good morning, Elizabeth," Eric said as he approached my desk the next day.

"Good morning."

"How are you?"

He seemed more chipper than usual, so I raised a brow at him. "I'm well, thanks. Why are you in such a good mood?"

Eric smiled. "Any messages?"

I reached for the pile, remembering a message I had taken that morning from a young sounding woman. "Does your mood have anything to do with Briana?"

"You don't miss a thing." He looked through the short stack of messages and then tucked them into his pocket. "I met her at the gym. She's a law student."

"Ooh," I crooned. "Good for you. Takes care of her body and has a brain. That's a lot better than the last girl."

I really enjoyed how Eric and I had slipped into a natural

friendship. Things hadn't gotten too complicated or messy, so we had just continued to joke around and talk like we always had. He'd gone on a few dates since we'd ended things, and I could honestly say it wasn't weird at all for us to talk about them. That was how I knew Eric had never been right for me. I couldn't imagine talking to Spencer about the girls he dated like we used to. It made me sick just thinking about it.

"Yeah, Holly was better in the body area than the brains. But she was a nice girl," he allowed, always the gentleman. "So, have you got any big plans this weekend? That barbeque for your friends, right?"

I shook my head. "No, that's next weekend. I actually have a date of my own."

Eric tilted his head. "With Spencer? He's back?"

"Had his first day with his unit at Miramar yesterday," I confirmed.

Eric let out a whistle. "Are you nervous?"

"No, should I be?"

"You'll be fine. I hope it goes well. But don't forget what I said about not doing anything rash. Spencer is the kind of guy who doesn't think about consequences. I don't want to see you get hurt again."

It touched me that he cared, but he was wrong about Spencer. "I appreciate that. There's more to him than you think, though."

Eric adopted his usual stance with his arms folded on my ledge. "Look, I know you guys have a long history, and your friendship is a big deal. But don't let that history make this new part of your relationship more serious than it needs to be. Give yourself some time to adjust, you know? It doesn't have to be all or nothing."

"Maybe that's why he freaked out and pulled away in the first place. It felt serious really quickly. And honestly, that's why I didn't tell him you and I broke up. I didn't want to jump right back in."

Eric quirked an eyebrow. "How did he find out?"

"Olivia told Matt and Matt told Spencer."

Eric opened his mouth to reply but snapped it shut when my dad came slowly around the corner. "Is this what you two do all day?"

We froze, guilty expressions on our faces.

"It sounds like an episode of *The Young and the Restless* up here," he scolded. I could see the laughter in his eyes though, so I knew that he wasn't mad at us. "Get back to work, Eric."

Eric nodded at my dad and shot me a comically guilty grimace before quickly walking down the hall.

"So," Dad said, approaching my ledge, "you and Spencer?"

I smiled, sheepishly. "Looks like it."

Dad shook his head with a strange smile. "Huh."

"What?" I asked.

"His mother predicted that you know."

"She did?"

"Yeah, just before she died. She told Mike that you two were meant for each other. Your mom and I always wondered if she was right."

I couldn't help the goosebumps that rose up on my arms.

## 26

## SPENCER

On Saturday morning I let myself into my dad's house and took a huge whiff of the strong scent of coffee coming from the kitchen. I made my way there first to grab a cup and then set off to find my dad. It was weird living in the barracks right down the street from my own house. I'd thought maybe I would feel more grown up after I was out of my dad's house, but living in the barracks was like living in a frat house with camo instead of Greek lettering. It was ridiculous. One major perk to being married was having your own place out in town. I thought of Mills and his townhouse every time a bunch of idiots played war with broomsticks in the hallway.

I stood in the doorway of my dad's study. He was sitting at the computer with his back to me, playing solitaire. He'd been retired from the Marine Corps for a couple of years now, and this was how he spent his

Saturday mornings. I cleared my throat. He turned around, and surprisingly, had a bit of a smile for me.

"Hey kid."

I nodded, sticking my hands in my pocket. "Hey."

"You're up early."

With a frown, I studied my watch. "It's nine fifteen."

"That it is. But pre-Marine Corps you wouldn't have shown your face until noon on Saturday."

I chuckled. He had a point. But after getting up at the crack of dawn for the majority of my time in the Corps, I couldn't imagine sleeping until noon. I guessed my Friday night partying habits had changed because of recent events, too. That was probably the main reason it was so easy to get up early on the weekends.

"Did Ellie bring you by? Is she here?" He started to get out of his chair but I shook my head so he lowered himself back down.

"I took an Uber... but uh, are you busy today?" I shuffled my feet.

He shook his head. "No plans."

"Well," I stammered, "I've been spending a lot on Ubers... and since my unit is a training unit, we won't be getting deployed. So, I'll be in San Diego for the next few years. I was thinking about getting a truck..."

"Okay."

I shuffled my feet again. "Do you want to come with me? And maybe co-sign for me, too?"

"I'd be glad to, son." I didn't miss the happiness that shone in his eyes when I asked, and it made my stomach tighten.

I wondered if my mom could see me making an effort with him. All of this was just as much for her benefit as his or mine. If she could see me, I hoped she would be proud. I hoped it would make up for the way I so harshly judged her without even knowing how she felt. In fact, knowing what I know now, I was pretty embarrassed about the decisions I'd made in her name.

I let out a breath. "Thanks, Dad. Do you think it'll take very long, though? I have a date later."

"It better be with Ellie."

I grinned. "It is."

My dad stood from his chair and grabbed his wallet and keys off the desk. "Good job, son."

~

When I pulled up to Mills' house, I honked the horn a few times. They came outside and I jumped down from the cab of my new 1994 Chevrolet Silverado. "Nice, huh?"

Mills whistled and held his arms out, admiring the black truck with its tinted windows and lift package. He hopped into the driver's seat and looked around. "Very nice. Is it eating up all your pay?"

I shook my head. "Nah, man. My dad gave me a decent down payment as a late graduation present, which seriously helped my payments. I think we figured it'd be about a year until I have the rest of it paid off."

"Really? Didn't see that one coming." Mills said, referring to the down payment.

"Same. And he was a killer negotiator. He got the guy to double the military discount since he's a vet and I'm on active duty."

"You're the worst," Mills groaned, leaning his head back against the seat.

Olivia laughed from behind me. "Congrats, Spencer. Matt's just mad I won't let him get a truck because he's gone so much this year."

"Yeah," Mills confirmed as he played with the radio. "She's making me drive her car or get rides instead of getting my own. It sucks."

I put my arm companionably around Olivia's shoulders. "Sorry, bro. Your woman has a point. I wouldn't have gotten this truck if I wasn't in a training squadron."

"Whatever. I'll just borrow it every now and then."

I went over to the open door and pretended to pull him down from the seat. "The heck you will."

He glared at me. "You want to crash in my guest room whenever you want? Then you'll let me use your truck."

"That's low."

"Okay, guys. Take it easy," Olivia joked. "Spence, we were just putting some stuff together for the house. Can you help Matt put the TV up on the wall? He doesn't trust me to lift it."

I nodded. "Smart man. Yeah, I'll help. I need your advice on my plans for Ellie tonight, anyway."

Olivia let out a girly squeal and clapped her hands. "I'm so glad you guys are going out. We're getting our nails done in a few so she'll be all done up."

"Ah. I probably shouldn't talk to you about it then. I

know how you girls are when you get your nails done. You get all gossipy. You're just going to tell her everything we talk about."

Olivia huffed indignantly but Mills hopped down from the truck and came to her rescue. "Apparently, Olivia is more of a steel trap than we would have thought. Think about how long it took for us to find out about Ellie and Eric breaking up."

"Good point," I allowed. "Thanks again for that, by the way."

"No comment." Olivia turned and headed toward the house, so I locked the truck and followed her and Mills up the drive.

"What do you have planned?" Olivia asked as she plopped down on the couch.

Mills and I hung the TV on the wall as I answered. "Well, I'm going to pick her up in my new truck, and then we're going to this hole-in-the-wall pizza place I heard about downtown."

Olivia frowned. "Seriously?"

I grunted under the weight of the large flat screen. "What's wrong with that?"

"I don't know, I mean, you guys are finally going on an actual date and you picked a place you're describing as 'hole-in-the-wall?' I figured you'd take her somewhere a little... nicer."

"Look, I won't screw this up by being someone I'm not. This is our kind of place. I need to remind her of how great it was between us before it got so complicated. This is the perfect place for that."

"Just saying, The Melting Pot wouldn't be a bad choice either."

We got the TV securely fastened to the mount on the wall, and I faced Olivia. "This isn't my first rodeo. Trust me."

"Fine. But where are you going after dinner? And please don't say a movie. That'd be super lame."

Mills rolled his eyes. "Olivia. Take it easy."

"No, she's right about the movie." I laughed and patted my friend on the back. "That would be super lame. I guess you better remember that."

Olivia waved her hand with a smile. "No, he doesn't have to remember that. We're past that point. I love going to the movies with him. You and Ellie just have too much to talk about to waste time in a movie."

"Girls are so complicated," Mills said. He moved into the dining room to screw the legs of their dining room table on, so I followed him in there to help.

Olivia rose from the couch and sat cross-legged in one of the dining room chairs. "Well, if not a movie, where are you going after dinner?"

I took the screwdriver from Mills' toolbox and got to work. "Fiesta Island. I'm gonna grab some firewood on the way to pick her up so we can use the fire pits on the beach."

Mills shook his head with a laugh as Olivia squealed, "That is so romantic."

"It's a good thing you bought the extended cab truck," Mills noted. "It'd be pretty pointless if you didn't have a back seat."

I shrugged. "There's always the truck bed."

"Okay, stop right there!" Olivia waved a hand. "Have your guy talk when I leave."

"In all seriousness, the Fiesta Island thing is for a reason," I admitted, helping Mills turn the table right side up now that we were finished attaching the legs. "Before I left for bootcamp, Ellie had invited all of our friends to a bonfire at Fiesta Island as a going away party for me. It was the first time I realized I had feelings for her. So, I thought it would be cool if we had our first official date there."

Olivia sighed. "Ah, that is amazing. I'm really happy you finally got your head out of your butt, Spencer."

"Gee, thanks, Olivia."

## 27

## ELLIE

I heard three short beeps from outside, so I ran down the stairs and peered out the front window. There was a shiny black truck at the curb, not quite new, but not beat up either. Spencer hopped down from the driver's side and rounded the back of the truck. He looked handsome in jeans and a flannel button-up with the sleeves rolled up to his elbows. I looked down at my short, black dress and heels. Something told me I wasn't dressed for the same kind of date that he was.

I opened the front door, and he grinned as he lowered the hand that was about to knock. "Hi."

I smiled back at him and held the door open wider. "Come on in."

"Thanks." He scanned me from head to toe, and I could feel myself blush under his gaze. "I hate to break it to you, E, but I think you might need to change."

"I thought you might say that."

"You look gorgeous, though," he covered quickly, extending his palms out. "It's just that I don't think you'll be very comfortable later."

Shaking my head, I turned toward the stairs to change. He grabbed my arm and yanked me to him, pressing his lips to mine. I leaned into him, relishing in the feel of his hands on my back and in my hair. I knew I'd worn it down for a reason. Finally, he drew away and touched his forehead to mine.

"Sorry, I just had to do that. You really do look amazing."

I swallowed and managed a small smile. "Thanks."

"Anytime."

"So... What should I wear? It's kind of hard to pick out an outfit for a mystery date, you know."

He released his hold on me and pursed his lips. "This is a date for jeans and flip-flops."

Curious, I cocked my head. "All right then. Be right back."

Back in my room, I grabbed my favorite jeans out of my drawer and wriggled into them. I pulled on a royal blue tank top and slipped into my most comfortable black flip-flops. Couldn't get more basic than that. I wondered what he had planned for us. It was fitting we'd be wearing such comfortable clothes on our first official date though. There was no one on Earth I was more comfortable with than Spencer. Even after everything that happened recently, he was still *my* Spencer.

Ready to get the show on the road, I shook off my lingering nerves and went back downstairs. Spencer was standing with one foot on the bottom step and his hand on the rail. I headed down and stopped when I was standing on the last step, inches from him. The vibes between us were electric. How had we stayed platonic friends for as long as we had? We stood there for a moment, just looking at each other until I heard my mom clear her throat from behind him.

Spencer turned and faced my mom, hands in his pockets. "Hi, Carol. How are you?"

My mom narrowed her eyes at him, but not without warmness. "I'm well, honey. It's good to see you back in San Diego."

"Thank you, I'm glad to be back." He smiled easily at her, and then at me.

"Mom, we're going out. We might be kind of late so don't wait up." I didn't miss the sudden rise of Spencer's eyebrows when I told my mom I might be out late.

My mom nodded. "Okay. *Be safe.*"

Her last two words made me cringe inwardly as I grabbed Spencer's hand and headed out the door. I really hoped the double meaning I'd heard wasn't intentional on her part. Judging by the fact that Spencer silently followed me out of the house instead of attempting to say goodbye to my mom, led me to think he'd heard the significance of what she'd said, too.

Spencer pulled himself together and opened the truck door for me, but his smile was off. "Staying out late, are you?"

I grabbed the handle on the doorframe and hoisted myself into the truck. Feeling a sudden burst of confidence, I winked. "That depends on if you play your cards right."

He shut the door and snickered. I could tell he was just as affected by me as I was by him.

When Spencer found a parking spot in the popular Gaslamp District of San Diego, I had a moment of panic about my outfit. Most of the shops and restaurants in the area were upscale. Was I underdressed? Was he setting me up?

I sighed as I hopped out of the truck. No sense in pestering him about where we were going. When Spencer got it in his head to plan out a date and surprise a girl, he was a steel trap until he executed all the phases. It was weird to think about that now. I wasn't his confidant. I was his date. I peered over at him as he walked next to me along the bustling sidewalk. Did he think of me as just another girl on one of his mystery dates?

After a few blocks, we stopped. The bright fluorescent lights of the tiny pizza shop spilled out onto the sidewalk from wide windows. The interior was relatively busy for such a small place. I grinned up at Spencer.

"What do you think?" he asked, his eyes searching mine for approval.

"It's perfect," I replied. The restaurant choice had answered my question. I wasn't just another girl on a mystery date. He'd planned this date especially for me. This was *our* kind of place.

We went inside and approached the counter. An older Italian woman appeared from the back and beamed at us. "What'll it be kids?"

I didn't bother looking at the menu. Spencer would know my order. He asked the woman for two slices of combination pizza for himself and one slice of pepperoni for me. My favorite part about these authentic New York pizza places was that the slices were huge and thin, just how I liked. He also ordered two fountain drinks, handing them to me to fill with ice-cold Coca-Cola.

We took our pizza and drinks to the bar seating along the windows. We faced a busy section of the Gaslamp District, so we could "people watch." That was another one of our favorite things to do. The date couldn't have been more perfect so far.

"So, I talked to my dad about the accounting thing," I told him through a mouthful of pizza.

"And?"

"And, you were right. He seemed really happy for me."

Spencer leaned in and gave me a brief kiss. "I'm really happy for you, too."

"Thank you."

My lips tingled from his kiss, and it took me a second to remember to eat my pizza and not just stare at him. Dating Spencer was fun.

"When do classes start?" he asked, turning back to his dinner.

"They already did. It's an online program so new cohorts start every week."

"What do you think so far?"

I took a drink of my Coke to wash down my pizza. "So far, I love it. It's nice learning at my own pace without having to sit in an actual classroom. Plus, I can do my homework when I have nothing to do at work, so it helps my days go by faster and I can still just relax when I get home."

"Which means even with a full-time job and school, you'll still have time for me."

I smiled and leaned in for another kiss. "And more perfect dates."

"Oh, just wait. It's going to get even better," he promised, brushing my hair back behind my ear and rubbing his thumb over my cheek.

For the rest of the meal, the conversation was light and flowed easily. It was almost as if nothing had changed between us and we were still the same friends we'd always been. Except for those brief moments when he would stop me mid-sentence for a quick kiss. Not to mention that once in a while our legs would brush under the table and it felt like a shock ran through me.

As we walked back to the truck, we strolled along the city streets hand in hand. We passed both tourists and locals heading to the various bars and clubs in the area. A group of girls we knew from high school came out of a restaurant and danced onto the street, laughing and having a great time. Spencer's hand tightened in mine.

"Ellie, Spencer," one of the girls, Laurie, hugged us both. "Good to see you guys!"

"Hey," we greeted them, having naturally let go of each other's hand while we hugged the girls. Our high school was enormous, so I didn't know them well, but I'd had some classes with each of them over the years. Plus, we'd all hung out at the same house parties. Spencer clearly knew Laurie better than the rest of them and thinking about them hooking up made my stomach flip.

Laurie put her hand on Spencer's arm. "How's Marine life? Are you like, back on vacation or something? We should get together."

"I'm actually stationed here now," he replied, casually stepping closer to me and taking my hand again, letting hers fall from his arm.

The girls had matching expressions of shock on their face as their eyes looked from our joined hands to our faces and back again. My stomach tightened, uncomfortable with their judgment.

"Are you guys *together*?" Laurie's eyes were wide as she gaped at Spencer. "Seriously?"

I wanted to crawl into a sewer drain and disappear.

"Seriously," Spencer confirmed, putting his arm around my waist and squeezing me against his side. "Why so shocked?"

Laurie shared a short laugh with her friends. "I don't know if 'shocked' is the right word... I mean... I always wondered. You guys were *way* too close to be just friends."

The other girls nodded in agreement and one said, "I think it's great."

"Thanks," I said shyly, smiling up at Spencer, grateful he'd made it clear we were together. He smiled back at me. He looked almost... proud?

"You guys are so cute," Laurie said, not an ounce of malice in her tone.

"Oh, we're adorable," Spencer joked and kissed the top of my head. "We'll see you guys later."

We said our goodbyes, and he steered me around the girls, confident as ever. Happy, as ever. In fact, it was practically radiating from him. I'd always known he stayed cool with all the girls he hung out with. He didn't give them false hope of a relationship; he kept it light and casual, no feelings period meant no *hard* feelings. But watching a past fling react well to seeing him happy with another girl was a good feeling. He may have made some dumb choices with our relationship, but Spencer was a great guy. I was immensely proud to be on his arm.

"Everything okay?" He squeezed my hand as he said the words, concern in his voice. "Are you having a good time?"

I nodded swiftly. "Yes. Definitely. Best date ever."

"Like I said, it's not over yet. I have one more item on the to-do list."

We'd reached the truck by then, and he gestured to the logs of firewood in the back of the truck. Recognizing they were there because we were going to Fiesta Island, I squealed and clapped my hands.

Spencer rolled his eyes at me and opened the truck door, offering me a hand up. "Girls."

I hopped into my seat and glared at him. "What do you mean, '*girls*'?"

"When I told Olivia what I had planned for tonight,

she had almost the exact same reaction. I just thought it was funny."

"Well," I said, smiling down at him, "that's what you get for picking such a romantic date spot."

"No pressure or anything." He closed the door with a laugh and crossed to his side of the cab.

28

# SPENCER

The ride to Fiesta Island from downtown was brief. I pulled onto the narrow road that wrapped around the small island. It only held a dog park, a running trail, and cement fire pits along the beach. We'd come here every summer for the past five years, bringing a ton of friends, good music, and food. This would be the first time I'd ever been here with just a girl. Everybody knew this spot was for couples or crowded bonfires, one or the other. I had no idea why, but no girl ever seemed to fit this spot for a date. Until Ellie.

We pulled up to a pit, and I backed up the truck until the bed was in a good spot to sit on in front of the fire. Ellie kicked off her flip-flops and jumped onto the beach below. I made my way to the back of the truck and pulled logs out of the back, tossing them into the pit. It would be a few minutes until the fire was lit.

"Wanna put on some music?" I asked Ellie. I couldn't

help but watch as she climbed back into the truck. She had a great butt. We should have started this a long time ago. I shook my head and got back to work on the fire while she found the country station.

"Hey," she popped her head out of the truck, "is this cooler for tonight?"

"Yeah," I called back. "There's some drinks in there, help yourself."

"Wow, you're prepared."

I reached in the truck bed for one more log and winked at her. "Have I ever come out here unprepared?"

She laughed and went for the cooler as I tossed the log on the fire. In all the years we'd been coming out to the pits I'd always made it a point to bring anything we'd need. Drinks, food if we were grilling out, stuff to eat with, trash bags for clean up. Just because it wasn't a bonfire with friends, didn't mean I'd prepared any less.

Ellie got out and joined me on the beach, two water bottles in hand. The fire was between us, and as I poked the smoldering logs with a stick, I watched as the firelight danced across her features. It was captivating.

"Perfect," I said, not sure if I was referring to the girl or the fire. Brushing my hands on my jeans, I walked over to the back of the truck and dropped the tailgate. In one swift movement, I lifted her by the waist and placed her on it. With my height and the slope of the beach, it put us face-to-face. I couldn't bring her lips to mine any faster if I'd tried, and she responded with just as much urgency.

When we were both breathless, I broke away and jumped onto the tailgate next to her, putting my arm around her shoulders. We sat in silence for a few moments, just staring out at the ocean or fire. I forced my breathing to even out, my heart rate to get back to normal.

"Best date ever?" I asked, trying to think of something other than laying her down in the back of the truck.

She nodded.

"It's a gift."

"Yeah, you practically wrote the book on fitting the date to the specific girl. I'm not surprised this one fits me."

I pulled back to look down at her. "You know it's different with you, E."

She said nothing for a moment, letting my words hang in the air. I was serious. It really was different. I'd been on plenty of great dates. Amusement park dates, zoo dates, country dancing dates, dinner dates, breakfast dates... all tailored to the girl or the situation. But I've never been on a date that fit me just as much as the girl. We fit.

"I'll have to get used to this."

"What?"

"Being more than just the girl you talked about your dates with. Being the girlfriend instead of the best friend."

I rose an eyebrow at her. "So, you're my girlfriend now? I don't remember making anything official..."

She elbowed me in the gut.

"*Ow*. I was kidding! It's official."

"I guess I could have let you ask me," she said, shrugging.

"Eh, isn't that a little cheesy?"

"Well, it might have been fine to just let things progress without a label... but we kind of already tried that and you ended it before we got the chance. So maybe we should take the time for details."

"Burn," I drew the word out.

"Too soon?"

"Just a bit."

We both laughed quietly, then fell into silence again.

"Ellie," I started, keeping my tone light, "will you be my girlfriend?"

She grinned. "No."

I threw my hands up. "I can't win."

Giggling, she pulled me closer. "Of course I will."

"Good." I kissed her firmly on the temple and then looked out at the fire again. "I've never been out here without a big group of people before."

She stiffened. "You've never taken a date out here?"

"Nope. Guess this was just meant to be our spot."

More companionable silence. I thought back to that night at Camp Pendleton and how we'd spent the weekend keeping things light and sharing comfortable silences like this one. It was nice, but the memory made me feel uneasy. Maybe we really should have talked things out back then. Maybe things would have been different... if I'd told her how I'd felt at the time, about why I'd held back for months and why I was scared to keep going, maybe we'd have never broken up.

"So, is there anything else we need to talk about before this goes any further?" I asked.

She looked startled. "What do you mean?"

"Well, everything might not have gotten so messed up

before if we'd ironed things out before jumping in. I don't want to make that same mistake again."

"I guess we could."

I smiled and rubbed my hand down her arm like I was trying to warm her up. "You know what?"

"What?"

"I've been pretty honest with you. I've talked about my feelings so much I don't even recognize myself anymore. And, I bet Olivia knows more about how you feel than I do."

She shrugged. "I actually planned on telling you how I felt tonight."

"Good. 'Bout time you poured your soul out, instead of leaving it all to me."

"Well, maybe I was just enjoying the role reversal of you being the sensitive one for once."

I poked her side. "Well, spill. Everything. From the beginning."

"Okay, you asked for it." She took a sip of her water and put it back on the tailgate next to her. "When you punched Tim in the nose at that bar, I thought it was probably the sexiest thing ever. Until later in the hotel, when the sexiest thing ever was how you had me up against that wall."

My hand tightened and then released on her. She had my attention.

"Then," she continued, "every minute we spent together after that was amazing. And right up until you dumped me on the side of the road, I was completely sure we were in a relationship and it was going to be a great one."

Again, my hand got tighter on her arm, but for a different reason. "Hold on, I did *not* 'dump you on the side of the road.' C'mon."

She blinked at me. "Did you dump me?"

"I guess."

"And were we standing on the side of the road at the time?"

I rolled my eyes. "You're ridiculous."

"*Anyway*... When I was dating Eric, and you were home for Winter Break, I tried to convince myself we should be friends. But that day on the boat when we had that moment by the bathroom, I had to work really hard to ignore what I felt for you."

"Interesting. Because you were kissing Eric when I came upstairs."

She narrowed her eyes at my tone. "Like I said, I tried really hard to ignore my feelings."

"Yeah, well, that was hard to see." I ran a hand over my head, almost like I could wipe away the memory. I remembered standing in that tiny bathroom, staring at myself in the mirror, thinking I might actually have a chance to get her back. Then when I'd come up the stairs and saw them kissing, that hope shattered like glass and all I felt was white-hot rage. Not at her, not even at him, but at myself.

She cringed. "I felt terrible. And not just because you saw it, but because it was wrong of me to lead Eric on when it was *you* I should have been kissing."

I felt a pull towards her, almost like I needed to kiss her to punctuate what she said. Her lips were soft and warm. I brought my hand up to her chin and circled my thumb along her jaw. I could feel heat rising up my spine in a slow, steady burn. Just like before, I pulled away before it got too far.

"I'm not sorry I saw it," I said, tucking her tighter against my side. "It was exactly what I needed to do whatever it took to be with you."

"Okay, well, our little chat after the wedding, and that kiss... it really messed me up. I was at lunch the next day with Eric and he told me he didn't want me to settle for him if I was actually in love with you."

I stiffened. "And, are you?"

"What?" She played dumb, meeting my gaze.

"Are you in love with me?"

I stared at her. She'd said she wanted to tell me about her feelings tonight, but was she ready to say those words? I knew she'd said them to Tim. And I knew it was nothing compared to this. I could see it all over her face. She'd never once looked at Tim the way she was looking at me. This feeling was so much stronger, so much deeper, than that. I knew it. But did she? And even if she did, would she admit it?

Disappointed in the time passing with no answer, I looked out at the water again.

She put her hand under my chin and turned my face back to hers. She nodded with the barest hint of a smile. "Yes, I am."

The relief and happiness I felt in that moment made me feel light as I wrapped my arms tightly around her, kissing her deeply. I smiled and kissed her one last time before she nuzzled into my chest.

"I love you, too, E," I whispered, my cheek resting on the top of her head as I held her in place. "I think I always have."

She lifted her face and kissed me again, and I used the arm behind her back to lift her onto my lap. She had a knee on either side of my thighs, our eyes locked in place. Her hands were on my chest, pressing her fingertips into my muscles through my flannel shirt. I watched her eyes as she made her way through the buttons down the front and pulled the shirt from my shoulders. I had a black tank underneath it and she splayed her fingers over my shoulders and arms as I ran my hands along her thighs.

I kissed a trail down her neck and onto her chest. The cut of her tank top was low, and I moved my lips along the spot where the top of her breasts rose out of the shirt. The night was quiet around us, the lull of the ocean waves being the soundtrack to this moment. I brought my lips back to hers, my hands in her hair, loving the way her hands gripped my shoulders. I took the kiss deeper and deeper as she pressed herself against me, feeling like I couldn't get close enough to her. Something inside of me felt like it was about to snap, and I knew I needed to slow this down.

I pulled away, resting my forehead against her chest, letting the feel of her breathing settle me. I wanted to pull her into the bed of the truck and keep going, but I knew we shouldn't. A hook-up at a known hook-up spot felt... not good enough for Ellie. If and when we ever took things to that next level, I wanted to take my time with her. I wanted her to feel special. I brought my head up to look at her. She was stunning. I was never going to let her get away from me again.

Before I even opened my eyes, I smiled. Memories of my date with Ellie last night flashed in my mind. It had been perfect. We had been perfect. We'd gotten everything worked out, and now that I was here in San Diego in a training squadron, none of my fears from before were going to get in the way of being with her. I rolled over, pressing my face into the pillow. This girl had me messed up.

After dropping Ellie off, *late*, just as she'd warned her mom, I'd crashed at Mills' place. We were all supposed to hang out today anyway, and I really hated the idea of going back to the barracks in case my loser roommate had all of his friends over playing World of Warcraft again. It just seemed like a lame ending to such a great night.

I'd slept in my boxers, so I got up and found my jeans and shirt, pulling them on. I opened the door and stepped into the hallway. The smell of coffee hit me, and I inhaled deeply. I'd definitely need some of that.

"It was amazing."

I stopped at the top of the stairs when I'd heard Ellie speak. It was wrong to eavesdrop, but I didn't care. I checked my watch. She'd come over early. I wondered if that meant she was as eager to see me again as I was about seeing her. I braced my hand against the wall as I stood there listening to the girl talk.

"Honestly," Ellie continued, "I had some pretty high expectations, but the whole night was just incredible."

I smiled and crossed my arms over my chest, proud of myself for planning such a good date.

Olivia laughed. "Those are some pretty major adjectives, Ells. Seriously though, you seem really happy. I'm glad."

I started to take a step, but then Ellie spoke again, and I hesitated.

"I really am. I was nervous though... thinking we'd have this perfect date and then maybe he'd freak out again and end it."

My stomach tightened.

"Ouch," Olivia said. "And how do you feel now?"

I waited anxiously for Ellie's response, holding my breath.

"After last night and everything we talked about, I think he'd be pretty freaking stupid to ruin it. Honestly. This is it, we're together. He's not getting rid of me that easily."

I smiled widely.

"Jokes aside," Ellie continued. "I trust him."

My chest swelled with pride again, but it was more because I was proud of her. She knew what she wanted and wouldn't let me get away with anything. It made me love her even more.

"Good," Olivia said. "Trust is huge. Matt and I have

never really broken up. I couldn't imagine if he dumped me and then I had to trust him not to hurt me again."

Figuring I'd done enough creeping on their conversation, I padded down the stairs.

"Matt would never do that. I think you're safe," Ellie said.

"Yeah," Olivia agreed. "But I think you're safe now too. You have Spencer completely wrapped around your finger at this point. Trust me."

"I think you're right about that, Olivia," I said from the foot of the stairs, making them jump. I walked over to the couch and sat next to Ellie, taking her hand.

"Good morning," Ellie greeted me, squeezing my hand. "How did you sleep?"

"Fine. You?"

Ellie laughed and leaned in to kiss me. "Great."

I returned her quick kiss and winked. We'd woken up in the same house countless times over the years, either her crashing at my house or me crashing at hers, so I was used to seeing her first thing in the morning. Now, sitting here with her after the night we'd had, I realized we probably wouldn't be able to spend the night in the same house anymore and have it be a "just friends" thing.

It hit me suddenly that maybe I was willing to grow up fast like Matt and Olivia. I wanted to wake up to Ellie, in our own place, every day. The reality of that would have scared me only a few short months ago. Now, it just felt right.

~

I walked into the shop on Monday morning and inhaled the scent of jet fuel and machinery. I patted the pockets of my olive-green coveralls to make sure they were empty. I'd accidentally brought my phone onto the flight line on Friday and had gotten blasted by about six NCO's. Satisfied I hadn't made that mistake again, I put on my red cranial helmet and jogged into the bright sunlight.

"Happy Monday, Boot," Corporal Rodriguez called over the noise of a turning jet. "Master Sergeant needs to see you."

I swallowed. "Yes, Corporal."

"He must have heard about the phone thing," Corporal Rodriguez called after me as I clipped back to the hangar.

Wracking my brain for reasons I'd be in trouble so early in my time at III, I crossed from the wide-open hangar into the dim offices at the back. The higher-ups' offices were on the second floor. I passed the ready room and saw some guys from night crew milling about before they left to sleep the day away.

I really didn't want to get yelled at again. Bringing my phone onto the flight line was stupid, I knew, but I'd already been lit up for it. Did Master Sergeant really need to keep hammering it home? I understood why FOD, or foreign object debris, was an issue. The pull from the jet engine was so strong that if you dropped something on the flight line and the engine sucked it up, you'd break a multi-million-dollar piece of machinery. Not to mention the risk of an object getting lodged into the flaps of the jet and then not functioning properly while the jet was airborne. No one wanted to be responsible for a pilot having to dump the plane.

Master Sergeant's door was open, and he looked up as I approached. "Hawkins, come on in."

"Thank you, Master Sergeant." I stood in front of his desk at attention.

"As you were," he directed, and waved a hand to the chair next to me. "Have a seat."

I sat in the chair and barely stopped my knee from bouncing before it gave away my nerves.

Master Sergeant held out a folder. "You've got orders out of 111. They need more guys for their upcoming deployment, and those guys usually come from training squadrons."

I took the folder with wide eyes. "Thank you, Master Sergeant. What squadron am I going to?"

"You're headed to 303. They're good guys over there. They've got good leadership. They're about to start a work-up cycle to prep for deployment. You'll have an exercise over the summer on the boat, called RIMPAC — Rim of the Pacific. Then you deploy in January."

Unsure of what to say, I nodded and glanced into the folder. It held my orders, a checkout worksheet, and all my paperwork from last week. "When do I report to 303?"

"Wednesday. You'll have the rest of today and tomorrow to go through your checkout process here with us, then show time at 303 is at 0730 in your Service Alphas. Any other questions?"

I shook my head. "No, Master Sergeant."

"Good," he said. "It was nice having you for a minute. Sorry we couldn't keep you. Even if you did bring your phone on my flight line."

Thankfully, I saw the humor in his eyes before I could get too stressed out. It was a shame to leave his squadron since he seemed like a cool dude to work under. "Thank you, Master Sergeant."

I pulled up to Ellie's after work and turned off the truck. For a minute, I just sat there staring at her house. It had been a little over seven months since I'd gone to boot camp. In only seven months, I'd gone from eager poolee, ready to get on with my life as a Marine deployed to foreign countries... to a new boot, crazy in love with his best friend, afraid to leave her. Afraid to hear what she'd say when I told her I was leaving. Afraid she only risked being with me because I was in a training squadron. I had no fear over a combat deployment, but these thoughts about a girl were twisting me up inside.

Ellie opened the front door and tilted her head.

I hopped out of the truck and shoved my hands in the pockets of my jeans as I crossed the driveway to the porch. "Hey."

She wrinkled her nose. "You look weird. What's up?"

With a sigh, I sat on the top step of the porch and leaned my back against the pillar to the side of the steps. "Come sit."

Warily, she closed the front door behind her and

crossed the porch to sit with me. She chose the wall across from me to lean her back against, and she straightened her legs in front of her crossing them at the ankles. She wore black yoga pants and a hot pink tank top. Her blonde hair was in a bun high on top of her head and I loved the way the style accentuated the lines of her face. Her face was calm, but I could see in her eyes I was making her uncomfortable. I figured it would be best to just blurt it all out instead of continuing with the dramatic silence.

"I got transferred to Mills' unit today because they need more guys for deployment."

My words hung in the air between us and even as I said them, I wished they weren't true. That exact sentence would have made me so happy only a few short months ago. Having a good friend in the same squadron, going on deployment, seeing the world... instead of being stuck in a training squadron with no cool stories to tell when I'm retired.

"Okay," she finally said. "Are you excited?"

I raised a brow. "Excited?"

"Spence, honestly, are you forgetting who you're talking to? We used to talk all the time about how you wanted to deploy. It's okay if that hasn't changed."

"Yeah," I allowed, "but that was before."

She gave me a small smile. "We'll be okay. We didn't finally get together just to be broken by something like deployment. The fact that you were at a squadron that didn't deploy had nothing to do with our decision to be together. Yes, it would have been nice to have you here all the time and not worry about separations... But you're a Marine. The whole 'Leave it to Beaver' thing stopped being appealing to me that first weekend we kissed. I'm *here* for *you*."

"Come here," I said and crooked my finger at her.

Ellie got up from the porch and I shifted so she could sit on my lap. I took her hand and interlaced our fingers together. She felt perfect in my arms, and I knew I needed her to be mine forever. Yes, we were young. Yes, I'd made fun of Mills for getting married. But everything he'd tried to tell me back then made all the sense in the world to me now. All I had to do was figure out the right time to make it happen. At some point, before I left for deployment, I was going to ask her to be my wife.

"It won't be easy," I told her.

She kissed my cheek. "Being with you is easy, remember? We'll figure out the rest as it comes."

## 29

## ELLIE

We stepped out of the elevator and onto the deck of the luxurious ship. Everywhere I looked, there were Marines in dress blues and women in gorgeous flowing dresses. I smoothed my hands over the satin bodice of my long black dress, relishing in the feel of it.

The Marine Corps Birthday was a big deal, always celebrated with a fancy birthday ball around the tenth of November. The ball's location apparently changed every year, and each unit had their own ball. This year, Spencer's squadron had chosen to host their ball on a dinner cruise in San Diego's harbor. I'd been looking forward to it ever since Olivia had first told me about it. It wasn't every day a girl could dress up like Cinderella and go to a real ball, so if this was what life was like in love with a Marine, I was completely down for it.

"You look amazing," Spencer whispered in my ear as

we gazed out over the water. The sun was close to setting, and a beautiful pink glow fell over the white of the ship's deck.

"Thank you." I smiled shyly at him. "You look great, too."

Spencer adjusted the alignment of his gold belt buckle and pulled at his collar. "I better. This is so uncomfortable."

I chuckled, smoothing a hand over his chest. "Good thing you look so hot in it. Take it from us girls, beauty is pain."

Spencer grabbed me around the waist and pulled me to him, nuzzling my ear. "You think I look hot?"

"Yes," I said through a soft giggle, enjoying the chill that ran up my spine as his warm breath tickled my neck.

"Easy, you two," Matt said as he and Olivia walked up to us. "Don't want the CO to see you getting all cozy out here, do you?"

Spencer relaxed his grip on me, shifting so that I was tucked closely to his side. "It's her fault."

I swatted him on the arm. "Hush, you. Olivia, I love your dress."

"Thank you, same to you." Olivia said, giving the blue tulle of her skirt a little fluff with her hand. "I could definitely get used to twenty years of Marine Corps Balls."

Matt rolled his eyes. "You'd think this was the only reason she wants to be with a Marine."

"It doesn't hurt," I said, nudging Spencer. "This is amazing."

The deck of the ship was decorated with Edison bulbs

strung over our heads, and I knew they would be ridiculously romantic once night fell. Couples milled about, drinking champagne or beer or soft drinks. Waiters in tuxedos flitted around the room, allowing people to take hors d'oeuvres off their silver trays. There was a dance floor in the middle of the deck, surrounded by circular tables covered in white linens with rose petals scattered on top. The places were set like the dinner scene from the Titanic, and I suddenly realized I would have no idea which fork to use first. It almost made me giggle to picture what Spencer's reaction would be to them. I knew he'd be just as confused as I was.

I continued scanning the deck while my friends chatted away. Beyond the dance floor was a DJ, who seemed to be the source of the soft rock ballads coming out of the speakers at a low volume around us. There was a section at the end of the deck where a photographer was set up taking prom-like photos of couples. There was a line of couples waiting for their turn. An American flag and a Marine Corps flag stood straight on each side to frame each couple, with the ship's railing and the ocean as the backdrop behind them.

Spencer caught me watching the scene. "Let me guess, you want a photo."

I glared at him. "Obviously."

"Fine. Let's get it out of the way now, so we can enjoy the rest of our night."

Olivia and Matt shared a meaningful look, but I didn't know what it meant, so I turned back to Spencer. "What's going on?"

"What?" Spencer asked, a puzzled look on his face.

"You look like you're up to something," I replied.

"Not me. Mills, are you up to something?"

Matt shrugged. "Not today. Olivia?"

"Never." Olivia smiled. "Ellie, lemme get your phone. I'll take a pic of you guys behind the photographer. That way you can still have the pic even if you decide not to buy the whole big photo package."

I tilted my head at her, but handed over the phone. "Okay, yeah. Are they that expensive?"

Spencer made a face at Olivia. "C'mon, let's just go."

The four of us made our way across the crowded deck to the area where the pictures were being taken. While we stood in line, I looked around at all the other couples. Some Marines had a ton of medals and stripes on their uniforms. They all looked older than Spencer and Matt, and I imagined one day, years from now, we'd all be at a ball together and our guys would have that many decorations on their uniforms, too. Unease settled in my belly. I hoped the four of us could stay together and keep going to these balls year after year, but in the Marine Corps, it seemed like staying together wasn't very likely. Matt could get transferred and he and Olivia could move away. Or, worse, Spencer could get transferred. And since we weren't married, I wouldn't be able to go with him.

"Ready?" Spencer asked.

I'd spent so long thinking about years to come that I hadn't realized it was our turn to take a photo. I smiled, pushing away my fears about the future. We were here now, and I needed to enjoy it. I took his hand as he led me over to the rail of the ship where we were supposed to stand. He positioned me with my back to his chest, his arms falling around my waist. We smiled, as prompted by the photographer. I caught sight of Olivia behind him. It looked like she was taking a video, rather than pictures, with my phone.

"Excuse me," Spencer said to the photographer, "Can we have one more pose?"

The photographer smiled. "Absolutely, go ahead."

"Thanks," Spencer said to her, then turned me around in his arms so I was facing him.

I let him move me, thinking he was just posing us for a picture, his hands in mine. Then, he dropped to one knee, and all my breath left my body. When he pulled out a small black box and opened it to reveal a stunning ring, my hand flew up to my mouth. The flash of the photographer's camera lit us up momentarily, and I blinked away the tears that threatened to spill onto my cheeks.

"Ellie Burton," Spencer began, his voice smooth and confident, "I've known you forever. You're my best friend, and you always have been. I know I always planned to leave. But after everything we've gone through in this last year and a half, I can't imagine leaving you. I want you to come with me. I can find you a house with a white picket fence... you might just have to move to a new one every three years or so."

He paused while I laughed, smiling up at me. I couldn't believe this was happening. I was barely aware of the crowd of couples around us, or that the photographer kept snapping photos.

Spencer squeezed my hand. "Ellie... Will you marry me?"

I beamed at him. Nothing in the whole world had ever surprised me as much as this. But, it was also the easiest choice I'd ever made. "Yes."

The crowd cheered around us, just as they had for Matt and Olivia during their very public proposal. Spencer grinned wildly and took the ring from the box, his hand shaking slightly as he placed it on my finger. Then, he stood from his position on bended knee and threw his arms around me, spinning me around and kissing me fiercely. The camera flashed again, the light as bright as the stunning future that laid ahead.

# EPILOGUE

OLIVIA

"I still can't believe it," Ellie smiled as she gazed wistfully at her engagement ring. She tilted her hand from side to side, watching it sparkle in the sun. "If you had asked me last year if I thought Spencer would ever get married I would have laughed at you. Especially if you said he'd be marrying *me*, of all people. This is so surreal."

Ellie and I were relaxing by the pool on base enjoying the San Diego sun. We'd been out here too many times to count in the few weeks since our guys had shipped out. "I'm so happy for you guys, Ells. You know what I just realized? You never told me exactly what he said when he proposed!"

Ellie gaped at me from the lounge chair next to mine. "Are you serious?"

"Yes! I guess with the holidays and them leaving for deployment we just never had a chance to talk about the details. I was too far away to actually hear anything from where I was standing. So, what did he say?" I nudged her with my elbow.

Ellie blushed. "First of all, I know hindsight is twenty-twenty, but I had a feeling something was up that night."

"You did?"

"When we first walked out onto the deck of the boat, I said I was cold, and he made some dumb joke about how he would offer me his coat but he couldn't take it off since it was part of the uniform. Then he laughed really awkwardly. That was my first clue something was up. Just the way he said it. He's normally a lot smoother than that, ya know?"

I chuckled. "Yeah, I can see that."

"And then a couple times I kept catching him looking at me with this weird expression ... at one point he even got kind of choked up."

"Really? That's so cute!"

Ellie giggled. "We're such girls."

"Whatever. We're not girly enough if we're just now talking about this. Go on."

She reached for her tanning oil and starting reapplying it to her legs. She seemed like she needed something to do with her hands. I knew how she felt. Talking about Matt with him being gone was hard because it only made me miss him more. I was always trying to fill my time to keep from missing him. I never had idle hands.

"He started with calling me his best friend," she continued. "Then he said that even though he'd always planned to be a Marine and leave San Diego, he didn't want to leave me. He made a joke about getting a house with a white picket fence but that we just might have to move every three years. It's kind of an inside joke with us. Then he got down on one knee and asked me to marry him."

"That is so sweet."

Ellie handed me the bottle of oil and I started reapplying my own coat of it. "Come to think of it, I don't know how Matt proposed, either. I was also too far away to hear anything."

I instantly got butterflies thinking about that beautiful day by the water. Unlike Ellie, I couldn't remember if he'd acted strange beforehand. I'd been so nervous to see him after the three months of boot camp that any signs that he was about to propose were completely lost on me until he'd actually dropped to one knee.

I smirked. "It was much less sappy."

She swatted me on the arm. "Hey!"

"I'm kidding! But really, Matt just told me how much he loved me and promised to love me forever. He was so nervous I'm not sure he could have said more than that! It was really sweet. At the time I thought he was going on and on because I was so excited to say 'yes,' but it was really short and simple. To be honest, I don't remember the exact words, just the way they made me feel."

Ellie sighed, her hand on her heart. "I think it's pretty cool that we both got to watch each other's engagements from afar."

"Me too."

Ellie flopped back on her chair. "Man, I can't believe we're only a few weeks in. This sucks."

I nodded. "Yeah, it really does. But it helps that I've been so busy with my nursing classes. And I don't know what I would do if I didn't have you! My friends at school all think I'm crazy."

"What do you mean?"

"None of them know what it's like to be with someone in the military, so the separation seems really weird to them."

Ellie frowned. "I'm sorry."

"I mean, don't get me wrong, I know they just don't know what it's like to have half your heart on the other side of the world."

"Yeah. It's definitely a unique problem to have. It's a good thing we have each other, then."

I smiled at my friend. "It sure is. So, how's work going?"

"Good. Eric is dating the manager at the Starbucks on the corner, so I've been getting free lattes all week instead of our yucky break room sludge."

"Nice! Hopefully this one sticks around a little longer than the last girl."

Ellie waved a hand. "I doubt it. He's too picky."

Before I could comment further on Eric's taste in women, my phone vibrated on the glass end table between us. The number was blocked so I started to ignore it, but like every wife of a deployed service member, I had an unrealistic hope that it would be Matt.

My stomach tightened as I sat upright and put the phone to my ear. "Hello?"

"Hey babe."

I hadn't heard the sound of his voice since the day they left. The Marines on the ship didn't get to use the phone unless it was an emergency. My heart was beating out of my chest fearing that this was, in fact, an emergency.

"What's wrong?" I asked breathlessly.

I was slightly aware that Ellie had bolted upright next to me, obviously alarmed by the call.

"Nothing. Why would something be wrong?" He sounded confused.

I waved a hand at Ellie so she knew it wasn't a tragedy and she leaned back in her seat and opened one of the bridal magazines we'd brought. I got up from my chair and started to wander along the pool deck. He always made fun of me because I had to pace if I was on the phone.

"I was worried because you said you wouldn't get to call unless there was an emergency," I explained.

"Oh." Matt sighed. "Well, this isn't an emergency. But I do have something to tell you."

My heart kicked it up a notch again. "What?"

"I'm in Afghanistan."

I stopped pacing. "What do you mean? Like, the ship is ported there or something?"

"No, I flew off the ship and into Qatar, then flew here."

One frustrating thing about my husband was that I always had to drag things out of him. He could never just explain something to me all at once.

"Okay. Why?"

"I guess they needed a couple of guys to work here in Kandahar in case one of the jets needs to land for maintenance while they're out on missions. So I'll just be here waiting for jets to come in. But the Air Force is here too, and some militaries from other countries, so I'll be working with them on their jets if they need me."

I considered this. "So, you won't be on the ship anymore?"

"Not for a few months. I'll probably get back on it right before we come home."

I had no idea what to say. Was this a good thing? Was he happy about it? Should I be happy about it? I had to fight the urge to yell at him to tell me more. If he were standing right in front of me I would be shaking him by the shoulders by now.

I wasn't replying, so he cleared his throat. "Are you still there?"

"Yeah."

"Are you okay?"

"Yeah, I'm fine, but I'm just confused. What does this mean? Is it safe there?"

"It's safe, don't worry at all. This will be cool, Liv. We'll get to talk on the phone every day if I have time and I can even video chat sometimes, too."

My spirits lifted. The idea of getting to talk to him every day had my heart singing. I had no idea going into this life that the daily chats about our day would be so important to me.

"Okay, now I'm happy!" I squealed. "You said they needed a couple of guys. Is Spencer with you?"

"No, he had to stay on the boat. I'm here with Brooks."

"Oh, great."

Ellie and I had only met Catherine Brooks a few times, but once would have been enough. She was super sassy to us at a spouse barbecue once, and we pretty much wrote her off after that.

"He's really cool, babe. I'm sure his wife will grow on you. He said she can be kind of a pain in the butt at first but once you get to know her she's nice."

I rolled my eyes. "I'm not really interested in getting to know her, Matt."

He sighed. "I hope you don't mind, but I told him about that barbecue you went to where she was rude to you guys. He said they'd just had some rough stuff in their personal life and to give her a break."

Guilt and embarrassment swam through me. "I'll make an effort. But I don't want to spend this time talking about Catherine Brooks. How long do you get to talk?"

"I actually have to go. We just landed and I have to go check out my tent and get settled. Then we're going to the gym. But I'll try to call you later."

I couldn't help but feel disappointed. Even though I wouldn't even be talking to him if he were still on the boat, I selfishly wanted more time. But the hope that he'd be able to call me back later was amazing.

"Okay, I love you."

"I love you, too, Liv."

I hung up and clutched my phone to my chest. So

many emotions swam around in my head that I felt shaky. It was like a breath of air after drowning to hear his voice after weeks of strictly emails. But the crushed feeling after ending the call made me feel childish and greedy.

It occurred to me that I was going to have to tell Ellie that I would be able to talk to my husband all the time now while she still couldn't talk to Spencer. A new level of emotions settled over me. Would she be jealous or happy for me? Would I blame her if she *were* jealous?

There was only one way to find out. I took a deep breath and started back to our chairs by the pool.

"So, that was Matt," I said, biting my lip.

"I gathered! What's going on? I thought they couldn't call unless it was an emergency."

I nodded. "He's not on the ship anymore. He's at Kandahar Airfield in Afghanistan."

Her eyes widened. "Seriously?"

"Yeah. I guess they needed a few guys to work there in case their jets needed to land for maintenance."

"Is Spencer with him?"

I knew that would be her first question. "No, he had to stay back. It's him and Brooks."

She wrinkled her nose. "Yuck."

"I know. He seems to really like him, though. He wants me to get to know Catherine."

"Double yuck."

I laughed. "Apparently they were going through some personal stuff when we first met her at the barbecue so we need to give her a break."

"Fine," she replied, rolling her eyes. "I guess we all

have our bad days. Anyway, does this mean you'll get to talk to him more often now?"

Feeling insecure, I nodded.

I didn't want to seem too excited so I dampened my feelings. I settled back onto my lounge chair after realizing that I was just standing there like an idiot. I really didn't want my new access to Matt to get in the way of my friendship with Ellie. If she showed any signs of bitterness towards me, I wasn't sure how I would handle that. A good friend would be primarily happy for me, rather than only thinking of herself.

"I'm so excited for you!" She clapped her hands, and I searched her face for any sign of deceit behind her wide smile. Finding none, I relaxed. Ellie was a great friend. Of course she would be happy for me.

"Thank you. I'm really excited, too. He said he was going to get settled in and go to the gym with Brooks and then call me later. I don't think I'm ever going to remove this phone from my hand now that there's the possibility of him calling."

Ellie chuckled and held up her phone. "Honey, I haven't let this thing out of my sight in weeks."

"Me neither." I conceded with a grin.

"So ... Afghanistan, huh? Sounds kind of ... *sorry*. Ignore me," Ellie said, waving a hand and going back to the wedding magazine.

"Sounds kind of scary?" I asked.

She peeked at me over the magazine. "Yeah."

"He said it's safe there. Safer than the boat, even." The words felt hollow, like there was no truth to them. But I knew there must be. How dangerous could it be if he was able to video chat and was headed to the gym? It sounded like any other base ... just in the middle of a war zone. *Ugh.*

Ellie's eyes widened and she flopped her head back. "We have a tough job here, Liv."

"You know what they say," I said, holding up my air quotes to mock the mugs and stickers at the store on base, "*Marine Wife: Toughest Job in the Corps.*"

My friend busted out a laugh and picked up a bridal magazine from the stack on the table between our lounge chairs. "Come on, let's stop thinking about deployment and plan my wedding."

"Sounds good," I replied.

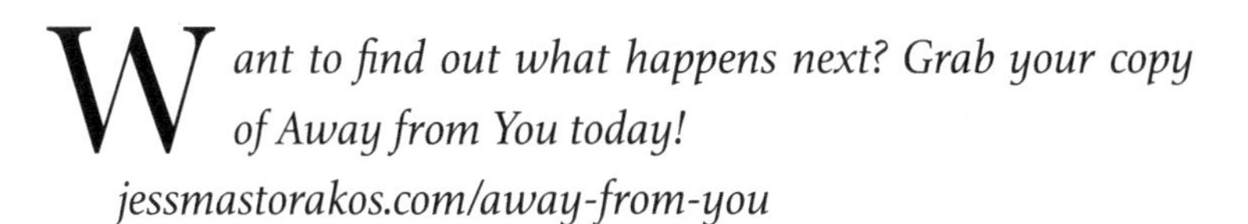

*Want to find out what happens next? Grab your copy of Away from You today!*

*jessmastorakos.com/away-from-you*

## ALSO BY JESS MASTORAKOS

THE FIRST COMES LOVE SERIES

A Match for the Marine (Dex & Amy)

A Blind Date for the Marine (Mateo & Claire)

A Princess for the Marine (Huck & Zara)

THE SAN DIEGO MARINES SERIES

Forever with You (Vince & Sara)

Back to You (Spencer & Ellie)

Away from You (Matt & Olivia)

Christmas with You (Cooper & Angie)

Believing in You (Jake & Ivy)

Memories of You (Brooks & Cat)

Home with You (Owen & Rachel)

Adored by You (Noah & Paige)

SAN DIEGO MARINES SPIN-OFF

Trusting in You (Eric & Lucy)

THE KAILUA MARINES SERIES

Treasured in Turtle Bay (Roman & Molly)

Promises at Pyramid Rock (Mac & Ana)

Stranded at the Sandbar (Tyler & Kate)

Romance on the Reef (PJ & Maggie)

Heartbeats in Honolulu (Hunter & Nora)

Christmas in Kailua (Logan & Tess)

## THE BRIDES OF BEAUFORT

The Proposal (Paul & Shelby)

## CHRISTMAS IN SNOW HILL

A Movie Star for Christmas (Nick & Holly)

Christmas with the Boy Next Door (Jack & Robin)

## ABOUT THE AUTHOR

Jess Mastorakos writes sweet military romance books that feature heroes with heart and the strong women they love. She is a proud Marine wife and mama of four. She loves her coffee in a glitter tumbler and planning with an erasable pen.

instagram.com/author_jessmastorakos
bookbub.com/authors/jess-mastorakos
goodreads.com/author_jessmastorakos